Saving Shepperd

A BOMBSHELLS OF BRENTWOOD NOVEL BY

VICTORIA BLUE

This book is an original publication of Waterhouse Press.

This is a work of fiction. Names, characters, places, and incidents either are the product of the author's imagination or are used fictitiously, and any resemblance to actual persons, living or dead, business establishments, events, or locales is entirely coincidental. The publisher does not assume any responsibility for third-party websites or their content.

Cover Design by Waterhouse Press
Cover Photograph: Shutterstock

Paperback ISBN: 978-1-64263-402-0

A BOMBSHELLS OF BRENTWOOD NOVEL BY

VICTORIA BLUE

For David,

your love and support is everything.

CHAPTER ONE

SHEPPERD

A quick glance at my phone while rushing into the building told me I was late again. No matter how much time I gave myself, it seemed like I couldn't get to my summer job on time. And my boss knew it.

The asshole had been riding my case since the week I started, and now I was his favorite target. All his pent-up hostility and frustration from his failures in life were taken out on me.

Dramatic? Maybe.

But I'd become the queen of overreacting lately. My fuse was so short, I was set off by every little thing. If the man even looked at me sideways today, I'd be fired from this place too.

Unfortunately, my bad attitude hadn't been serving me well in the workplace. I was on my third job in as many months. Of course none of the terminations were my fault. Somehow, I managed to gain employment in three separate places with the exact same mansplaining type of boss who expected me to do all the things he didn't want to do while he took the credit.

Maybe I wasn't cut out for the whole work thing. I didn't get along with most of my coworkers either. If I was let go from this one, I already decided I wouldn't look for another. I'd wasted my entire summer on this merry-go-round of attempted people-pleasing, and it just wasn't for me.

Was this what the world was turning into, though? Maybe. If these three dipshits were my only interaction with men, I'd have lost all hope in the gender all together. It also didn't help that three of my four sisters had found amazing men to partner with and those constant in-my-face examples of high-quality men were setting the bar impossibly high for me.

"You're late," my boss said by way of a greeting.

I had just set my bag on my desk when he pounced. "I'm aware," was all I could offer. How many more apologies could I give?

After logging in to my computer, I got busy. The company processed medical billing for a bunch of plastic surgeons in the area. In this town, there was no shortage of specialists. The amount of money spent on physically altering bodies was astronomical. Maybe I needed to reconsider my major.

I had one more semester until I graduated. My twin was already done with her four-year degree and was just awarded a scholarship for our university's graduate program. I had no interest in continuing beyond what our parents expected, though. Honestly, I was lucky to have made it this far.

I hated school. I hated the original thirteen years of grade school and high school and the college experience too. None of what everyone else had such fond memories of appealed to me. Sororities, parties, learning...all seemed like a waste of time to me. I learned best by doing. This summer was proof enough that was all you really needed to be capable of landing a job. As long as you could sell yourself during an interview, the rest could be learned on the job.

My cell phone vibrated on the desk where it sat screen-side down. Daryl, my boss, didn't mind if we had our phones on during work hours as long as we got the work done. I snuck a peak at the incoming text and felt the first genuine smile of the day try to break through.

Hey, lady.

After a quick look around the office to ensure Daryl was busy and not monitoring my activities, I shot him a reply.

Hey, yourself.

Can I see you tonight?

Work until 6. After that?

A few minutes passed, and I worried he might not respond. I just met the guy after shamelessly flirting with him for most of the summer. We worked out at the same gym, and it was months of eye-fucking across the room before he finally asked me out.

We'd gone out twice so far, and I was really into him. Still waiting for the other shoe to drop, though, because it always did. It didn't make sense that the guy was single. He was the most beautiful man I'd ever laid eyes on and was funny and charming as hell, too.

Something would ruin it all. It always did.

Sounds great. Call me on your way home,
and we'll figure out the details.

I turned my phone back over and got busy. As long as I

got the enormous stack of papers on the opposite corner of the desk dealt with, I'd be finished on time. If I sat there mooning over a guy for too long, I'd have to stay late until I was through it all. Perfect! That motivation would keep me focused.

Two hours later, my eyes were crossing from looking at so many numbers, and I wanted to crawl under my desk and take a nap. I stood and stretched my arms high above my head and told my coworker I needed a break.

"I'm going to get some caffeine down the hall. Want anything?"

She backed away from her keyboard and stood too. "Mind some company? I could use a break too."

"Free country," I replied with a shrug and then winced. I was so used to being snarky around my family, the answer just fell out of my mouth when I opened it. "Sorry," I mumbled when she looked at me with a confused, unimpressed stare.

"Really," I said, stopping her with a hand to her forearm. "I'm sorry. That was super shitty, and you don't deserve the attitude. I had the worst night's sleep and am just a little punchy today."

The part about not sleeping well was one hundred percent true. I never did. Plagued with night terrors most of my life, I adapted to function on as little as two or three hours of sleep each night.

I used to talk to my parents about the bad dreams when I was little but stopped sharing what I suffered through by the time I was ten. They knew something was terribly wrong with my psychological and emotional health, though, but were at a loss with how to deal with me. Because I was twenty-two, they couldn't force me to seek professional help even though we all knew that was what I needed.

Joy gave me a sweet but brief smile. "I get it. Don't worry about it. Let's get some coffee."

The girl was just a year or two older than me and had been working here close to a year. She had naturally curly hair that fell in perfect spiral ringlets down her back. She was taller than my five-foot-six-inch height and was the poster girl for office-casual in linen trousers and a white T-shirt.

When the air conditioner kicked on, like Daryl made sure it always did, she'd throw on the denim jacket that rested over the back of her chair and looked like she'd stepped out of an ad for the Gap.

"So," she said while we stirred our cups, "are you seeing anyone?" She looked a little sheepish after asking and quickly followed up with, "There's a reason I'm asking. My boyfriend's best friend is fresh out of a long-term thing." She took a sip from her mug, keeping her eyes pinned to me over the rim. "He's been moping around, driving us crazy," she said with a solid eye roll, "So I was wondering if you would want to double some time?"

I lifted my cup to my lips, even though it was way too hot to drink, just to buy some time to come up with an excuse. I was definitely not the girl for her goodwill mission. Whatever was going on with Law was way too new to consider him my boyfriend, but I definitely didn't want to deal with a rebound guy.

The grin that spread across my lips couldn't be helped. Every time I thought of that man, I felt like someone turned up the heat suddenly, and I got flushed and breathless.

Joy tilted her head and matched my smile. "Honestly, he's a really nice guy. I didn't do a good job of selling him just then, did I?" She lifted her shoulders in a quick shrug and added,

"But it's true, he's driving us a little crazy. His ex really did a number on him. And he's a good guy. Totally didn't deserve what she did to him."

"Cheated?" I asked. Keeping her on the topic of her friend was better than my having to explain my own relationship status.

"You guessed it. Why are some people so heartless?"

I was hardly an expert on relationships. Of any kind. But I did have some experience with being heartless. Although, that didn't seem like the right information to inject into the conversation.

"It's probably better it happened now than, say, after they got married. Right?" I offered. "Or brought kids into the world."

She nodded and said, "So true. The whole thing has been so scandalous in their friend group because she got together with another close friend. So not only did he lose his high school sweetheart but a close friend too."

"Ouch." I winced. "That definitely makes it worse." I finished my coffee in record time, rinsed my mug, and grabbed some paper towels to dry it. "Guess we should get back," I bemoaned.

"Yeah, I suppose." Joy sighed. "That stuff isn't going to enter itself," she quipped.

I liked this girl, and lately that takeaway was getting rarer and rarer.

The rest of my shift went quickly. About twenty minutes before quitting time, I messaged Law to see what the plan was for the night.

Leaving in about twenty minutes.

Hungry?

If he only knew.

So far, one of the best things about this guy was that he didn't give me shit about my eating habits. He was totally into working out and looking his best. Not one single comment about being too thin or an under-the breath remark about my needing to eat more.

Sure. I could eat. Want to meet somewhere?

I was thinking I'd cook for us.

I don't want to put you out. Are you sure?

I enjoy cooking. Especially for a beautiful lady.

Sounds great. Can I bring anything?

Just your sexy self. I'll send you my address and see you soon. XO

Hmmm, that XO at the end kind of threw me for a second. This guy was not the cutesy, lovey-dovey type of guy. At least I didn't think he was. Not to mention, we were only on our third official date. Interesting that he went with that sign-off.

But I decided not to overthink or overanalyze it like I normally did with things. Despite what everyone in my family thought, I was trying to improve myself every day.

The drive to Law's place wasn't very long. It helped

immensely that the greater portion of evening commuters had already made it home, so that decreased my drive time as well. Looking at my phone—twice—to ensure the front door I stood before was the right one, I lifted my hand to ring the bell just as the large walnut panel swung open.

"There she is!" the sexy man said with that mischievous grin I was getting used to seeing on his handsome face.

With my hand at my throat, I gasped, "Holy shit! You surprised me."

"I have cameras," he said and opened his arms wide to greet me.

I stepped into his embrace and let my eyes flutter closed as his intoxicating scent enveloped me. Even while working out, this man smelled so freaking good I wanted to climb him like a tree.

He planted a quick kiss to the side of my head while we hugged and he quietly said, "I'm so happy to see you." His voice was deep and scratchy beside my ear, and goosebumps erupted on my arms and thighs from the vibration.

When he released me from his arms, I looked up and smiled. Surely, my eyes were glassy, betraying the arousal he just flooded me with and still, the smile was an actual, genuine one. It felt good to hear someone was happy to see me, and I soaked in the feeling.

"Thank you for the invite."

"Well, I hope you brought your appetite," he said while tugging me through his spotless home to the kitchen. "Can I get you something to drink while I get everything to the table?"

"What are you having?" I looked around the various counters to spot his beverage of choice, not wanting to ask for alcohol if he was drinking something else.

"I have a beer I've been nursing while I cook, but there's a great bottle of wine to go with dinner breathing on the table."

"Mmm, that sounds great. I can help myself, though. Or do you need a hand with anything? Let me just wash up real fast," I offered as I made my way to the sink to wash my hands. "Your home is lovely. Is it just you here?" I called back over my shoulder.

The place was beyond lovely. I was totally trying to play it cool. Ironically, he didn't live that far from my parent's home in Brentwood. I wasn't completely sure what he did for a living, but obviously it was something lucrative because the rent in this area was outrageous.

His decor was right up my alley too. Simple and clean, and everything neat and tidy. I couldn't stand cluttered spaces. Messy homes made my brain short-circuit. You wouldn't know that by the room I shared with my twin. Well...used to share with my twin. Now that she'd moved in with her boyfriend, Andrew, I had the room to myself.

But I hated that house. I hated everything there except my twin sister, as a matter of fact. This place of Law's, though? Serious goals. Maybe if this budding romance we were getting into didn't work out, I could just move in and be his housekeeper. The thought made me chuckle to myself, and unfortunately, I must have laughed loud enough that he'd heard me.

"What's so funny over there?" he asked over his shoulder while tossing an enormous salad.

"Oh my God, Law." I bugged my eyes wide at the size of the salad bowl. "Are there more people joining us? There's so much food here!" A quick wave of panic swept over my entire body. I mean, I said I would eat, but there was so much food on the island. What the hell was he thinking?

"Nope, just us," he said with a hint of embarrassment. "You see, I come from a very big family. They're the only ones I ever cook for, and I'm used to needing enough for a small army. I didn't do a very good job of scaling down for just two, did I?"

I climbed up onto a stool across from where he was working. "How many siblings do you have?"

"There are ten of us. Plus Mom and Dad, of course." He grinned at my wide-eyed reaction.

"Your poor mother," I said smiling into my glass. After tasting the wine, I moaned into the glass and went back for another taste. "Wow, this is fantastic."

"Woman," he said in the most serious tone and completely stopped what he was doing to stare at me. Luckily he didn't hold the quiet pause long enough to truly make me panic and said, "Do not make sounds like that when I'm standing this close to you. We won't make it to the meal." He quirked one brow higher than the other, and I giggled.

Freaking giggled. Like a silly little schoolgirl. Instantly I felt heat crawl up my chest and neck and then fill my cheeks with a flush I knew he would notice.

Law continued to stare at me, and the blushing just got worse.

"Sorry," I said and studied the movement in the countertop stone. It was either marble or limestone, I wasn't sure which, but had interesting veins of gray and beige throughout. The earthy colors were picked up in the cabinet finish and other decorative accents around the room.

He moved with a grace I don't think I'd witnessed in a man. Law was in front of me before I could make sense of his relocation, and he bent at the waist to be eye-level with me.

His eyes were soulful and intense, and his gaze flitted around my face and neck before he finally spoke.

In a dark, raspy tone that settled right between my thighs, he said, "You are the sexiest woman I've ever seen. This heat moving over your skin is mesmerizing." He gave me a slow, perfect kiss that left me breathless when he stood tall again. "Now stop trying to distract me, or I'm going to burn something," he said with a wink and was gone and back to his tasks on the other side of the island.

When I was sure sound would come from my throat that wasn't just a helpless whimper, I said, "Thank you. I think I'm just going to call you Danger moving forward."

He laughed a deep, hearty laugh that made my grin spread wider. "Danger, huh? I've been called a lot of things in my life, but never that one. Big points for originality, lady."

I executed a quick, seated curtsey at his compliment and took a moment to soak in the vibe of being near this guy. It had been so long since I'd felt playful and lighthearted that I almost had trouble identifying what I was feeling. Being around Law created a buoyancy in my heart and mind, and it felt really good. Addicting.

Yeah, the nickname Danger suited him perfectly. Spending time with him was dangerous. Dangerously alluring and dangerously enjoyable. If I were wise, which I could plainly admit I typically wasn't, I'd end things with the man before they got started.

I couldn't be hurt if I didn't put myself at risk, right?

CHAPTER TWO

LAW

Confidence was something I had in abundance. The word swagger had been thrown my way a time or two. That was fine. I could own both those traits. Who didn't appreciate someone who knew what they wanted and had the balls to go for it?

"Does your family call you Lawrence?" Shepperd asked.

"Not if they expect me to respond," I chuckled. "Of course, no rules ever apply to our mom because she is the queen of the castle. She does whatever she wants, and we all give in to her every request," I answered after finishing my wine.

The bottle was empty, and our stomachs were full. I knew going into the evening that the woman ate like a mouse. She had to with how small she was. Like a dumbass, I made way too much food. Now I'd be eating the leftovers for every meal for the rest of the week.

"I'm a bit embarrassed to ask you this," she said while looking adorably shy. Not a look I had seen before on the sassy siren. But I kind of liked it, or more so that I brought it out in her.

"I'm an open book," I assured her and sat back more comfortably on my seat. "Ask away."

"What do you do? For a job, I mean?" She set her fork down and groaned. "I can't eat another bite. Honestly, that was incredible."

"I'm glad you liked it. Next time I'll know to leave out the olives." I snuck her a quick wink so she wouldn't feel self-conscious about the little mound of black olive pieces pushed far to one side of her plate.

"Sorry," she apologized and set her napkin over the offending pile.

"No need to apologize, darling," I reassured. "I didn't know you didn't like them, so my apologies as well. As far as employment, I lead the sales team for one of my father's companies. My education was focused on marketing, and it just kind of dovetailed into the spot I'm in now."

"Do you enjoy it?"

"For the most part. It's not easy being in his shadow all the time, but it has been incredible learning from him. Seems like I'm constantly screwing something up, though. He's a very tough guy to please. Seemingly impossible standards."

"That must be parents' inclination. I go through much of the same with mine. Though not with regard to my employment." She shrugged. "They don't even know I have a job."

"Are you not close?" I asked, trying to learn more about her.

"Hmmm, that's a complicated subject," she said but didn't explain further.

I tilted my chin slightly and waited, hoping she'd open up a bit. The woman intrigued me more than any I'd associated with lately. She was smart and damn clever. When we had light, joking back-and-forth exchanges, she gave as good as she got. I appreciated it when a person didn't take everything so seriously. Made me look forward to talking to her.

Shepperd finished the last of her wine and exhaled heavily. "There are seven in my family. My parents and five girls. I actually have a twin." She gave a rare, genuine smile after that detail and quickly added, "And no, we don't sleep with guys together, so don't even ask about your chances."

"Damn," I teased. "Just when I thought I'd get to cross something off my bucket list!"

"You'd be shocked how many times I've had to address the topic," she said with one of the best eye rolls I'd ever seen.

"No, I know guys are pigs. Add to that how gorgeous you are, and I'm guessing you're beating guys off with a stick all the time."

"Well, that's probably overstating things a bit, but my sisters are all beautiful. We all look very similar, and since we're so close in age, people tend to notice us," she shared while carrying her plate to the sink.

"Let me clean up since you cooked," she insisted.

"You're my guest," I said, taking the dish directly from her hand. "I'd much rather sit and talk more. Let's get comfortable in the next room, and I'll clean this up later."

She looked like she wanted to protest, and I appreciated her wanting to help. I'd cooked for women in the past who didn't lift a finger or even offer to. They'd just expected to be waited on, and it was a turn-off. I loved taking care of a woman in all ways. But it meant so much more when it was appreciated, not expected.

"How about an after-dinner drink? More wine?" I offered before we took seats on the sofa.

"Hmm, as nice as that sounds, I'm driving. Better not," she replied with a frown.

"One more and we'll see where the night goes?" I asked

hopefully. I thought she was way more at ease now that she had a few glasses of wine in her, and I really didn't want the night to end. I wouldn't presume she wanted to spend the night, but I definitely wouldn't turn her down if things went in that direction.

"See? This is why I'm going to call you Danger. You're very tempting. Seductive without trying." She looked down with that shyness again. Her age became noticeably younger in that moment.

So I asked the dreaded question. It was the point a guy either became completely freaked out or way more interested. And God, I wanted the second option with more hope than I should feel about a girl I barely knew.

"Can I ask how old you are? I think we've all gotten a little too used to these online dating apps where you get a fact list about the person before you even start talking to someone. Since we met in person first, some of these things seem awkward to just outright ask. So, I'm sorry if I'm coming across as bold." It felt like I was rambling out of nervousness and was acutely aware of not liking the feeling.

She studied me before answering. "I'm twenty-two. What about you? I'm thinking you're at least five or maybe seven years older than I am."

"Does that bother you?" I asked rather than admit I just turned thirty.

"I wouldn't be here if it did, would I?"

I grinned at her sassy reply. "No, I guess you wouldn't. I don't get the impression you do anything other than exactly what you want to do. Exactly when you want to do it."

"Hmm, well, sometimes I do. I used to be a major pushover." She shook her head and said, "Not anymore, though. Those days are done."

She finished that comment with solid conviction, and I wanted to ask more questions. It seemed like something in particular brought about the change, but I didn't feel comfortable enough yet to get that personal. I'd store it away, though, for another time. There was a sadness lurking in her, and that comment brought it to the forefront.

An uncomfortable silence grew between us, and I scooped her hand into mine and gave it a soft squeeze.

Finally, she met my eyes again, and unexplainably, I said, "I'm sorry."

With a slight tilt to her head, she asked, "Sorry? For what?"

"I'm not sure," I forced a small laugh. "You looked sad all of a sudden, and I thought if it was something I said, I should apologize. It was the last thing I was going for," I assured her.

"No, I'm not sad. A little tired. Maybe that's what you're picking up on," she lied. Terribly. I knew the difference between sad and sleepy but decided to drop it and move on. I wasn't looking to ruin the night.

"Well, you're more than welcome to spend the night here. I have several guest rooms, so you don't have to drive if you're too tired."

"That's very sweet of you," she said but gave no hint if she'd take me up on the offer. "You never answered my question," she reminded as she wove her fingers through mine and waited.

"You were very close. I'm thirty."

"I'm a little surprised you haven't settled down already," she said with a smile, but I wasn't sure if she was teasing or not.

"Most of my friends are still single. I have a couple in long-term relationships, but other than that..." Why did I feel like I was defending my life choices here?

After giving my hand a gentle squeeze, she said, "I meant because you're obviously a very eligible man. I'm surprised some woman hasn't staked her claim on you already," she hurried to explain, maybe sensing my defensiveness.

"Sorry, I didn't mean to sound so defensive. I get a lot of shit from my parents about not finding a nice girl to settle down with. I think the minute I hear anything that sounds like that, I shift into a defensive posture. But you didn't deserve all that."

She put her other hand on my forearm and looked me right in the eye while saying, "Law, it's fine. Stop apologizing for everything. I'm not the kind of girl who takes everything the wrong way. I knew what you meant while you were saying it."

"You're very smart for such a young lady." *And please don't stop touching me.* Both spots where her hands made contact with my body were noticeably heating up.

"Does our age difference bother you?" she asked pointedly. Fair enough, I had asked her something similar only minutes before.

"No, not at all," I replied without thought. Because honestly, it didn't.

We sat for a few beats and just took each other in. The woman was so damn beautiful, I couldn't decide where to settle my gaze. She smiled while lifting her refilled glass to her mouth, and I tracked her slow movement. I wanted to taste the wine on her lips more than anything else.

After setting my own drink on the coffee table, I slid across the cushion that separated us, took her drink, and set it beside mine.

"Can I kiss you?" I asked, intentionally letting my voice settle deeper in my throat.

"Mmm, yes please," she said and tilted her chin toward me. "I was hoping you would after the way you were just looking at me."

Threading my fingers through the hair at her nape, I gripped the back of her neck and tugged her closer. Our mouths met gently at first. Tentatively. She tasted like the wine we were sipping...and sin. Or at least what I thought sinning with this sexy little thing should taste like. Arousal surged through my body and thickened my cock. Damn, I should've done this earlier in the night so I might be inside her body by now.

That particular thought encouraged my tongue's exploration. She was so delicious, I immediately had fantasies forming about tasting her everywhere. We parted, and I watched her slowly open her eyes and grin.

"What is that grin about? Looks very mischievous," I teased.

"Truth?"

"Always," I answered easily.

"I was letting my imagination run free," she whispered. The husky tone of her voice intensified with her arousal, and the sound made my blood heat.

"Care to share?" I asked, appreciating her honesty and bravery.

But she slowly shook her head and tapped her temple. "No. I think I'll keep that particular one to myself. For now."

I was getting addicted to her smile. Every version of it. She said so much without saying a word. I could watch her all night.

"You know, I hope I don't regret saying this, but I really like you," I admitted.

"Why would you regret saying that? And thank you. I

really like you too."

I shrugged. "I don't know. I don't want to seem clingy or creepy or anything."

She chuckled before saying, "Oh, gorgeous man, you are the furthest thing from creepy. Trust me."

"Had your share of creepers, have you?"

"Hasn't every girl? Internet dating seems to bring them out of the woodwork. Or at least that has been my experience." She shook her head slowly and rubbed her forehead.

"That comment sounds like there's at least one entertaining story behind it. Spill it," I teased and poked an index finger into her side.

Shepperd shook her head and squirmed out of reach while giggling. "No way."

I launched myself at her and tickled her sides, and she burst with the most delightfully sultry, rumbly laugh I'd ever heard. The resonance of the sound vibrated through my entire body and made my dick spring right back to attention. From a woman's laugh? Couldn't say that had ever happened before.

"Tell me," I insisted and tickled her sides again while she squirmed beneath me. Playfully I pinned her arms down at her sides, and something switched, like a circuit being blown. Her face went from light, giggling playfulness to sheer terror in the blink of an eye.

"No! Stop!" she shouted and began thrashing beneath me. I released the hold I had on her immediately and sprang to my feet, presenting my hands out in front of me so she could see them both.

"Okay. Okay." I don't know why I repeated the word, but I was so thrown at the mood shift I couldn't get my brain online quickly enough to say anything else. So I said it a third time.

"Okay."

And then silence. Neither of us said a word, but the woman's panicked breaths sawed in and out of her body in a way that had her entire torso racked with the effort.

Cautiously I said, "I'm so sorry. I'm not sure what just happened, but I assure you it wasn't my intent. I was just playing around." I kept my voice quiet and calm and slowly eased back down to the sofa. With my careful movement and quiet voice, I hoped she'd snap out of whatever she was experiencing.

But her wide, wild eyes just darted back and forth. I didn't want to say anything that would set her off again but couldn't take the silence. I wanted to hold her and comfort her but instead left plenty of space between our bodies.

"You okay?" I asked. Maybe if she'd talk a little, she'd calm down. When she didn't reply, I tried, "Shepperd? You good?"

The woman sprang to her feet like she just popped out of a jack-in-the-box. I didn't miss the tears wetting her cheeks. I didn't know how to make up for my monumental screw-up. Shit, I wasn't even sure what I did wrong.

"I should go," she blurted. Her movements were erratic and frantic, and there was no way in hell I'd let her drive in her current state.

"I think you should settle down before you get behind the wheel, sweetheart. I'd never forgive myself if you were injured or, God forbid, hurt someone else. Want a little more wine to calm your nerves?"

"I'll be fine," she clipped and whipped her head back and forth clearly looking for something.

"What? What are you looking for? Please don't rush off. I don't think you should drive so upset. Please." I stepped in front of her while repeating my concern. I reached for her hands, but instead of allowing me to hold them, she quickly drew them in close to her body.

Okay, that hurt a little bit.

"Listen. I'm really sorry. Can we just calm down and not end a great night like this?" I tried again and was starting to lose my patience. I mean, for Christ's sake, how many times did I have to apologize? I still wasn't one hundred percent clear about what I did wrong.

In one long, rushed sentence she gave a brief explanation. "You don't have to keep apologizing. It's me. My baggage. Where the fuck did I set my purse?"

Apparently that was all the explanation I would get.

"I believe it's in the kitchen." I was about to offer to get it, but she beelined out of the room to fetch it herself, and I stood there like a helpless idiot and watched her.

At the front door, she finally paused. I'm not sure she would've if I hadn't physically put my body between her and the exit.

"I had a great time. Thank you for cooking for me. It really was delicious," she rushed out and punctuated the platitudes with the fakest smile I'd ever seen.

What in the actual hell was going on? The woman's entire personality transformed from the person I just spent the evening with to this wild, spooked colt.

"Uhhh, you're welcome?" I replied with a questioning tone. I continued to hold out hope that she'd snap out of whatever she was dealing with. But then I had a flash of clarity and stepped out of the way. I'd had my share of dealing with crazy girls in the past, and if that's what was happening, she could go. I didn't have the time or the inclination to get involved with a nutcase again.

And what a bummer of a realization that was. I watched her hurry down my front walk and jump into her car like she was a trauma surgeon rushing to meet a patient in the operating room. Until her red taillights disappeared around the bend in my street, I stood on my sidewalk and watched her go.

When I came back inside, I locked the door behind me and, just for a moment, rested all my weight back against the thing. I had a sink full of dishes to clean up and a second bottle of wine I had just opened to finish while I did so. Not at all how I hoped the night would end, but, well, here I was. I decided to call my brother Jacob to talk while I did the chores so I wouldn't stew in my head.

His phone rang three times, and I was about to end the call when he picked up.

His deep voice blasted through my phone. "Hello?"

"Whatcha doin'?" I asked with uncharacteristically lazy language.

"Law?" he asked in reply, already confused by my unusual greeting.

"Yeah, man?"

"What's wrong?" Just from the tone of my voice, my brother already knew something was bothering me. It was the plus and minus of our close relationship. When it came to me, his bullshit meter was finely tuned.

"Why are you asking me that? Can't a guy just call his brother to say hi?" I tried to infuse the retort with lightness instead of the annoyance I was harboring. He had nothing to do with any of the feelings upending my normal calm, and it would be unfair to pin them on him.

"I suppose a guy could. It's just that you wouldn't. So out with it," Jake carefully demanded.

"Seriously, nothing. I was just doing a little check-in," I tried again. I couldn't quite put my finger on why I wasn't just spilling my guts about the real issue. Probably because I didn't quite know myself.

"You're so full of shit," my brother teased. "Okay, what's her name?" Without realizing it, he'd hit the bullseye of my issues with one question.

"Shepperd." I sighed while scraping her uneaten portion of dinner into the trash. "She's that hottie from the gym I've been telling you about."

"Daaaammnn," he drew out like a teenage girl.

"What?"

"It's been a long time since a female had you this turned around. You've been talking about this one for a while. Normally you've conquered and moved on three times over in this amount of time. Either she's something special or you're losing your game, brother," Jacob teased, and the assertion rubbed me wrong. Probably because it was really close to the truth.

"Well, we played cat and mouse for longer than I usually put up with, that's true. Tonight, she finally came over for dinner. And yes, before you ask, I made pasta. It's all I have in the skillset unless she wants boiled chicken and steamed brown rice."

"Isn't it early for her to already have left, then? Can't help you with your blue balls, dude. You're going to have to handle that on your own."

"Ha, funny. Blue balls I can handle. Mind fucks, not so much," I admitted.

"Okay, tell me what happened," Jake sighed with the brotherly understanding I was hoping for.

"Dinner was great. Food was good, conversation was good. And then we were sitting on the couch, just talking. Well, and a little kissing, but nothing more. She said something, and I playfully tickled her, and in a split second, she totally went mental on me." The whole scene replayed in my head while I explained the events to Jake. It didn't make any more sense as I recalled the scene than when it actually took place.

My brother scoffed, probably thinking I was leaving out key information. "From being tickled? Something else must have happened."

I rubbed my forehead where I typically held tension. If I didn't work through this, I'd end up with a migraine. "I don't know," I bemoaned. "I honestly don't know what happened. She shouted something like, 'No, stop,' and of course I did. Immediately. When a girl gets that crazy look in her eyes while you're touching her, you know to back way the fuck up, you know?" I asked, looking for validation.

"No, on this one I can't say that I know. But from what you're describing it sounds like she got spooked," Jacob offered thoughtfully. Then added, "Triggered maybe?"

"Triggered?" I'd heard the word before, but it usually sounded like psychobabble, and I instantly checked out. But because I really thought this girl could matter, I added a couple follow-ups. "By what? Being tickled?"

I could hear Jacob shifting around, maybe getting comfortable in a chair or something. "Listen. Here's what I know. Since Vela was abducted, I see the strangest things set off panic like you wouldn't believe. It can be a sound, a smell, or some combination of words no one else understands would be an issue but her. But then she flips out, and it can take hours to calm her down."

I could physically feel the pain I heard in his voice as if it were my own. His new family had been through so much since they'd gotten his daughter back from her captor.

I didn't really know what to say. "*Ooosh,* dude. That sounds rough. But it also sounds like you were in my living room this evening. How often do you deal with something like that?"

"Just depends. Some weeks we go without it happening at all. Then there will be one particular day she's like a giant exposed nerve and gets triggered by five different things." He sighed heavily enough that I felt his emotion from my end of the call. "It's exhausting. For everyone."

"That poor kid," I muttered but felt an ache from the information right in the center of my chest. Between our niece, Stella, and now my brother's kid too, it pained me to hear about little ones suffering at the hands of adults.

Our oldest sister, Cecile, had married a monster. They created the world's most adorable child, Stella, before she knew his true colors. For years, the asshole ex physically abused their daughter for his own kicks. The bastard cleverly hid what he was doing to her until she started acting out aggressively with her classmates.

Through Cecile's amazing mothering and a handful of mental health professionals, it came to light that he'd been hurting his own daughter for most of her life. She didn't know better to tell anyone and said she just thought that's what parents did to their kids.

So fucked up.

Stella's abuse was deeply disturbing for all of us. It made me vow to never bring a child into this messed-up world. If parents couldn't be trusted to care for, love, and nurture the very humans they created, how on earth did you trust the rest of the world?

"You there, man?" Jacob asked quietly.

"Yeah, sorry. Just thinking a hundred different things. I like the girl, but I'm not sure I want to get involved if she's got head problems. Don't know if I have the capacity to deal with all that, you know?"

"Law, of course you do. Look how much you love Stella. Think how unfair it would be if Stella or Vela got labeled not worthy of the effort it might take to love them. Especially since they were victims. They didn't ask for their lives to be forever changed, did they?" His comments were valid but probably not what I wanted to hear at the moment. I was already feeling guilty about my selfish thoughts without him adding that icing to the cake.

And it still didn't automatically mean I was the man for the job. If I didn't want to invest more time and energy into seeing if there was really something between me and Shepperd, now would be the perfect time to pull out.

"Hey, I gotta go," Jake said, interrupting my browbeating. "I hope that helped. At least a little. All I can advise is to be patient. Talk with her. See if she can outline her triggers for you so you don't unknowingly set her off again with an innocent comment or gesture."

"Yeah, I hear you. Thanks, Jake. Thanks for picking up and all you shared about Vela. You guys are so strong and amazing. Not sure we all remind you of that enough."

We hung up, and I finished loading the dishwasher. I had abandoned the task when our conversation took that serious turn because I wanted to give the topic my undivided attention.

Being alone with all these thoughts was the last thing I

wanted or needed. It was too late to hit the gym, my favorite way to work through something. Plus, I was exhausted. After the kitchen was spotless, I headed to my bathroom for a hot shower. It wouldn't kill me to crawl into bed before midnight once in a while, and it looked like that was my best option.

By the time I finished in the bathroom, I could barely walk the few yards to my bed. The steam and pounding water relaxed my muscles enough to release a lot of the tension I'd been holding, and the minute my head hit the pillow, I was out. I didn't move a muscle through the entire night, and for once, I wasn't exhausted when I got up the next morning.

I felt energized and ready to take on a new day. Good thing, too, because I had a packed schedule for the rest of the week. I'd made up my mind to put the Shepperd situation on the back burner. I'd leave the ball in her court, and if she wanted to reach out, I'd be happy to talk to her. Maybe even see her again.

But I wouldn't pursue her. Like I told my brother, I didn't have the energy to deal with a woman that came along with a full set of baggage. That's why I typically kept my female interactions light and noncommittal. I was in the phase of my life where I needed to focus on my career and getting ahead. The personal-life stuff was extra—for when and if I had the time and inclination.

So why did I keep checking my phone throughout the day? Why was I thinking about that sexy blonde every free minute? Why did I have to repeatedly coach myself to set the phone down and walk away. Don't text her, don't call her, no matter how many well-intended excuses I came up with. They were all bullshit, and I knew it.

The girl was under my skin. There was no better way to

describe it. It was unfamiliar territory, but I could recognize it for what it was. I was interested in her—in getting to know her better. Interested in spending more time being goofy and laughing. And I was most definitely interested in getting in her pants. But not if I needed to decipher a code to figure out what the hell she was dealing with.

Maybe Jake was right. We needed to have a conversation. I should give her the opportunity to explain what happened, what happened that saddled her with these unusual reactions in the first place. Was that some random reaction, or had she flipped out on a guy like that before? If she wasn't willing to open up and try to explain things to me, I would know we had no future, and I could move on.

Solid plan. When and if she did reach out to me, those would be my conditions. That didn't mean I'd necessarily lay them out for her in a bulleted PowerPoint presentation, but having them in mind gave me a sort of outline of how to handle her.

The rest of the week went by in a blur. Shepperd wasn't at the gym at the usual time we both went, and I started to worry. What if something happened to her on her drive home? I knew she was too agitated to drive, but she wouldn't hang out and calm down. Friday afternoon came and went, and I still hadn't heard from her.

I had plans to hit a local pub for happy hour with two coworkers, and just as I parked in the lot downtown, my phone buzzed with an incoming text.

Hey there! TGIF!

The message was from Shepperd. I stared at the screen

for a minute or two, trying to decide the best way to handle her. Were we going to pretend that episode at my house never happened? I couldn't even lie to myself and say I didn't want to see her again. Hell, she was filling every free moment in my mind. Maybe I just needed to sleep with her and put her in my rearview mirror. I'd get the curiosity out of my system and get some much-needed sexual tension released too.

Yeah, I liked the sound of that plan. So I texted her back before getting out of my car.

Hey yourself! How was your week?

I locked my car and set the alarm before dropping the key into my front pants pocket. I confirmed that I had my wallet and headed toward the bar's front entrance. Parking was a bit challenging because the weekend was getting started, so the closest lot I found was a few blocks away. While I slowly walked to meet my buddies, I watched the bouncing ellipses on our text thread, waiting for her next message.

Glad it's over, I'll say that much. What are you doing tonight/this weekend? Want to get together?

Bingo! Just the message I was hoping for. Or at least judging by my body's reaction to reading her text, it's what I was hoping for. The dumb part of my plan however was that it didn't extend past that point. I knew I wanted her to reach out to me, and now that she had, I was torn about how to respond. Truthfully, I knew I wanted to accept her invitation.

That wasn't what I was confused about. The uncontrollable excitement and happiness I felt was throwing me off my normally cool game. How was I already so into this girl?

If I admitted to the non-virtuous side of myself, it was likely infatuation. The thrill of the hunt maybe. Since I hadn't conquered this particular prey as of yet, there was a level of challenge to it all. That had always been what led me astray when I had a perfectly fine woman in my life. Another one would catch my eye, and off I'd wander.

I wasn't a sleazy guy who cheated on women. I simply never committed in the first place. I kept my options open knowing damn well I'd get bored and start looking for the next great thing.

It was an awful pattern and definitely the fatal flaw in my life's plot. I'd probably lost potential quality partners because of my fear of committing to one woman. My brother insisted that I just hadn't found *the one* yet. He assured me that when I did, the thrill of the hunt would evaporate.

Meeting some work buddies for a couple atm. Tomorrow?

The response bubble popped up and throbbed for a few seconds and then disappeared. I was inside the bar ordering my first round when I felt my phone vibrate against my thigh. Once I told the friendly guy behind the very busy bar what I wanted, I pulled my phone out to check her reply.

Sounds good. Just text or call, and we'll set something up. Have fun tonight. XO

I'd like to say that was the last I thought of the woman for the rest of the night. I'd like to say the curvy redhead at the end of the bar didn't give me her number along with a very detailed description of how she'd like to spend the evening. But both would be untrue.

I could've worked out the week's frustrations between the sheets with that gorgeous siren, but instead, I drove home alone after a couple of hours. While the redhead was tempting, I couldn't shake thoughts of a specific blond bombshell.

I stared at my phone when I crawled beneath the cool sheets debating if it was too late to send a message.

Just one couldn't hurt, right? If she was already sleeping, she'd likely have the thing on do not disturb and would wake to my message and know I was thinking about her all night. If I were lucky and she was still awake, I could just say good night and be done with it.

But instead, I wrote three different messages and deleted them before settling on something that was simple and heartfelt.

Sleep well, gorgeous girl. I hope you dream of me.

Quickly I stabbed the Send button before I changed my mind again. I was putting way more thought into a damn text than necessary. I reread the message twice while no indication came through that she even saw it. So, with a heavy sigh, I tossed my phone onto the bed and turned on my side to get more comfortable.

Lying down gave my body permission to relax a bit, and the exhaustion of a trying week crept in. Just as I was drifting off, my phone's screen lit up the room with a soft glow. Like a teenager, I scrambled to find the device within the covers and stared at the screen until my eyes adjusted enough to read her reply.

Thank you. You too. But of me, of course. I hope you had a good time tonight with your friends.

I could have left the conversation end there. It was a perfectly natural place to end things and get the sleep my body was begging for. But now an excitement swirled in the pit of my stomach, and then I actually scoffed into the dark room. Why the hell was I acting the way I was? Over a text message. And what was it about this girl that had my interest so peaked? None of it made sense, and the longer I lay there and tried to figure it out, the more wired I became.

Fuck it. I'd text her one more time and then sleep.

Yeah, it wasn't bad. Kind of boring, though, so I left pretty early.

Oh, I'm sorry.

No, no need to be. I think I'm just tired. Normally I have a blast with the crew, but something was off tonight.

What do you mean?

I'm not sure. Two of the five of us are married, and one is in a serious relationship. In fact, he spent the whole night talking about his girlfriend and was scrolling IG for proposal ideas.

How funny. I can't picture it. Sounds like you all are at different stages of life.

Definitely. I'll let you sleep, just wanted to say good night.

You're sweet. Night. XO

XO

Finally, with a dopey smile on my face, I fell asleep to thoughts of Ms. Shepperd Farsay. Even though we didn't set a solid plan for tomorrow, I was already looking forward to seeing her. Hopefully, after a good night's sleep, I'd be able to make more sense of these unfamiliar feelings I was having about the girl.

CHAPTER THREE

SHEPPERD

While I lay in bed waiting for the communal bathroom in my family's home to be free, I reread the messages from Law for a third time. A strange expression was consuming my entire face, and it wasn't until there was a quiet knock on my door that I realized I was smiling.

Seriously, what the hell? From reading a handful of text messages from a guy much too slick for my own best interest. When I gave the guy a few minutes of head time, I knew I was falling for him and didn't like it one bit. It was way too quick and not a place I was comfortable. *Caring for someone.* That just led to problems and eventual pain. I had way too much baggage to ever get involved with someone long-term, and I knew it.

Shit, all I had to do was reflect on that disaster from the other night at his place. What normal person freaks out the way I did? From being tickled?

I knew the answer, but it wasn't one I typically cared to share with anyone. First, I wasn't normal. Second, it wasn't the tickling that set me off.

I was a girl with a dark secret. Even my family didn't know the deal. No one did. Okay, not true. One other person did because he was the monster that haunted me in my dreams.

Hell, on really bad days, I didn't even have to be asleep to be tortured by the memories. And even though the worst of it all happened when I was in grade school, the nightmare film reel that played in my mind was as fresh as the latest blockbuster.

It started when I was eight. Maye and I just started third grade, and we were the sweet little blond twins that everyone cooed and gushed over. Our mother still dressed us the same, everywhere we went. Even around the house, our play clothes matched right down to our little fold-over socks. The thing that really amazed all the adults was how much we looked like our two older sisters, too. Clemson, our youngest sister, has a bigger gap in age between us and her, so she always escaped the fascinated stares.

One vile, awful-smelling man at our school took particular interest in the Farsay girls. Later, I found out he started with my oldest sister, Hannah. I never had the courage to ask her how far he took his sick, inappropriate attention with her, but I knew that knowledge was the birthplace of the deep resentment I had for her.

In my mind, if that janitor hadn't been so interested in her to begin with, he wouldn't have come for me. Several times while I was pinned beneath the grimy scumbag, he would talk about Hannah with sickening reverence. Like it wasn't bad enough he was molesting a child, he had to talk about his obsession with my older sister while doing it.

Scars. I had big, incurable, mental and emotional scars from years of abuse by a trusted adult at the school our parents shipped us off to, day in and day out. Like many child predators, he was clever with his threats. I was terrified to tell anyone what was happening, so I retreated inward and became very angry. Now, no one knew why I was so hateful and nasty, but there were hours of horrific details that gave me every right to feel the way I did.

All in all, I was doing damn good for what I was hiding. I had some trust issues, but not with humanity overall. Now, I could spot a creep from a mile away. There was a certain vibe that evil people put off, and my senses were finely tuned to it. Shockingly, many really bad people lived and worked among us every day. You just had to know when to turn and go in the other direction.

The area of my life suffering most was my personal relationships. There were a couple of trusted souls I could confide in, but I knew opening up to someone would just saddle them with a lot of crap they didn't want in their head. Plus, then there would always be the weight of my abuse hanging in the air between all our interactions, and I didn't want that either. So I continued to keep my shit exactly that. Mine.

This thing with Law was knocking me off my normal course, though. I couldn't quite put my finger on what or why, but I'd never let myself be triggered while being intimate with someone like I was the other night. And all we were doing was kissing!

If I could figure out what was so different about the guy, I was sure I could get a handle on the reaction. In the meantime, I tried to feel him out to see if I would need to address what happened at his house or if we'd sweep it under the rug and never mention it again. Of course, that was my preference, but I didn't know him well enough yet to know if he'd push for more of an explanation or not.

When the knock on my bedroom door was more insistent, I realized I'd been so lost in my thoughts, I'd completely ignored whoever wanted in the first time I'd heard it. Likely my mom, but she normally barged right in after knocking.

"Yeah?" I called out, and the door opened cautiously. Oddly, it was my dad in the doorway, but then I remembered it was the weekend.

"Morning, Shep. Sleep good?"

"Not bad, what's up?" We didn't make small talk these days, so his trepidation immediately set me on edge. The majority of people in this house had sleeping problems, so even asking how I slept was ridiculous. He knew damn well how I slept. With one eye open so the nightmares could only get half as bad.

If I hovered in that first stage of sleep, I didn't wake up screaming and cause panic through the whole house. It happened enough times when I was young that I trained myself to not sleep deeply. The drama after one of those episodes could be worse than the episode itself. Everyone got all beside themselves, and I ended up shutting down because I was consumed by guilt for upsetting everyone.

"Nothing really, just saying hi and seeing what you're up to today. Got plans?" While he restlessly shifted from foot to foot, my mom joined him just inside the door.

"Not at the moment. I need to get some laundry done, and I'm thinking of rearranging the room now that Maye moved in with the nutty professor," I replied and did my best to keep emotion out of my answer. The truth was I was devastated when my twin recently moved out. She was the closest friend I had, and I missed her more every day.

"Be kind," my dad reminded, but I didn't miss the little grin on his lips at the use of the nickname I'd been exercising since she brought the man around. In my heart, I was happy for her. Over the moon, as a matter of fact.

Maye was the most amazing human on the planet. Her heart was big and generous, and she authentically enjoyed sharing her joy with the people around her. Like our two older sisters, Hannah and Agatha, she fell in love quickly. Though her Prince Charming appeared in the shape of one of the professors at the college we attended.

Maye moved in with him a few weeks ago, and I was left here in the family home to fend for myself. When we were little girls, our mom always told us when you meet the right man, you'll know it. Personally, I never believed in that nonsense but now that it happened to Maye, I considered maybe I just hadn't met my Mr. Right yet.

My parents weren't thrilled with the whole relationship at first, but they seemed to be warming up to the man.

"I'm thinking about doing some fishing at the pier. Want to come along?" my dad asked, pulling me out of my thoughts and back to the conversation.

"I don't think so, Dad. Thanks for asking, though. Why don't you ask Clemmie? She likes that kind of thing." Honestly, no matter what activity he had up his sleeve for the day, I wouldn't be interested. Hanging out with him all day would make me miserable.

He had a way of getting me to open up to him without even knowing it, and I didn't have the energy to be on high alert all day. He didn't hide his disappointment at my rejection, but I wasn't in the mood to be guilted into spending my time making other people happy either.

Why didn't anyone spend their time worrying about my happiness?

"Can you shut the door on your way out? I think I'm going to try to sleep a bit more while the house is quiet," I asked, not being subtle about being finished with our little chat.

But instead, they came into the room farther and each took a seat at the foot of my bed.

Great.

"Can we talk?" he said while she studied me like a science project.

"Is that not what we've been doing?" I sassed back while sitting up against my headboard. My typical mouthy attitude always fell into place when I felt defensive. My dad tilted his head to the side and sighed. He had the lowest tolerance for my shit out of everyone.

"Your mother and I are worried about you, Shepperd."

"Can we not—"

"You've lost so much weight, honey, and we're worried. We wouldn't be doing our jobs as your parents if we sat by and watched you make yourself sick. We'd like to help you, but you have to let us." He finished with a heavy sigh as though those were the hardest sentences he'd ever spoken.

"Look," I began with very little patience. This conversation had gotten so old. "I'm fine. I eat every day."

But as if I had zero input here, they charged ahead.

My mom spoke up next. "We think maybe talking to someone, a professional, that specializes in eating disorders would be a good place to start."

"No."

"Listen. As long as you live under my roof," my dad said, falling back on his favorite threat since playing Mr. Nice Guy wasn't yielding the desired result, "you'll do what is asked of you. And this is in your best interest. Mom has been researching doctors in the area, and there are some of the finest in the world right here in Los Angeles."

"You guys, *no*," I said again and furiously squeezed my eyes shut to keep the damn tears that were welling up from spilling out. "Really, the answer is no. It's an unnecessary waste of your money. If I don't want to go, I won't. I'm an adult, and you can't make me." I crossed my arms over my chest in a defiant stance, truly coming off the furthest from an adult as possible.

My dad took a calming breath. "Actually, we can. As the people supporting you financially, we make the decisions. If you aren't going to take proper care of yourself, we'll do it for you. Your mother and I didn't want it to come to this. You understand that, right?"

"No!" I shouted then. How dare he play the *you forced our hand* bit with me. "I don't understand at all. I told you I'm fine, and I am! You both have plenty of other things to worry about. Take me off that list. I'm not going to a shrink."

He let out a slow, insufferable breath. "There's only one other option here, Shep."

"Oh?" I asked, ready to make any sort of concession. "And what is that?" Anything had to be better than seeing a shrink.

"There's an inpatient program that has an opening," he began, and I lost my shit.

Bolting up off my bed, the room spun while blinding black dots decimated my vision and made it impossible to gain my balance. I reached for the nearest piece of furniture so I didn't faceplant. I was livid that of all the times for that to happen, it was while they were watching so closely.

In a flash, my dad was on his feet too, gripping me by the elbows to steady me.

"Baby, this has to stop. You're going to kill yourself, and for what? Why? Who has put this notion in your head that looking like a damn skeleton is attractive or a healthy way to live?"

His plaintive tone nearly broke me. I knew what I was doing to myself. But I had it under complete control. But this... seeing that the way I abused myself was hurting other people... Well shit, that just added another layer to the fucked-up habits I'd developed. This was my issue, not theirs.

Frustrated, I tried to free myself from his hold, but he gripped tighter.

"You're hurting me," I said through clenched teeth as bile rose in my throat. "Let go," I gasped and barely registered the panic on his face as he witnessed the transition.

One moment, I was in my bedroom fighting for my free will, and the next I was mentally thrown back about twelve years to the dank janitor's room in my school.

"You're hurting me." I choked on vomit that came up while I fought to get away. This room at the far end of the building was dimly lit and damp. The smell of greasy rags and oil cans stung my nose and eyes.

I knew telling him that just excited him more by the way his breathing sped up. A wild, unforgivable plan lit his narrow eyes with an evil light and terrified me even more. Kicking and biting, scratching and pulling what little hair he had did nothing to make him stop. The one time I screamed for help, he choked me until the room went black. Never did that a second time.

"Shepperd!" my dad shouted, and I snapped out of the memory. My breathing was rapid and shallow, and I knew if I didn't calm the fuck down, I'd pass out. I skittered back from him until my back hit the narrow wall beside my bedroom door. Instinctively, my hands shot up in front of me to defend myself, but my parents weren't advancing toward me.

They were both frozen with confusion and panic to even think of physically consoling me at the moment. I was never more grateful for it because having to fend them off would possibly break me.

With his hands out front, mirroring my stance, my dad said, "Okay. Let's all calm down. Not sure what the hell just happened, but let's all just calm down."

"Shepperd," Mom said gently. "Honey, do you want to come sit down here? You look like you've seen a ghost," she finished and motioned to my bed. "Let's sit."

With jerky movements, I shook my head. "Just go," I choked out and then added in desperation, "please."

"No, honey. I don't want to leave you like this. Let's just sit for a few minutes."

Then I completely snapped. "I don't want to fucking sit! I want you two to get the fuck out of my room! Now!"

Oh, my dad didn't like that demand. At all. "Listen, young lady, I don't know what's going on here, but you're not calling the shots. You don't demand we leave a room in the house we pay for. Got it?"

Oh, I got it all right. If this was going to be his new battle cry every single time something didn't go the way he wanted it to, I'd put an end to the threats the only way I could.

"Fine. I'll leave. I'll move out. Then you won't have to worry about me and what I eat or don't eat. Or when I just want to be respected enough as a human to be afforded some fucking privacy!" I couldn't calm down while they confronted me. Like every other female in our house, my voice was downright thunderous when I was provoked.

"This isn't over," my father said quietly, likely just to have the last word.

"Nope. I'm pretty sure it is," I said, and the second they cleared the doorway, I slammed the thing shut behind them.

I flopped down onto my bed, face first, and cried for the next twenty minutes. I was so exhausted and so disappointed with myself when the tears finally stopped rushing out, I fell asleep.

It was close to noon when I woke up. My back was stiff, and my stomach was growling demands for something other than water or coffee. I didn't want to chance running into either of my parents in the kitchen, so I threw on my gym clothes, grabbed my keys and water bottle, and high-tailed it through the house out to the driveway. My dad's car was there, but Mom's was gone.

Damn, I must've really been sleeping, because normally, someone coming or going woke me.

I slid into my little car and started the engine. Immediately three different warning lights came on, and I thumped my head against the wheel.

One was gas. I could fix that. The other two were unfamiliar, and I had way too much pride and stubbornness to ask my dad to look at it for me. Especially after what had just transpired.

The gym wasn't too far from our house, so I thought I would hit the first food joint in between. I ended up ducking into a smoothie place and got one of my stand-by meal replacement combos. I was a sucker for anything mango and got an impressive brain freeze from the first gulp. As I squinted through the agony, I heard a familiar voice.

I popped my eyes open to see Law scooting into the booth across from me. That beautiful, sexy grin he wore did unreasonable things between my thighs. After a deep inhale as the stabbing head pain subsided, I pointed to my temple as though he would understand what was happening.

"Uh-oh. Either you're really unhappy to see me, or you're

on the tail end of a brain freeze. I love the drinks here and do the same thing every damn time." He laughed and reached across the table for my hand. "I really hope it's the second one," he said quietly.

Somehow the man even made a lack of confidence look good, and I couldn't hold back my smile. I was definitely happy to see him.

Alarmingly so as a matter of fact.

"Hey," I said shyly. "This is a pleasant surprise. On my way to work out." I thumbed over my shoulder in the direction of our gym. "But I needed some fuel first."

"What a coincidence," he said with a wink. "Same. I guess I shouldn't assume you want company here. Do you mind?"

After a little shake of my head, I said, "No, not at all. It's been a morning. I'll say that much." I rolled my eyes to punctuate the comment in case he didn't pick up on the sarcasm. "It's definitely great to see you. How did you sleep last night?"

"Not bad. Tossed and turned for a bit after we said goodnight. My mind was all over the place if I'm honest," he admitted and held my gaze for a few long beats after.

"Yeah?" I asked, deciding to tease him a bit. "Anything interesting? Do I know her?"

Law's smile widened, and he took both hands then. "She's pretty amazing actually. It's super new, you know? But I'm hoping to get to know her better. Can't stop thinking about her, and seriously, I'm crushing pretty hard."

"Oooh, lucky girl." Then I had no idea what came over me. Maybe I knew this guy could really be special—or maybe it was the bone-deep loneliness I was feeling before he sat down with me. I wasn't normally one to willingly discuss feelings but said to the incredibly handsome guy with no preamble, "I'm really sorry about the other night."

The moment the words came out, I wanted to rewind and handle the conversation differently. Namely, not have it at all. I liked Law's playful nature. He made me laugh whenever we spoke or spent time together. Now that I opened the door that little crack, would he want to dissect every problem I had one by one? Would I have to go into detailed explanation of every fucked-up thing I'd experienced as a little girl?

He squeezed my hands a little tighter and surprised me by lifting them to his lips and kissing my knuckles.

"There's no need to apologize. And one day"—he paused and met my transfixed stare—"when you feel like you trust me enough..."

I swallowed so hard it actually hurt.

"You can talk to me about what that was all about."

Uninvited tears filled my eyes, and it pissed me off, honestly. I wasn't a big crier, and that was the second time today that I was pulling a Hannah. Maybe my hormones were in overdrive preparing for a period. I hadn't had one of those in almost a year since my body weight dipped to an all-time low. But some months, my hormones still went through the motions anyway.

"Babe?" Law said, and I realized I'd been just staring at him for longer than normal. "Okay?"

I dipped my chin and raised it in two quick, jerky motions, and that was good enough for him.

He squeezed my hands one last time and said in a much lighter tone, "Good. Now, finish up so we can go. I'm ready to get to it."

He meant the gym, and I knew that, but a little naughty

voice in the back of my mind was shouting that I'd like to get to other things with him instead. The smile that spread across my lips gave away the mental conversation I was entertaining, and he grinned too.

"Oh, we'll get there too, baby," he assured with a devilish smile.

This man was big trouble. Judging by the way he lit up parts of my body that no one else ever had, I was deeply concerned about how irrationally behaved I would be willing to be with him. Definitely wouldn't be letting that slip out in a moment of weakness, though. I could barely handle his charm and charisma at their normal levels. If he knew he had me hooked, I'd be devoured whole.

Before I could answer his original question, the girl behind the counter shouted, "Sarah?" I stood to get the sandwich I ordered in a moment of weakness, and my companion was visibly confused. He put his hand out to stop me, probably thinking I heard her wrong, but that was the name I gave her when I'd ordered. Now I'd have to explain that weird little habit too.

These were just a few of the reasons I never had a long-term boyfriend. I had so many odd habits and rituals I went through in a day. Once I started spending more time with a person, they were exposed to them. I didn't like feeling defensive or having to explain the reasons I did things. Truly, it wasn't anyone's business. I was on the *whatever it takes to get through the day* approach to life. Most people didn't realize it because, on the outside, I looked like I was pretty squared away. Or at least I thought I did.

At the counter, I thanked the girl for my order and carefully placed the food in my bag. I didn't really want the

BLT anymore and didn't want to keep Law from his workout. I plastered on a fake smile and turned to where he was sitting only to turn right into his embrace.

Fuck this guy smelled good. Instinctually, I slid my arms around his waist and let him hug me for a moment. No harm in enjoying this feeling for a few beats. Over his shoulder, I could see the employee staring at us with envy and what could I say? I liked it.

That's right, sister. This one picked me.

Now I just had to stop acting like a nut all the time so I wouldn't scare him off.

CHAPTER FOUR

LAW

The gym was quickly losing its appeal. Holding Shepperd in my arms felt so right. Such a perfect physical fit. I loved the way she felt so small and fragile, but I knew she was anything but. Also, there was the minor problem that we were blocking people from their food orders, and I didn't miss the looks she already got when she walked up to the counter in the first place.

The woman was a head-turner. It was that simple. Even though her face was completely free of makeup, and her golden hair was piled in some messy nest on top of her head, she was every American boy's wet dream. An image of the woman in a pair of short cut-offs, sexy cowboy boots, and a vest with nothing else made my dick swell. She was my perfect image of the girl next door.

With my arm around her waist, I tugged her out of the way before the hangry patrons turned feral.

"As much as I want to keep holding you, there are some restless people behind you," I muttered beside her ear. At the same time, I was mentally celebrating that she didn't shy away from the public display of affection. I was a hands-on kind of guy. Always had been. Physical touch was the most satisfying way to express how I felt about someone, and that was our first public go at it and it felt really good. It felt right.

I wanted to check with her, though, to be sure I didn't overstep. "Thank you," I said quietly as we headed toward the exit.

"You're welcome?" she asked while smiling through the question. "For what, exactly?"

"It was presumptuous to just touch you like that in public. I'm grateful you didn't mind it happening," I explained with a grin.

She looked up at me for a long second and then treated me to the most beautiful, genuine smile. I'd seen the fake one she used as a weapon, and I'd seen the equally fake one she used as a shield. This smile was neither of those.

"No." She shook her head slowly. "I didn't mind that at all." An unexpected giggle burst out of her as we left the shop. "I think the girl behind the counter just had kittens, though."

I tilted my head with confusion, and she went on. "She was checking you out. Big time. When you hugged me, she was giving me the death stare over your shoulder. Quite entertaining, actually."

"What's this?" I teased. "Feeling territorial?" And why did that thrill me instead of freak me the fuck out like it normally did? Thoughts for another time.

"There are times being part of one gender or the other is downright embarrassing, you know?" Shepperd asked.

"What do you mean?"

"Sometimes the way women behave, especially to each other." She paused. After a shrug, she added, "I don't know, it makes me not want to be in the club I guess." She looked up at me again, and the vulnerability on her expression sucked the air out of my lungs.

Abruptly, I stopped walking and pulled her into my

embrace again. Yeah, I could totally get used to holding this little doll.

"Maybe we should start our own club?" I offered with a slow smile. "We're the only two members, so we make all the rules."

She leaned back in my arms to meet my gaze. "I like the way you think, mister." Her smile suddenly faded, and she looked away.

"What? What just happened?" I asked quietly.

"I just realized...I don't even know your last name. And my bad if you've told me because I definitely don't remember you doing so." She looked away again, and I squeezed her closer to my body.

"It's Masterson." I said it with the likeness to a mike drop. This was the part where things always got weird with new chicks. I watched as the facts lined up in her mind, and she swallowed so hard I saw her throat constrict.

"Masterson? Why does that sound familiar?"

She was either doing a great job covering her natural reaction or was one of the five people in the city who didn't know of my family's fortune and fame.

"Let's have the rest of this conversation over dinner tonight," I said as an invitation.

"Are you asking me out?" she asked with a mischievous smile. I really enjoyed this playful side of her. "Or telling me what to do?" By the way the temperature dropped around the woman, I knew what my answer better be if I had any hope of seeing her tonight.

"I'm sorry, where are my manners? My mother would smack me in the back of the head for acting so presumptuous." With formality completely unfitting of our surroundings I asked, "Would you do me the honor of your company at my home this evening? I'd be happy to cook, or we can order in," I offered with a sexy smile.

"I would love that. Any girl who turns down your cooking is a damn fool," she said, and I held my tongue regarding how little she ate the last time I cooked for her. If that was how she dug into a meal she enjoyed, I'd hate to see the effort she gave toward something unpalatable.

"Perfect!" I grabbed her hand to hold while we walked across the strip mall's parking lot to our gym. "Let's get a workout in and then hit the grocery store," I said, excited to spend the afternoon with her too. "If you're up for that?"

"I would love that, but I'll have to go home to clean up. I don't want to sit in my sweaty gym clothes all evening."

"You're welcome to shower at my place after the market. Up to you, but the offer stands. I don't want to be pushy here." I didn't mean a word of it. I totally wanted to be pushy. I wanted to tell her she was spending the day and night with me, and I wouldn't take no for an answer. Wisely, I held my tongue.

"Okay, let's see how it plays out. Fair enough?" she asked as I held the door open for her and followed her into the gym.

"Perfect. Now let's get this done. I'm on legs today," I said as we checked in by scanning our membership cards.

"I think I'm going to take it easy today. Maybe some cardio and floor work. I had a terrible night's sleep, again, and the morning from hell with my parents. If I didn't want to get out of that damn house so badly, I probably wouldn't even be here today," she rambled as we walked through the massive fitness center.

That was the most personal information she'd freely offered up—well, ever.

"Do you want to talk about it? Get it off your mind?" How did I get it through to her that I was a safe space? That she could vent to me as easily as she could tease me.

Time. It was probably the answer to a lot of things. Especially in a new relationship. I just needed to work harder at being patient. It had never been my strong suit, but over time I would prove that I was present and interested in what she had going on. Eventually, it would be the norm.

Well, look at me thinking mature thoughts.

Thoughts beyond the quickest route to get into a girl's panties. With age really did come wisdom. I also knew that telling her repeatedly that she could confide in me wouldn't make her trust me any sooner. That was a place she had to arrive on her own time.

I just had to continually remind myself to be a patient man. The reward would be worth it.

My workout went by in a flash knowing I'd have my hands on her again afterward. Every time I searched the weight room space for her, I'd find those incredible blue eyes watching me too. It reminded me of the months we spent playing I Spy with each other before I finally asked her to hang out. During those weeks, seeing her in the tiny little clothes she wore to work out was the highlight of my existence. I lost count of the number of times I had to jerk off thinking about her little ass in those neon-green shorts. Definitely my favorite of all the ones she wore.

We left the gym and headed to our cars. While working out, I came up with a simple menu for dinner and a mental list of things I needed to pick up. We agreed on stopping at the grocery store on the route to my house, and I couldn't resist tugging her close before we parted ways to drive our separate cars.

"I'm sweaty," she said. "Fair warning."

Twelve typical guy comments about how I'd like to make her sweat flashed through my mind before I spit out, "I don't mind." So, fine, not my smoothest line of the bunch, but I was a little scrambled by the woman.

I was thankful she had pulled on a loose pair of joggers before we left the gym. If she strutted around the market in those little shorts the way she did the gym, I'd be in a fistfight before we made it out of the produce aisle.

We chatted as we walked the aisles, adding items to the cart as we went.

"So what's the longest relationship you've been in?" I asked while she was reading the label on a box of crackers. "And what are you looking for? Do you have food allergies?"

"No, I can eat pretty much anything. I was looking to see how many carbs were in a serving. I hate working out, believe it or not." She paused a moment and looked up from the package to catalog my reaction to that statement. "If I have to spend all that time doing something I don't love, I'll be damned if I'm going to undo the hard work with a bad food choice."

"Fair enough." It was just a hunch, but I assumed she wasn't looking for the typical automatic response about not having to watch her weight.

Although, when she finally finished examining every detail on the damn box, she put the crackers back on the shelf and started off down the aisle. I grabbed the box she just replaced and tossed it in the cart.

She looked back with a frown and pointed to the cart. "I decided against those."

"Do you mind if I get them? They look good. Love salty

snacks."

She shrugged and started walking again. "What's the longest relationship you've been in?" she asked instead of answering the question herself.

After thinking for a moment I said, "Probably my high school sweetheart. We were together over a year, but since then nothing more than a few months. Maybe four, tops. What about you?"

"I've never really dated the same guy for long. A few dates and I cut bait typically."

"So am I defying the odds here?" I asked, making it obvious with my expression that I was teasing.

She smiled then too. "Definitely an outlier."

We finished getting what we needed plus two bottles of wine. She put on an adorable pout when I refused to let her pay. If the girl had a clue how much money I had, she'd know how ridiculous she was being. Instead of explaining things in the middle of the checkout line, I stole a quick kiss from her irresistible lips and guided her toward the door with my free hand. The large reusable bag we brought in from my trunk was full and slung over my opposite shoulder.

"At least let me carry something, then," she insisted, and I shook my head.

"Darling, this bag weighs more than you do, you'd topple right over," I said playfully, but she flashed a glare my way. Luckily, it was gone as soon as it appeared, but I wanted to smack my forehead for saying something so dumb. I didn't want her to think I was bagging on her weight, so I rambled on.

"Plus, my mother raised us to be gentlemen. She'd smack me upside the head if I did something so rude."

As we strolled to our cars, she asked, "So you grew up

with nine other kids in the house. What was that like? It must have been chaos at times." She smiled as though imagining the circus that was my family home.

"There were times it was pretty crazy. But there's a big span of years between the ten of us, so some of my siblings were already out on their own when the youngest few were born." The usual smile that took over my face when I spoke about my brothers and sisters appeared.

"Do you all get together regularly?" Shepperd asked as I loaded the bag in my trunk.

"For holidays at least. My mom insists we all spend Christmas at the family's place up north and now that my oldest sister and my brother Jake have daughters, I'm sure she'll go all out."

Shepperd muttered to herself, "Jake Masterson... Why does that sound so familiar?"

"He's a bigshot architect here in town. He actually uses Jacob Cole for his work, though."

"He designed that new building for Sebastian Shark, right? The one downtown?"

"He sure did. He's busier than ever now that the project has wrapped up and everyone sees how talented he is. How do you know about Shark?"

She dismissed my question with a wave of her hand. "Kind of a long story. But that's so cool, and that explains why your name sounded so familiar."

I closed the trunk and pulled her close to me. "Okay, you want to follow me to my place or are you headed home first?"

"I think I'll take you up on the shower offer when we get there. If you're still good with that plan."

"Works for me," I replied with a quick peck. "See you in

a few minutes." I released her before she felt the way my body responded to holding her close combined with mental images of her in my shower—or, even better, joining her there.

We worked together to put the groceries away, and I couldn't help but notice the way we moved around my kitchen with ease. Shepperd was smart and independent and wasn't the kind of girl who needed explicit instructions on every task.

I asked her to deal with the produce while I got us drinks, and she set about the task without another question. After handing her a gin and tonic and watching with rapt fascination as she took the first sip, I pressed her against the island and kissed her. Her lips tasted crisp from the drink, and I pushed in for more.

When we parted, I held her close and drowned in the depth of her blue eyes. "I like you here. In my home. It feels good," I admitted and hoped it wasn't too much. If the truth scared her, I'd dial it back, but something about this woman made me want to open my soul for her to see all its parts.

"Mmmm, I think you're right. It feels really nice to be here with you," she replied. "Thank you for inviting me over."

I didn't really have more to offer to the conversation, but I was quickly getting addicted to kissing her. Touching her.

We kissed a little more before she pulled away and said, "Will you direct me to the shower? I'll feel so much better once I've freshened up."

After I got her set up in one of the guest bathrooms, I went back to the kitchen to marinate the meat we were having for dinner. The recipe was simple to throw together and I had just returned the meat to the refrigerator to tenderize when I sensed Shepperd behind me. She moved like a quiet little mouse, so I didn't hear her, but I felt her energy in the room before I turned around.

"How was it?" I asked and nearly stuttered on the words when I saw her. Her hair was damp and in a long, loose braid over one shoulder. Her milky skin was fresh and dewy, and she looked so incredibly young. I had laid out an old concert T-shirt that was soft and worn and a pair of flannel pajama bottoms that completely swallowed her tiny frame.

"Showers are one of my favorite things. I could stand there for a full hour and not even realize how much time passed. And that shower in there..." She thumbed over her shoulder toward the ensuite she used. "Well, that was magnificent. Are all your bedrooms and bathrooms that luxurious?"

"Would you like a tour?" I asked and immediately wondered if getting her near my own bed would be a mistake. At the very least, it would be a monumental test of my will.

But when she let out a delighted little squeal, the plan was solidified. Playfully, I offered my bent arm for her to clasp like we were setting off on a leisurely stroll.

I placed my hand on top of hers where her delicate fingers clutched the crook of my arm. She had already seen the kitchen and living room, so I guided her toward the master suite. Beating down every thought of sweeping her into my arms and stalking down that same hallway, I rambled nervously about the art I'd hung recently and the woman who created the lively piece.

Shep stopped to stare at the painting for a long moment but didn't say a word. Finally, I asked her what she was thinking while studying the image. The breath was knocked from my lungs when she turned to me, quickly dashing tears from her cheeks.

"It's so...so...incredible. There are so many things to look at individually, like here"—she motioned to a section of the art—"and here. But then it's something completely different when you look at it as a whole. You know?" She looked back and forth between the painting and me and waited for my response.

"I know exactly what you mean. That's what I loved so much about it too. From the first moment I saw it in the gallery. And now, every time I look at it, I swear I find a new detail to marvel at. She's really a gifted painter."

"Wow. I'll say. There's so much emotion captured here." She stared at the painting again and finally asked, "Do you have other pieces by this same artist?"

"No, this was my first of hers. But now that I know how talented she is, I will definitely be looking for others. As you've probably noticed, I have a lot of wall space to fill."

We continued through the hall and into my bedroom. I made my bed every morning out of habit from childhood. It was always something my mother insisted we did ourselves. We had plenty of staff in our home, but she encouraged us to take pride in our own spaces. The message reached home for some of us, but a few of my siblings were complete slobs. Now, they had their own homes and armies of help to clean up after their careless habits. I just couldn't live that way.

"I appreciate how tidy you are," Shepperd said with a little sly smile. "This space is so calming and relaxing. I think I can picture you in here after a long day, just relaxing and thinking."

"You're exactly right. This is where I go right when I come home. I want to get some sort of sofa or something for over here"—I motioned to the empty corner of the room—"but I'm having a hard time finding just what I want."

"Well, it may be forward of me to offer this, but if you ever want company or a second opinion while furniture shopping, I love decorating. Well, at least in my mind I do." She gave a sweet little shrug like she was embarrassed about what she had so honestly offered.

I turned to her and pulled her up against my body with two hands on her hips. The woman was so small, I could move her around with little effort.

"I would love that," I said sincerely. But now, holding her so close, the last thing I was thinking about was furniture shopping. I bent over her slowly, making sure she didn't get spooked. That last episode was still too fresh in my mind.

"I really want to kiss you," I said, my voice low and resonant.

Her huge, beguiling eyes gave me permission to dip closer. I continued the slow advance until our hungry lips met. This woman was magic and tumult and measured energy in an entrancing little package. How were so many big emotions contained in such a small body?

Unleashing her passion and spirit quickly became my end goal. I knew in the depths of my soul, and possibly my heart, that Shepperd Farsay had so much more to give of herself...if she would just let down her guard and let me see all of her.

In my arms, her body relaxed in increments. Slowly, she melted into me and surely felt my mounting desire now pressed between us. But I continued to remind myself to go slowly and carefully. Respectfully. I could be a patient man when focused and motivated, and she deserved those things from me. From everyone, really, and I had a distinct feeling she wasn't getting many of her emotional needs met by the other people in her life.

That was okay. I could be the things she needed. There

was a moment while we kissed that I wondered where all these noble, considerate thoughts were coming from. I was a pretty typical guy usually. Satisfaction, gratification, and release were the main objectives of my actions and efforts. But in that uncharacteristic moment, Shepperd's tentative touch made me want to do better. Be better.

We kissed for a few minutes, and my body grew restless. I wanted to playfully scoop her into my arms and stalk toward the bed. There were a million fantasies playing out in my busy mind until I finally broke our connection.

"Christ, girl," I rasped with my forehead pressed to hers. "We need to relax for a minute or I'm going to do something stupid again."

She stared up at me for a long moment while clutching my hands in hers.

"Can we talk about that?" She motioned through the air in a random gesture, and I grinned. I liked that I was becoming familiar with her little quirks, and adding to her verbal dialogue with quick, choppy hand motions was my favorite. "About what happened the other night?"

"I would like that. Want to sit in here or go back out to the living room?"

"Here is fine. I like being in your space. Probably more than I should."

"I like having you here too," I replied, hoping it would put her at ease to know the feeling was mutual. "Probably more than I should."

We sat on the edge of the bed at first, but then I scooted back against the mountain of throw pillows against the headboard. "Will you sit with me here?" I gestured for her to nestle between my legs. My arms encircled her slight frame, and it felt so good...so right to protect her that way.

"How's that? You comfortable?"

"Mmmm, so comfortable. I could fall asleep right here I think." She rubbed her nose into my chest like a little kitty, and I smiled.

"I would like that very much," I said but left out the rest of what I was thinking. How perfect the position would be after fucking her senseless while we enjoyed the afterglow of our passion. It was all right there in the air between us. I couldn't be the only one feeling the electricity between our bodies, but we needed to have that conversation.

We lay for a few minutes while she gathered her thoughts and finally spoke just as I was going to say something silly to break the tension that was building.

"I'm going to start by apologizing for the other night. Mostly for the way I handled the situation. It was immature of me to just bolt out of here the way I did. I was so worried I'd messed things up between us. Already."

"Do you prefer to get it all out, and then I comment, or would it be better to go back and forth as you say what you need to say? Because I already want to tell you that you have nothing to apologize for. I felt like maybe I was too pushy that night, and you just weren't on the same page or ready to be physical."

She twisted between my thighs to look up at me. "You are one of the most considerate men I've ever met. You weren't pushy at all. And I like this back and forth"—she waved between our chests with a slim hand—"as you described it. Feels more like a conversation and not a presentation."

"Good. Me too. I just have to remind myself not to bogart the conversation as I tend to do." I gave her a quick wink so she knew the self-deprecation was lighthearted and not a fishing expedition for her to stroke my ego.

"I'll keep you in line, don't worry," she answered with a playful sparkle in her deep-blue eyes.

"Fair enough." I smiled and kissed the top of her head.

She took another deep breath, and even if she hadn't done that again, the stiffness in her frame told me just how uncomfortable she was. Based on her reaction the other night, whatever she was about to share with me wouldn't be easy.

"Take your time," I encouraged gently.

"Some...bad stuff happened to me when I was a little girl. Bad, bad stuff." She shook her head and then rubbed her forehead.

I wanted to smile at the gesture because I did the exact same thing when stressed, but now wasn't the time to be smiling.

"I don't want to burden you with the details," she said, "but let's just say, it's made me a little jumpier than some."

"Thank you for sharing that with me." I wanted to dive deeper into what happened but knew that was for her to share at her own pace. "Please don't consider anything you tell me a burden. I feel honored that you confided in me."

"Law, you have to understand it's been a while since I've met someone that I've felt a connection with. Most of the guys I've gone out with have been pretty casual hookups—nothing more. I just haven't felt like they'd understand what having a history like mine can do in here." She tapped her temple a few times before saying, "Nor would they want to put in the time and effort to work through the damage." She threw her hands up between us as if to stop me from speaking even though I was in full listener mode.

She went from the defensive posture to cradling her face in her palms in the next second. I just waited for her to work through it all.

"I guess that makes me sound like a slut, that I just hook up with every guy I meet, and that's not how it's been. Honestly."

"I wasn't thinking anything close to that, darling. Please continue," I said after taking her hands in mine so she couldn't hide her beautiful face while we spoke. This raw, honest version was even more breathtaking than her usual mien.

"So, while I don't have trouble with the straight-up physical part of being with a guy, when my head starts getting involved—that's when things can go sideways. I feel vulnerable I guess?" She looked at me for understanding, and I nodded that I was following. "That's when I guess I lose that tight grip I normally have on things. Because my head wants to think more than the normal talk track that reassures me it's all okay."

She paused for only a second before adding, "I'm not sure if that even makes sense. The way I'm explaining it. Or trying to explain it, I guess." She forced a laugh and a smile that stabbed me in the chest.

I gave her a little squeeze against my body until she relaxed a bit. If my physical presence could make her feel safe instead of panicked, we'd both be happy campers. I was a touchy person when I had a woman to call my own. Now, I almost held my breath while waiting for her to go on. If she told me she didn't like being touched outside of the bedroom, it would be a real letdown.

"It makes perfect sense. Are there certain things that trigger panic like the other night? Things that you know? Or does it happen randomly?"

"Definitely certain things set me off all the time. Once

and a while, though, something will trigger me that never has before. Those are really hard to recover from, because it's like, just when I think I have a handle on it all, and that fucker has stolen all he will ever take from me, he wins again."

"Can I ask, was this person charged or prosecuted? Are you in danger?" I wouldn't hesitate to fuck someone up who hurt women—and especially little girls. I felt nearly homicidal at the thought of her being abused.

"No," she said quietly and couldn't hold my gaze. I'd be damned if she'd be ashamed on top of it all. At least if I could help it. She continued before I could say anything, though. "He was a seasoned predator. He knew just how to threaten me so that I never told anyone. I was terrified he'd hurt my family. And I was a child, so I didn't understand that he was manipulating me."

Instinctually, I pulled her into my arms. I wanted to comfort her and erase the pain from the bastard who hurt her. While I cradled her in my lap, I pressed my lips to the side of her head. With my face buried in her silky hair, I quietly said, "I'm so sorry you went through what you did. If I could take it away, I would, baby."

I could feel her facial expression change beneath my lips. "Thank you. That's very sweet." The response seemed so trained that it irritated me rather than comforted me.

Again, though, this wasn't about me. I had to keep reminding myself of that, and somewhere in the back of my busy mind, another self-observation was filed away. How had I become so selfish?

"Shepperd, look at me. Please."

It took longer than I would've preferred, but she finally turned in my arms to meet my waiting attention.

"Thank you for sharing that with me. I'm serious right now. I'm not trying to placate you or give you some verbal pat on the head and send you on your way. I want to know all there is to know about you. I want to be a person you're comfortable enough with to share your feelings. All of them."

I stopped there because I felt precariously close to making an ass out of myself. I didn't know where all that just came from. I never said stuff like that to a woman. It wasn't something I was interested in. But things about this girl were burrowing deep into my psyche in ways I hadn't experienced before. And the craziest part of all of it? I liked it.

CHAPTER FIVE

SHEPPERD

God, I hoped I didn't just fuck everything up by telling him all that. Not that I even scratched the surface of my issues. But now, Law had this look in his soulful eyes that I couldn't make sense of. Was that pity? The last thing I wanted was pity. Definitely something was different between us now and I had to think that was reasonable given what I just shared with him. But had it been a mistake?

My first inclination was to bolt. To flee the scene and reassess the situation from a safe space. But I saw where that got me the other night, and I didn't want to go back there again. I was truly scared I had driven the man away before we had a chance to explore what could grow between us.

"Don't..." I started to say but pulled myself back immediately when I heard the tone in my voice. "Sorry," I said much quieter. Much kinder.

"Don't what?" he asked, thankfully absent of the defensiveness I expected. My own voice would've held that inflection if I were in his shoes.

"I'm sorry. That was a knee-jerk response to what I'm seeing here," I explained, drawing a circle in the air a few inches in front of his face. "I'm trying to get better at not reacting like that. At least with you," I finished with a shy smile. This gentle openness was harder than the biting, acidic, defensive style I usually communicated with.

"Can I tell you something about my family?" he asked, and I couldn't make sense of why he asked permission first.

"Ooohhhkaayy..." I drew out with a head tilt, not understanding where we were going with the conversation.

"It will make more sense in a minute," he explained. "I didn't want to just blurt out something about me after you shared such personal information. I don't want it to come across as me minimizing your experiences or that I'm only capable of talking about myself."

I was definitely picking up a pattern. The man had either been accused of being self-centered and didn't like it, or he truly recognized a personality flaw and was trying to improve.

With focused sincerity, I said, "In that case, yes, please. I'd love to get to know things about your family and your life."

"I'm one of ten children. I know I've told you that before. My oldest sister, Cecile, was married for a few years and has a little girl. Stella."

His eyes danced with the kind of love that could make my ovaries swell if I allowed the energy to penetrate my guard. I already knew he adored this child before he said another word. I could feel his emotions in the air around him like warm, rich cake batter. The atmosphere was comforting, safe, and filled with familial loyalty.

"I have a feeling Miss Stella is one spoiled little lady."

Law's features quickly changed to abashed. As predicted, my lower abdomen clenched with a hormonal surge. Christ, this guy was dangerous for my carefully controlled existence.

"Guilty. We all are. But she's an angel. Honestly, I know everyone thinks their kid or relative is the cutest thing ever, but she really is. She has this mop of bright-red hair and little chubby cheeks you just want to take a bite of. My brother Jake has a daughter the same age, but that's a story for another day. We're all still getting to know her."

"Do you have pictures?" I asked, sitting forward a bit, but he quickly closed his arms tighter around my waist.

"Where do you think you're going?" he teased.

"I want to see them. I assumed you'd fish your phone out and show me."

"In a second. I want to tell you the rest, and I'm enjoying holding you like this too much to move." His voice turned low and serious on that last part. By the way it suddenly became hard to swallow or even take a full breath, it was like he was staring directly into my soul.

Oooh, serious Law was even sexier than playful Law. While I usually avoided intense conversation at almost any cost, this one was worth engaging in. Not sure how I felt so confident about that, but my gut was rarely wrong.

He went through the sad details of Stella's abuse, and I listened as open-mindedly as I could. Oftentimes, when I shared even a hint of my history with someone, they did exactly what Law was doing. By sharing their own experiences, people assumed we instantly had some sort of connection or bond, and they were automatically qualified as a person I could trust and open up to. Not always the case. Also, if I told a person about my past, which I rarely did, the best thing they could do was listen and be compassionate. But for some reason, this seemed to be the go-to response.

Hearing about another victim suffering out in the world didn't make me feel united with them. It made me angry. Angry that another person was robbed of joy and innocence by a predator.

Because I knew how that felt. Once something like that happened, you never really got over it. Every person looked suspicious or threatening, every situation looked like a trap.

Law's intentions were pure, though. Based on what I knew about the guy so far, in his heart, he told me this information for the right reasons. He wasn't trying to take over the conversation or shift the focus to him, or Stella. He was just trying to bond with me through a painful experience.

Normally, I would've ended this type of conversation after the first few lines, but I saw the amount of love he had for this child. Instead of feeling frustrated like I normally did, I wanted to comfort him in return. I wanted to give him the reaction I wished for on the rare occasion I shared my pain with someone.

Sitting up taller on his lap, I wrapped both arms around his neck and pressed my body into his. I squeezed him close to me, and we breathed together for a long moment.

Finally, I pulled back. "I'm sorry you and your family know what that kind of pain and betrayal feels like. It breaks my heart every time I hear about another person being taken advantage of by someone who should have loved them or cared for them."

"You're so brave," he said into my hair. I had to consciously hold in my scoff. "I can feel the way your body just tensed in my arms that you want to refute that."

Wow. The man saw things most people completely missed. Or if they did see my reaction to their comments, they ignored them and plowed ahead with their own agendas.

A soft smile played at my lips instead. "You're very observant."

"I can be. When something matters, or rather, someone matters. I want to learn all I can about that person." He paused for a moment, and I could only guess he was trying to come up with a tactful way to ask something. That assumption was confirmed when he finally spoke again.

"I think you're brave because you've been dealing with the trauma alone. And you go out in public every day, face the world, strangers...hell, maybe even the bastard who hurt you, and you haven't told anyone what happened." He maneuvered his body so we were looking directly into each other's eyes again. "That's incredibly brave, Shepperd."

Before he even finished, I was shaking my head. He had it all so backwards. How could he not see that?

"I'm not brave, Law. I'm a coward. Instead of dealing with what happened, I bolt. I've been running for so long, I'm out of places to hide."

"You don't have to hide from me. And whenever you want to hide from the rest of the world, run to me. Okay?" He held my gaze until I dipped my chin in agreement.

"Do you see the guy still?" he finally asked quietly.

"No, it's been years," I said, always careful with the amount of information I released.

"An old neighbor? Distant relative?" he fired one after the other.

Why did he need to know? It's not like it would change anything.

"No. No one like that."

He just stared at me, seeming to encourage me to tell him without asking again.

And for some reason, I wanted to tell him. Maybe it would feel good to let the secret out. It's not like he'd go down to my old school and find the guy. It was my understanding he'd died years ago.

"It was a janitor at my school. I think he molested my oldest sister, too," I blurted and waited for the earth to open up and swallow me. For so long I was terrified to say the words out loud. Convinced something tragic would happen when I released my truth. Now that I had, and literally nothing changed, I was incensed. There was no monumental sense of relief, just stifling heavy air between us. I tried to bolt, and damn the guy for already having my number. He wrapped his arms around my waist a little tighter and just stared.

"What?" I bit, pissed that he wouldn't let me stand.

His voice was gentle and soothing when he said, "Calm down, darling. I'm right here. Nothing's changed. I'm still right here."

I tried to stand again, and that time, he released his hold on me. I shot to my feet, stumbling from the extra force I used. Law was on his feet in a second steadying me with large, confident hands on my hips.

"Was that the first time you told anyone? Ever?"

I couldn't speak. I'd already said enough anyway. I looked down at my feet and studied the pattern on my socks.

"Shep?"

Finally, I just nodded. Tears were fighting to break free and backflowing into my throat. I knew if I used my voice, it would be like turning a dam's release valve, and it would be hours before I felt in control again.

Without another word, Law stepped closer and pulled me into his arms. He didn't need me to explain or embellish, he was content with what I already shared. Being in his arms felt so good. So safe and comforting. Quickly the peace I felt turned into exhaustion, and I could barely stay on my feet.

"Hey, hey?" He ducked down to be at eye level. "What's going on? Do you want to lie down? Are you okay?"

Again, I just nodded, and then a third time. He guided me to the bed and stood at the side while I climbed onto the mattress. Watching him through half-closed eyes, I could see the indecisiveness in his posture but couldn't muster the strength to alleviate it.

Finally, he asked, "Can I lie down with you? Hold you more?"

Seeing this normally confident, dominant man so unsure of himself turned me on more than hearing him direct me. He showed me vulnerability, and I found it extremely attractive. Made him more real and attainable. Up until that point, I went back and forth trying to figure out what the man saw in me. What could a broken, screwed-up me offer a put-together, confident man like him?

"I would like that," I mumbled, and he climbed onto his bed and fit his body against mine. He draped his long arm over my hip and clutched my hand in his. Within minutes we were both sound asleep.

Hours later I woke, completely disoriented. The room was lit only by faint lights that were built into the electrical outlets. Law had rolled onto his back in sleep, so just one side of my body was warm where we pressed together. The opposite side had the chill of the still air in the quiet room. My stirring woke him almost instantly.

"I'm sorry," I rushed out and stuttered as he turned toward me and wrapped me in his arms. The man was so handsome it was arresting. In the dimly lit room, the hard angles of his face were more pronounced where shadows played with his

Adonis-like geometry.

"What are you apologizing for? This is my idea of heaven right here." He grinned and crushed me closer. All I could manage in reply was a blank stare.

"Heaven?"

"Waking up and you're still here," he explained while his smile spread to my lips too.

He kissed me softly. At first, anyway. But now that we both had rested a bit and maybe felt a little bolder in the darkened room, the intensity of our connection ramped up quickly. He swept into my mouth with his tongue, and a husky whimper escaped when I parted more for his exploration.

There was a brief moment when my brain tried to ruin things and overanalyze what he might think of the sound I made. But as though he sensed me disengaging, Law ground his erection into my thigh, and I was instantly relieved to see—or feel, rather—that he enjoyed my unedited reaction.

We made out like teenagers for about twenty minutes, then I breathlessly pulled back. "Okay, Danger. You're earning your nickname with scary precision."

He laughed, and I was instantly aroused. I'm not sure I'd ever been turned on by a guy's laugh before, but Law's was so genuine and pure. It shot straight to my pussy and reverberated there. In an effort to not embarrass myself by giving in to pure desire and mounting him, I squeezed my eyes shut to block out the onslaught of stimulation.

"What's wrong?" he asked, fading from playful to serious with one question.

"My God, nothing," I sighed with a grin, eyes still closed. "Nothing at all. I can't even remember the last time I said that and meant it."

"Why are you squeezing your eyes shut like that?"

So I gave it to him. I just blurted out what I was feeling like I was overturning a wheelbarrow filled with thoughts and words right at his feet.

"It's hard to look at you," I word-vomited. "You're so good-looking."

He rolled his eyes, and I poked him in the abdomen.

"I'm not joking," I continued. "I'm being boldly honest. Looking at you makes my body feel ways." I paused there, trying to put words to the sensations but came up short. "I'm not sure what's even happening. It's terrifying and exhilarating at the same time."

Immediately I wanted to burrow under the sumptuous bedding and hide from all the thoughts I had just admitted.

His stillness and attentiveness were more unnerving than his usual animated feedback. Instead of saying anything to break the excruciating silence, he moved closer, then closer still until our mouths were less than an inch apart.

"Can I kiss you again? I was rather enjoying that," he asked in a voice so heavy with intention I had to swallow before my throat would cooperate and produce sound.

"Yes. Please do." I smiled and willed my erratically beating heart to calm the fuck down. My eyes darted from feature to feature on his beautiful face and tried to catalog the details for later.

Law moved above me while carefully watching my reaction. "Will it be too much if I lie on top of you? I want to feel you beneath me more than I can remember ever wanting something." Quickly he tacked on, "But I don't want to scare you, or trigger you. You have to help me here until we know each other better." A devilish smile spread from one corner of his mouth.

"It's fine if you do that. Lie on me."

So he did, and I took a few moments to revel in the feeling. His body weight pressing me deeper into the mattress, the warmth coming from his skin. Everything about the scene was incredible. As long as I stayed engaged with what was going on and didn't let my mind wander, things would be fine. Better than fine.

Law kissed across my jaw to the spot beneath my ear. I felt his measured breaths and his slick tongue as he lapped at my skin.

"You smell so good. I don't know what perfume you wear, but it drives me crazy. It suits you perfectly."

"Mmmm, feels so good," I hummed and stretched my neck to the side to let him explore. He moved my hair to the pillow above my head while keeping eye contact the entire time.

"I'm one lucky man," he said and gave his head a little shake.

"Mmmm," I moaned again when he returned his attention back to my neck.

He sucked my skin a bit harder as he made a path downward.

"I think I'm the lucky one here," I finally said.

He kissed down my throat to the hollow between my collar bones and spent some time nuzzling in the dip.

I spread my legs a little more, and he settled into the space I created. His erection was impossible to miss in that position, and he rocked into me a couple times as if testing the waters to see if I would deny him. If he kept up that motion, I'd take my own pants down and insist he do it properly.

To show him I was present and agreeable to what was

happening, I wrapped my legs around his hips and held his body to mine.

A low groan worked up his throat and vibrated against my own while he continued feasting on my skin.

He slid his hand under the hem of my shirt, and I arched into his palm. The movement sent a clear message that I was doing fine with what was going on, so he boldly went right for my breast beneath the fabric. I rolled my eyes back when he gave my stiff nipple a little flick, so he did it again.

"Sit up for a sec?" he asked while pulling his body back to give me room to accommodate his request.

I sat up, and he had my shirt off and tossed over his shoulder with a wicked grin.

"That's better." He stretched his arms behind my back to release my bra. He tossed that off the bed too and sat back on his heels to take me in.

I leaned back on bent elbows and watched his expression. The man looked like he was mentally mapping out a plan of where to touch but couldn't decide where to start. I cupped my breasts in my hands and gave them a gentle squeeze before pushing them toward the center in offering.

"You look like a little boy on Christmas morning."

He chuckled. "Apparently I've been very good this year, then. Fuck me," he said, shaking his head. "You're so stunning. I can't stop staring. Every single thing about you is perfect."

I was positive no one had ever said those words to me in my entire life. Yes, people told me I was pretty. Yes, people always commented about my long blond hair. But that's where the love usually stopped. Next I would usually hear that I needed to eat more, that you could see my bones right under my skin, or worse—what I always suspected in my insecure thoughts—

the comparisons between my older sisters or my twin and me. Some people were rude enough to vocalize the thoughts while the rest silently made their lists of my shortcomings.

But I forced myself to stay present with Law. So far, he wasn't like the other guys I'd fooled around with. If he said he appreciated something, he meant it. He was confident in the way he moved, and he gave me an immeasurable sense of security.

When I snapped out of my own thoughts and reengaged in the moment, his mouth was exploring the underside of my breast, where he sucked particularly hard on my delicate skin. Yeah, that was definitely going to leave a mark, and I secretly rejoiced.

"Fuck!" I yipped when he sunk his teeth into my body. "Feels so good," I preached straight up to the ceiling above me. "God, yes."

"You like that?" he asked, pulling back from his busy work.

"Yes. Definitely," I panted.

My sexy man got right back to work, and by the time he was done and we were both glassy-eyed and panting, I had a chain of bite marks from one breast to the other.

"No bathing suit for you for a few days," he chuckled while surveying the bruises. He ran his finger from one to the other and looked very pleased with himself. Blatantly, he rubbed the bulge at his crotch and made a strangled sort of moan.

"Need some help there?" I said as seductively as possible, and I saw immediately how my question surprised him.

"I don't want to push my good fortune by going too fast," he said, palming his dick the whole time. "I may need to handle this, though, or I'm going to go blind."

I burst out laughing. I hadn't heard that ridiculous wives'

tale in a long time. His boyish humor was so charming. So many things about the man were charming. Again, the word danger flashed in my mind. This time it seemed more like a promise than a warning, though, and I was feeling exceptionally bold.

Bold and horny.

"Do you have condoms here?" I asked rather than beating around the bush. I wanted it. He wanted it. I was completely ready to just go for it.

"I do." He carefully studied my face. "Are you sure? Maybe we should wait?"

I was almost shocked by the suggestion, and honestly, I was a little hurt. Quickly embarrassment rushed in like a flash flood. Had I really misread the situation? I was certain we were on the same page.

Law crawled back up my body until our noses bumped. While holding my gaze, he said, "I don't want to screw this up. I'd rather wait until you're one hundred percent ready so we both have a great experience."

"I'm one hundred percent ready right now," I protested. Any more of this talk, though, and I'd retreat. I had my dignity still, and I certainly wouldn't beg him to fuck me. Not in that way at least. "But if you're not, then that's cool. Seriously, it's fine."

I scanned the surrounding area on the bed for my discarded clothes. I was feeling more and more vulnerable by the second and wanted to cover my body. To shield myself from his assessing stare.

"Stop." His voice was stern and strong and undeniably in control.

I stopped shuffling through the bedding and looked up at him. "What?" I snapped when he didn't say more. "I'm sorry

I misread what was going on," I stammered while trying to control my temper. I was embarrassed now, and my go-to demeanor was bitch.

"Hey," he said quietly and somehow still seductive. "I wasn't saying no. I just don't want to screw things up here. You matter too much."

"Well, I feel like an idiot. Like I was being too pushy. I'm sorry."

"Don't apologize." He positioned himself so his back was against the headboard. "Here, come lie in my arms."

"Maybe I should just get going," I offered instead, and he jacked up to sit straighter.

"Shepperd. Come on. We've been having such a great time. Please don't leave." He sounded so earnest, it pulled me out of my mental tailspin. "Please don't."

The voice inside was telling me—no, more like yelling at me not to screw this up. I needed to swallow my embarrassment and stay. Work through it. No relationship was always smooth sailing. Or perfect synchronization all the time. That wasn't realistic. If I wanted to really give this thing between us a shot, some work may have to be put into it now and then. Especially in the beginning.

My shoulders dropped as low as they could go, and I sighed. I promised myself I wouldn't cry again as I crawled back onto the bed and into his waiting embrace.

"I'm sorry," I muttered into his firm chest. "I'm such a fucking idiot."

Abruptly he pulled back and stared at me. After much too long for my comfort, he said, "Don't say things like that about yourself. I don't like it. In fact, from this moment forward, I'm officially forbidding it. If you say negative things about yourself in my presence, you'll be punished." His lecture's intent softened the edge of his delivery. The goofy way he waggled his brows on that last part helped lighten the mood too.

I playfully smacked at his chest, and he snatched my flailing hand right out of the air.

"Careful now," he warned in that low, growly voice.

My eyes had to be the size of silver dollars by the time he was done. "Okay, Danger. That tone of voice may have to be registered as a deadly weapon," I teased. Then I grew serious. "Thank you for making me stay. And thank you for not making me feel stupid for throwing myself at you like that. I really didn't want to leave. It's such a habit...the flight instinct." I had no idea why I'd just confessed all that, but it might help him know me better.

"I understand, believe it or not. It's human nature to bolt in uncomfortable or unsafe situations. I'm glad we're taking it slow, though—"

He stopped abruptly when I gave him a skeptical look.

"I'm serious. I mean, my cock isn't very happy with me right now, but I think taking it slower will be better in the long run. Do I want to nail you to this bed twelve ways from Sunday? Hell yes. But really, your comfort and security are what's most important."

"You're really an incredible person, you know that?"

"Thank you, baby. That's nice of you to say that."

"Well, I'm not saying it just to be nice. I'm telling you the truth."

We lay quietly for a while before my stomach made a series of obscenely loud noises. The more I thought about it, the less I wanted to leave. Especially to end up back at my parents' house where they'd start right back in on me.

"Let's feed you, girl. You can't tell me you're not hungry when your stomach is growling like that." He pushed to sit up and get out of bed.

"I'd be fine with an apple or something," I said as I pulled my shirt over my head. Fuck the bra. I hated those things anyway.

"Let's check on the meat I have marinating. I'll throw it on the grill, and we'll be eating in no time," he said and tugged me by the hand toward the kitchen.

CHAPTER SIX

LAW

After dinner and cleanup, Shepperd ended up spending the night. I held the beautiful woman in my arms the entire time. The next morning, we both agreed we hadn't slept that well in a very long time. There was something so right about the way she'd felt in my arms, I'd be happy to hold her there forever.

Whoooaaa, dude. Who the hell was this guy, and where was the guy I'd known my whole life? Maybe the magic of the right woman had the power to show a man a version of himself he hadn't seen before. Or maybe I'd seen that version of myself before but only in short glimpses. Like when I was with Stella or helping my mom with her pet projects around the house.

Tapping into a gentler, kinder version of myself wasn't half bad. As long as I didn't lose the other parts of me I worked so hard to nurture too. But maybe that's what happened when you found the person meant for you. The good parts of your personality flourished, and the hidden parts were seen.

I made two cups of coffee while Shepperd took a shower, and I looked up as she walked into the kitchen. Her long hair was in loose waves down her back, and she had on one of my T-shirts tied in a knot at the bottom hem with the joggers she'd had on after the gym the day before.

"I feel like a million bucks. Your shower is heavenly, and

it's so nice to not rush. At my house, we all share one bathroom, and someone always wants in the moment I step under the water." She shook her head. "Never fails."

"Man, that can't be good. Especially with all those girls. One bathroom? I thought you said you lived in Brentwood?" I pushed one of the cups across the counter to her.

"Mmmm, thank you," she said and lifted the mug to her lips. "I do live in Brentwood. Not far from here, actually. But not all the homes in the zip code are enormous, you know? My parents have a bathroom in their bedroom, but the rest of us share the other one. Oh, and there is a half-bath for guests."

I couldn't miss how her mood had grown somber.

"What is it, baby?" I moved to stand closer to her. It was official: I was addicted to touching this girl.

"Honestly, I dread going home. I got into it pretty bad with my parents yesterday before I ran into you, and I just don't like being there."

"Do you want to talk about it? Have you thought about moving out?" The question seemed innocent enough until I saw the look she gave me in response. "What?"

"Of course I'd love to move out, but rent is really high—everywhere. I still have one semester of school to finish and would need to land a job that pays more than what I'm making now. A lot more."

"You know, I can't make any promises, but I can poke around the HR departments at my dad's companies and see if there are any openings. Couldn't hurt to look, right?" The offer was genuine, but I felt the air in the room cool the minute the words were out of my mouth.

"No, no way," she said abruptly. "Thank you, though."

"No strings attached. Honestly. What's wrong with just

looking into it?"

"I just don't feel right about it. I do appreciate the suggestion, though," she said more calmly than her original refusal.

"Well, I'll leave the offer on the table if you want to think about it. I don't like seeing you unhappy like you just were when talking about going home."

"I'll be fine. They get all worked up about my shit periodically, then something else happens and they forget all about me again. I just need to lie low until they focus on something else."

What the hell was going on with her parents? She made that comment as if it was a normal interaction between parents and their kids and then moved on like I should swallow that crap too. I had a harder time keeping up with those expectations than any of the other sensitive topics the girl had hurled my way.

And then, as if I had been possessed by aliens and lost complete control of my stupid mouth, I asked, "Why don't you just stay here with me?"

Yes. I really just said that.

And the dumbfounded look on her face verified I'd lost my damn mind. Where would a thought like that even come from? What the hell kind of magic spell did this woman have over me? She was making me do and say—and feel—things way out of my normal character.

"Law. Be serious," she deadpanned.

And the stupid just kept coming. "I'm one hundred percent serious." In fact, the more the idea floated around in my mushy gray matter, the more excitement buzzed through my whole body.

"Think about it, Shep. We get along great. So far, we really enjoy being around each other—"

"Lawrence. Masterson," she said in a voice that sounded eerily like my mother's. "Get a hold of yourself, man." She was laughing by the time she finished, and the grin on my own face was so big it hurt.

"Darling. The only thing I want to get a hold of right now is your sweet little body. But stop trying to change the subject. At least think about it. We can just be like roommates if you'd feel better about the whole idea that way." I stopped when she tilted her head to the side like I'd lost my mind.

"And how do you propose we do that? I mean with what's going on here between us? I don't know about you, but I don't think I can just pretend to be your roommate."

The way she made air quotes around the word *pretend* brought a full chuckle. She was so damn cute and sexy, I wanted to throw her down and bury myself inside her.

"Okay, you have a point there," I conceded once I got my brain out of my dick long enough to formulate a reply. "Like the job thing, I'm going to leave the offer on the table. I would love to have you here. Not just because it gets lonely by myself, or because I constantly cook way too much for one person, but because I like being around you."

She shook her head while grinning. "You're crazy. Do you know that?"

"Definitely crazy about you. Yes," I answered solemnly. "But would you think about it? At least a little?"

"It seems like a recipe for disaster. I'm an awful human, Law. You have to realize that by now. I'm snappy and bitchy and have more baggage than a Samsonite kiosk at the airport. What would make you sign up for spending twenty-four seven with someone like that?" She rushed all that out and then stood with her hands in little balled fists on her hips like she expected a legitimate answer.

I stepped right into her personal space and unclenched her hands. "I warned you, lady, about saying negative things about yourself. Didn't I?" My voice was low and serious, and I watched the exact effect it had on her. The exact reaction I was going for. She stared up at me while swallowing so roughly, I could see every muscle and tendon in her neck doing their jobs.

"I think I'm going to go before you do something that will make me want to never leave," she whispered.

"Will you think about it? Moving in here?" I pressed again.

"Yeah. I'll think about it." Then she muttered to herself, "Crazy fucker," as she backed out of my embrace and grabbed her bag.

"I heard that," I warned.

The smile I got in response was enough to carry me through the rest of the day. Before I knew it, the sun was low in the sky, and I had mentally rearranged my place five times to accommodate a new roomie. Now that the idea was in my head, it was all I could think about. I considered calling Jake to talk me out of it but never dialed the phone. I didn't want to be talked out of it.

In fact, I couldn't remember wanting something more than I wanted this harebrained plan to come together.

CHAPTER SEVEN

SHEPPERD

The only way to get the man out of my head was to call in some reinforcements. In my life, that list was damn short. One name, as a matter of fact, and as I dialed my twin's number, I hoped like hell she wouldn't pick up.

"Shep? You okay?" were the first words out of her mouth. Not "hello" or any other sort of greeting, but a panicked inquiry of my well-being.

And why was that? I knew the answer with more clarity than I cared to admit. Because denial had become a very comfortable space for me to exist within. I had pushed everyone who cared about me away so many times, they were trained to believe the only time I reached out was as a last resort.

I supposed it wasn't too far from the truth, though. Even now, I wasn't calling my sister and best friend to just bullshit or ask about her new romance. I was calling out of desperation that I was about to make the biggest mistake of my young life.

And I'd made some doozies already.

"Hey, Maye. Yeah, everything's fine. Calm down. Geeze," I replied with a touch of exasperation. I took a deep breath and said, "How's it going?"

See? That isn't so hard, is it? Normal, everyday, human interaction. It can be done.

"I'm good. Tired, but good." She paused for longer than I would have preferred and asked again, "Shep, what's going on? You're scaring me."

So I bit the bullet and laid on the touchy-feely stuff. I knew she related to the emotional crap very well, so even though it was manipulative, I hit her with the big guns.

"I miss you," I admitted with a legitimate wad of pain in my throat.

"If you don't tell me what's going on right now, Shepperd Farsay, I'm going to hang up this phone and come there right now."

"Please stop. I'm serious. I miss you, and I thought I'd see if you wanted to have lunch or something? A drink maybe?" I knew that would seal the deal. Anytime I offered to sit down to a meal with one of my family members, they'd move heaven and earth to make it happen.

"Sure. I have a few days this week that might work. I'm busy beyond anything I could've imagined with this grant-writing gig I picked up. What day were you thinking?"

Although it was a normal response from her, I felt like she'd stabbed me in the chest. I was so conditioned to have everyone bend over backward to accommodate my rare good nature. So now, to hear her doing me a favor by fitting me into her *too busy for you* schedule...well, it hurt. It just hurt.

Again, it was my own fault. And if I wanted things to change, I had to put in the effort. I'd had a long, honest talk with myself last night and decided I needed to make some changes in my life—in the way I treated the people that I cared about, especially. If I didn't, and my God was this conversation glaring evidence that I was right, I'd be completely alone.

"I was kind of hoping we could do it today," I said

cautiously.

"Hmmm," she said, and I could hear her shuffling around. "Let me just check what Andrew has planned. Maybe I could meet you for a drink. Hold on one second while I see what his schedule looks like."

She either muted the call or held her hand over the receiver, because I couldn't hear a sound from her end of the line. I even checked that we hadn't been disconnected.

But then she settled my mounting fear that she'd ditched my call and popped back on. "Yeah, okay, that should work out. What time were you thinking? If possible, I don't want to stay out too late because I have a meeting early in the morning that I need to be fresh for."

"That's my ever-practical twin," I teased.

"You know me."

"I'm pretty much wide open here, and as always, would be happy to get the hell out of this house at any time. So you decide when, and we can just meet at Charlie's if that works for you? That's pretty much halfway between here and there."

"Good plan. How about an hour from now? I just need to change quick and get over that way."

"Works for me!" I replied enthusiastically.

My mood had changed so many times on this short call, but I was glad I would be seeing my sister. I really needed someone to talk to about this fast-moving thing happening between Law and me, and Maye would give it to me straight. If I was being crazy and reckless even considering moving in with a guy I hardly knew, she'd be the one to tell me.

"Okay, see you soon. And Shep?"

Just as I was about to say good-bye, I had to course-correct and reply to her saying my name in that particular way only she could. I swallowed hard knowing she was about to drop a bomb on me just by the tone of her voice.

"Yeah?"

"I'm glad you called."

Fucking tears filled my eyes from the sincerity in her voice, and my own was rough when I said, "Me too, Maye."

An hour and half later, I rushed through the front door of the small bar near our school's campus. Luckily, I found a parking spot close by, because it was one of the darkest nights I'd seen in memory. Normally, the sky was clear and full of stars and a bright moon that helped light the way, but the air felt like a storm must be blowing in off the water, and dense cloud cover made the night extra moody.

My twin was always on time, so she already had a small booth secured toward the back of the little place and gave me a wave when we saw each other. Instinctually, I knew right where to look for her when I burst through the door and carried my momentum in her direction.

She stood, and we hugged briefly. Look, Rome wasn't built in a day. I wasn't a touchy-feely kind of girl, and no matter how many pep talks I had with myself about being nicer, more patient, and more available in general, some things would never change.

We took our seats on opposite sides of the little booth, and I tossed my bag on the bench beside me. Of course, I fished out my phone and put it on the table out of habit. If Law happened to message me while I was here, that would just be a bonus. He and I spoke briefly in the morning, but he had a full day planned with his niece, so I promised myself to give him some breathing room.

"You really scared me today, I'm not going to lie," she said right out of the gate.

"Would you stop with that," I scoffed.

"You and I both know you aren't a chatty Kathy. I'm used to there being sirens going off in the background when I pick up your call," she said with a grin.

"Ha! Very funny. That was one time, Maye. And you're never going to let me live that down, are you?" I matched her grin, and we stopped talking a few minutes while the server took our orders.

"So, tell me, what's new with you? How has it been around the house?" Maye asked when the adorable waitress walked off.

"I fucking hate that house. So basically, nothing's changed. Other than now you're not there to make it bearable." I paused there wondering if I should just launch into the half-baked idea of moving in with Law, or warm her up a little more.

"I got a really weird call from Mom yesterday. I was a little surprised I didn't hear from you sooner," she said as our server returned with our drinks.

I'm sure my face was twisted with confusion. What would a conversation between my mother and sister have to do with me? Then it hit me. I was exactly what their conversation was about. My mother was mounting her crusade to fix me and probably tried to enlist my twin in her project.

I gave a grand eye roll after sipping my cocktail. "Oh, the current house project is"—I made air quotes—"fix Shepperd. Again." I shook my head in disbelief and disgust that the woman actually bothered Maye with her nonsense.

Gently, as she had such a natural way about her, Maye asked, "Is there cause for their concern? You know they love you. They love us all. I don't imagine it's easy being parents.

Especially of five spirited, strong-willed young ladies."

"Are you seriously going to turn on me too?" I blurted and probably should have tempered my response a bit. But the words kept tumbling out if for no other reason than sheer panic that I was losing my only ally in the world.

"I can't deal with this if that's the case, Maye. I called you because I need help. I need some advice, and you're the only person who gets me, you know? But if I have to defend myself to you too, well, fuck it. I'm on my own, I guess." I gave a careless shrug that was nothing like I truly felt. I cared if my parents were driving a wedge between my twin and me more than anything.

"Calm down." She stretched across the table to pat my hand, but I pulled mine out of reach.

"Don't patronize me," I warned. "Seriously."

She waited a few moments while I settled down. The woman really knew me better than anyone. "Have you noticed how nothing gets your temper flared the way the mention of self-improvement does?"

Well, that stung. Of course, because it was the truth. But she kept going, completely disregarding the glare I offered in reply to her question.

"What are you so afraid of, Shep? Seriously. Is it letting the people who care about you down? Do you think you'll end up disappointing them? Or is it that there may be an actual problem that's gotten out of hand and needs some professional input?"

Her level, careful delivery just pissed me off more.

"I thought you were on my side," I choked through tears that arrived against every effort I made to hold them at bay.

"This isn't about taking sides, sister. This is about you

being the best version of yourself that you can be. And it's been very hard on all of us watching you starve yourself for"—she looked heavenward—"God, how long has it been now?"

I sat pouting for several minutes before I could even address this bullshit. I was fighting the urge to just fucking leave with every ounce of energy I had in me. But I had promised myself that behavior strategy was shelved.

"This is complete bullshit. You know that?" I spat her direction. Regardless of the war going on in my head and heart, my temper flared like dry brush. All my good intentions of having a productive, supportive conversation went out the window. Angrily, I swiped the tears from my cheeks and stared at her. "How can you be on their side on this? I'm not starving myself. I eat. Every day. I don't want to have to defend myself all the time, Maye. Especially to you!"

"I'm sorry, Shep. I'm not trying to attack. I'm really not. And I'm not on their side, as you keep accusing. I will always have your back. Always. But that doesn't mean I'm not worried about you. I have been for so long, and now that they've dropped the bag of crap in the middle of the table here, I thought maybe you'd feel more comfortable dealing with it with me instead of them."

I shook my head. "I just can't believe they'd stoop this low. Actually pit you against me like this. It's their lowest point yet."

Now she sat forward in her seat and hissed across the table. Her demeanor change was so abrupt, I reared back in my own seat. "Did you not just hear a word I said? I'm on your side. I want to help you. Stop being so fucking childish, Shepperd."

"Childish?" I uttered with disbelief. And then incredulously repeated the word. "Childish?"

She shrugged in response.

Something in me snapped. "You know what? Fuck this. This family is so fucked up, no one even knows the nightmare they're living in. We've all been lying to ourselves for so long, we believe our own bullshit."

My twin stared at me, confused, proving my point with precision. No one knew the real problems lurking in each other's minds and memories. Those secrets that kept us awake at every odd hour of the night. No one knew what we were struggling with in the plain light of day either. We were all so preoccupied with coping with our own demons, we couldn't tell the difference between reality and fantasy.

Angrily, I shoved my phone into my purse, slung the bag across my body, and left the bar. Maye called after me, but I was in a blind rage at that point. A person would've been downright foolish to get in my way in that moment.

Tears clouded my vision as I burst out the front door and onto the night's street. There were still plenty of people milling around on the sidewalks, making their way to and from their evening destinations. By the time I was behind the wheel of my beat-up car, I could barely catch a full breath. I never would've thought my twin would turn on me. Never. We always had each other's backs. That was the first time in our lives she took their side against me, and the feeling cut straight through to my sad, lonely heart.

I had no one. Absolutely no one. Not one person in my life believed in me enough to stand up for me, and the realization was so painful I actually moaned out loud inside my small car. The physical pain of my emotional despair was just as powerful as an actual wound.

Probably not making the wisest decisions in the moment,

I latched my seatbelt, started the car, and squeezed my eyes shut while the engine coughed and sputtered to life. Tears continued to cascade down my cheeks as I put the car into drive and pulled into traffic without as much as a glance over my shoulder.

I didn't care. See how they'd all like it if I were killed in a traffic accident. That would teach them to betray the ones they were supposed to fight to the death for, wouldn't it? No satisfaction came from the reckless thoughts, though, because I feared the reality way too much to sit with the imagined scenario for too long.

No one would even notice if I were alive or dead. If anything, they would be glad to get rid of me because it would be one less thing for them to worry about. One less person's life to try to control.

But where could I go now? There was no way I would go back to my parent's house. I steadfastly refused to go into some sort of treatment program for a problem I didn't have. No way.

Obviously, after Maye's fresh betrayal, her place wasn't an option. Hannah and Dah didn't need my bullshit in their happy little love nests either. Even if I could get up the balls to show up on either of their doorsteps, I knew I wouldn't be welcomed.

Mindlessly, I ended up in the last place I thought I would. I raised my heavy arm to ring the bell, and just like before, Law scared the daylights out of me when he whooshed the door open before my finger made contact with the button.

"Shepperd?" he gasped, and I wasn't sure why he sounded that way. Exhaustion was all over his face and posture, but his tone was directed toward me for sure.

Immediately, I wanted to turn and bolt. What the hell

was I thinking just showing up here? I barely remembered the route I took to get to his place and couldn't imagine how many traffic violations I committed in doing so.

"Hey? You okay?" he asked while bending at the waist to get a better look at my face in the dim light.

"I'm—I—can—"

He stepped closer and wrapped his strong, protective arms around me and pulled me to his chest. I completely crumbled against his body and had no doubt he was supporting most of my weight as he moved us inside his front door.

I clung to him like he was a life raft after the flight of my existence just crashed into an icy sea. My whole body shook with my sobbing, and he patiently waited for me to get through the emotional onslaught and explain what had happened.

Finally, when I felt calm enough to speak, I looked up into his caring eyes. "I'm sorry," were the first words that came out, whether out of habit for always hurting the people closest to me or because it was the emotion that fought its way to the front line.

"Baby, why are you apologizing? What has you this upset? Come on, let's sit down." He tugged me toward the living room. A grave and serious look washed over his face, and he swallowed roughly. "Did someone hurt you?"

Oh, my heart. His protective nature was so powerful and addicting. He had no idea how badly I needed someone to just care about my well-being right then. He couldn't possibly have known, but because he was the amazing, kind-hearted man that he was, it was his natural go-to response given the sparse clues he had.

Before I could get words out again, I shook my head to alleviate his fear. Finally, I said, "No, I'm fine. I'm fine." I inhaled a slow, full breath and blew it out between pressed lips.

He guided us to the sofa and sat right beside me. His muscular legs pressed against my much smaller ones, and he draped his arm across my shoulders, pulling me to him.

"Now, tell me what happened," he issued but then shifted to put some space between us. I wanted to protest—maybe even climb into his lap so he could cradle me there, but I didn't feel like I had the right to demand so much physical support from him.

"Do you want something to drink, baby? Water? Something stronger?"

"Maybe some water, if you wouldn't mind?" My voice was raspy from all the tears.

"You got it. Be right back." He planted a gentle kiss to the top of my head as he stood and headed to the kitchen. He returned with a bottle of water and unscrewed the top for me before handing it over.

After a few sips, I replaced the cap and set the bottle on the floor by my feet.

Law took my hands in his and angled his body toward me. "Now tell me what happened." His tone was gentle but still demanding and had a way of making me feel safe because I knew his concern was genuine.

"Well, you know I haven't been getting along with my parents," I said, and he nodded. "While you were busy today, I called my sister, my twin, to see if she wanted to meet for a drink. To catch up, you know?"

He nodded again, and I studied our joined hands for a long moment before continuing.

"We met at a little bar near campus, and almost the minute I sat down, she started on me. Saying the same bullshit that my parents have been. She even admitted that my mother had called her yesterday. And...well...I kind of lost it and stormed out." I shrugged my shoulders because explaining the situation out loud made the whole thing seem so petty. "And... yeah. Here I am."

But then all the uncomfortable feelings as a result of just showing up on his doorstep slammed into me, and I rushed out words before I could examine what I was saying. "I'm sorry I just showed up uninvited. I didn't know where else to go. I'm sorry. I'm not trying to make you feel bad for me or put you in an uncomfortable situation here. If you've thought about it since the other day and really don't want me here, I'd understand. Seriously. I just drove here on autopilot. I kind of surprised myself that this was where I landed." I forced out a chuckle that was so awkward, I winced.

Now he was the one studying our joined hands for an uncomfortably long beat. When I was about to shoot to my feet and rush for the front door, he must have sensed my mounting nerves.

"You're more than welcome to stay here, Shep. The offer still stands. You can stay for a night, or a week, or however long you'd like. I want you here."

Tears swelled in my eyes again and spilled down my cheeks like little rain drops. Hearing those words from his lips caused a riot of emotions I couldn't process all at once. He wanted me there. He wanted me, period.

"Are you sure?" I croaked, sounding helpless and hopeless and hating every moment of both.

"Positive," he said without pause and stretched his neck to look around me. "Did you bring anything with you?"

I shook my head and swiped my cheeks.

Law leaned forward and pulled out a handkerchief from his back pocket and handed it to me.

I marveled at the starched white cotton for a few seconds before using it to dry my eyes. The man carried a handkerchief? If I wasn't smitten before that discovery, I was now. What a gentleman. What a beautiful, kind, intelligent, sexy gentleman.

"Thank you, Law."

"My mom always insisted we carry them. I know it's old fashioned, but you'd be surprised how often it comes in handy."

"I mean for everything. For letting me stay, for being so sweet." I shrugged. "For everything," I repeated. Tears began again as I formulated an admission I never thought I'd utter aloud. "I don't have anyone to turn to. Anyone who cares." I dabbed my runny nose and couldn't meet his gaze.

With a thick index finger beneath my chin, he lifted my face to have direct eye contact. "You have me now."

CHAPTER EIGHT

LAW

I was no expert on family dynamics. Not by a long shot. And I'd barely had any personal relationships in my own life that lasted longer than a month. I had no experience to draw from regarding navigating this situation. So I let my gut take the wheel with Shepperd and knew there was no way she'd be leaving. At least tonight. We could reassess the situation in the morning when her emotions weren't so raw and come up with a gameplan that worked for us both.

I didn't like seeing her so upset that her entire frame shook while I held her. When I finally made enough sense of the little bits of information she was giving me, my offer remained as genuine as when I initially made it.

"Have you had dinner?" I asked, then quickly added, "I was thinking of ordering something right before you got here."

She gave her head the slightest shake. I would've missed it if I hadn't been watching her so intently. She looked so fragile sitting on my overstuffed couch, I wanted to just scoop her up in my arms and cradle her there for the rest of the night.

"I'm not really hungry," she finally answered. "But please, eat, if you are."

Mentally, I was compiling a list of bad habits I wanted to help her break, starting with her nutrition. But since that was also a hot-button issue with her and she'd already had enough people turn on her today, I said nothing. Whatever I ended up ordering or making for myself, I'd ensure there was enough for the two of us, and she could change her mind without feeling guilty.

"Do you like Chinese?"

"Yeah, it's not bad. I'm really not hungry, though," she said again.

"I know, but in case you change your mind," I said with a wink in hope of keeping the conversation light. Pulling out my phone, I made quick work of placing an order on the take-out app I used and put my phone on the coffee table when I finished.

I walked over to where she was curled up on the sofa, and I towered above her. I wanted to bend down and lift her into my arms but didn't have that level of comfort yet.

"Can I sit with you?" I asked hopefully.

She nodded and smiled. "I'd like that," she murmured in a tone low and sultry.

My dick perked up immediately. The woman had a spell cast on me, no doubt. I couldn't remember another girl who had that type of influence over my body.

After I got comfortable, I pulled her against my chest and wrapped my arms around her. She was so small and fragile yet so brave and mighty at the same time. With my nose pressed to her hair, I inhaled her fragrance and just let the scent move through all my senses.

"You know, as weird as it may sound, this is a perfect night to me."

"Getting Chinese takeout?" she asked while running her fingernails up and down my forearms.

"No, although good food is definitely an added bonus. I meant just spending a quiet night in, enjoying holding you in my arms. I could do this every day."

Shepperd just hummed in response, and I felt her body relax into my embrace a little more. Eventually she said, "I had you pegged all wrong."

"How so?"

"I thought you were more of a social butterfly. Or party animal, even."

"I've had plenty of time in both of those camps. Lately I just want to be here doing my own thing."

When Shep tried to sit up and break our moment, I held on tighter.

"What's wrong? Where are you going?" I rushed out.

"I feel bad. Like I'm totally intruding on your private time. It was selfish and inconsiderate of me to just show up on your doorstep and think you'd drop whatever it was you were doing to help me nurse my wounds."

I tugged her closer and crossed my arms over her chest. "You're misunderstanding," I said and waited for her to turn her face and make eye contact. I wanted to be sure she heard my next words clearly. "Your being here is what makes this perfect, darling."

She was speechless after that declaration, but a slow smile crossed her sexy lips.

"Really?" she whispered.

"Really." I planted another kiss on the top of her head. I would have much rather kissed her in truth, but the way we were situated made it impossible. Plus, I wanted to be respectful of the emotional state she was in when she first arrived. Even though her mood was slowly improving the longer we just sat together, I had the sense all the unaddressed issues weighing her down were still right there, just beneath the surface.

So we sat quietly and enjoyed the physical comfort of each other. I smiled where I sat behind her, noticing little things about her in our stillness. Some part of her body was constantly in motion. She toyed with the hem of my shirt, the dusting of hair on my arm, or intertwined and then unwound our fingers over and over. Her little frame had so much energy coursing through it, it seemed impossible for her to be completely at rest.

"You comfortable?" I asked softly.

"Yes. So good, I could sleep like this all night. Hell..." She chuckled. "I may actually get real sleep while wrapped in your arms like this. You make me feel safe."

And why did that light me up from within? It was exactly what I'd hoped for her to get from the cuddling. For her to verbalize her pleasure filled my chest with happiness. Contentment.

It was close to thirty minutes later when the security camera app on my phone chimed. I knew the delivery driver was approaching my front stoop, so I extracted myself from our cocoon and went to meet the guy at the door.

The delivery service didn't include a tip, so I gave the kid a ten-dollar bill and he was off. Shepperd was still reclined on the sofa where I left her, so I decided to eat at the coffee table. I set the food there and went to the kitchen for plates. Hopefully, they included chopsticks in the bag, but I grabbed silverware in case they didn't or Shep didn't like using the traditional utensils.

When I came back into the living room, she was kneeling at the low table, unpacking the bag. A surge of emotions swept through me again from seeing her there. What an odd thing to spark the reaction I was feeling, but instead of overthinking it, I just smiled and exhaled and enjoyed the scene.

She looked so at home here. So right. I wanted to tell her what I was feeling but didn't want to scare her off. Shit, if I thought about it too long, the ideas running through my head could freak me out too. Expressing these intense emotions this early in a relationship had the huge potential of making me look like a clingy loser, so I kept my mouth shut.

With an almost shy shrug, I said, "I brought you a plate too in case you changed your mind. Smells good, doesn't it? This is my first-time ordering from this place, so I hope it's not a letdown." I was rambling nervously, so I snapped my mouth shut while she studied my every move.

"Why did you stop so abruptly?" The girl rarely missed a detail, so I should've expected the question.

"I don't know." I shrugged again. "Sounded like I was rambling a bit, I guess?"

"I think it's adorable," she said, grinning.

"Adorable?" With one brow hiked high on my forehead, I mused, "Don't think I've been called adorable in a very long time."

"I don't know..." Now she was the shy one looking in the empty bag just for something to do other than hold my gaze. "I like thinking I've made the formidable Lawrence Masterson flustered."

I sat down on the floor across the coffee table from her and grabbed the white container filled with steamed rice. "You certainly have some sort of spell on me, woman. No doubt about it."

After the rice, I grabbed the box with the garlic shrimp

entrée I ordered and spooned a healthy amount on top of the fluffy grain. My mouth watered from the aroma, and I couldn't wait to dig in.

I placed both boxes in front of Shepperd, silently encouraging her to help herself. I didn't like eating in front of people who weren't sharing the meal, but I was starving. Any manners I should've had about not enjoying the food while she just sat there disappeared when the first bite hit my tongue.

"Damn, so good," I said between forkfuls.

"You know, when I was a little girl, I used to wish I was a witch with magical powers. I was obsessed with the idea for a while. Every time I saw a shooting star or my dad would give me his loose change for the fountain at the mall, that was my wish."

"I think you'd be a formidable witch for sure. Did you want to be a good witch or a bad witch?"

"Both." She smiled, excited to share her childhood fantasy.

I inwardly celebrated the way she was opening up to me. Even if they were little details, I hoped we were building a solid base that we could form something enduring upon.

This felt so right. I was tired of denying myself deeper connections with people out of fear of being hurt or hurting the other person. With Shepperd, I wanted to make the effort. Put in the work to be the best version of myself for her. Then, maybe, she would trust me enough to support her while she found what the best version of her looked like. It was something I really wanted to be a part of.

We ate and continued chatting. I avoided the topic of what landed her on my doorstep but hoped she would open up about it eventually. Even if it wasn't tonight, I had to keep building her trust in me.

She ended up taking a few shrimp from my plate but never made a plate for herself. When we were finished, we worked together to put the leftovers in containers that I could grab in the morning for my lunch. I was so tired of eating out every day and looked forward to having something easy to grab and go in the morning.

"Are you working tomorrow?" I asked across the kitchen island. "When do you start back with classes?"

Perched on one of the stools while I loaded the dishwasher, she dropped her face into her hands and sat that way for a moment.

"What is it? Did I overstep?"

Quickly, she looked up. "No, you haven't overstepped. I'm just realizing how shortsighted I was coming here tonight. I don't have any clothes with me, and I'm supposed to work in the morning. What the hell am I going to wear?"

"Ahh, yeah, that's going to be an issue, isn't it. Can you go back to your parent's place early tomorrow morning? Head to work from there? You said their place isn't too far from here, right? Just leave like fifteen minutes early?"

She thought about the idea for a few minutes. "That's not a bad idea. If I'm in a hurry, they might be less likely to start in on me again. My dad is a real stickler for being on time, so he wouldn't get in the way of that." She rubbed her forehead with the fingertips of one hand. "At least I don't think he would."

Her whole body had tensed from the conversation shift, and I felt like an asshole for asking what I thought was an innocent question.

"I'm sorry," I muttered.

"For what? It's not your fault my parents are overprotective and a little crazy." She forced a smile, and it pierced my heart straight through.

I didn't like that particular expression on her and was starting to notice a pattern. She put on that fake smile when she was trying to convince someone that everything was fine. But I knew damn well it wasn't and didn't want to brush another thing under the rug.

"Darling, don't do that."

"Do what?" she snapped, instantly becoming defensive.

"You don't have to try and sell me a load of crap. I know you're having a hard time right now with your folks. You don't have to put on a fake smile like everything is rainbows and unicorns."

She was quiet for a while. "You're right. It's a bad habit that I need to work on."

Her admission took me by surprise. I was expecting her to get pissed. Maybe even storm off like I'd seen her do a couple of times now.

I rounded the large marble slab in the center of the kitchen and scooped up her hands in mine. "I think you're pretty damn amazing the way you are. I just want you to know you can completely be yourself around me."

"You're so sweet," she said quietly, gulping roughly as though she was about to say something difficult. "I don't want to mess this up." She looked up to meet my gaze. "You know?"

After giving her knuckles a slow kiss, I said, "I do. I feel the same way. So far, I think we're doing a good job, though, don't you?"

"I know I'm trying. Probably more than I've tried at anything in a long time. You said I have a spell on you." She smiled shyly before admitting, "I think it's the other way around, honestly. You make me feel comfortable in my own skin, and I haven't felt that way in a really long time."

I glided my palms up her forearms and cupped her elbows in my hands. Her skin was the softest thing I'd ever touched, and I longed to have her laid out on my bed, completely naked and available for me to devour. My cock liked that idea too, and I tried to banish the image before I had a full erection.

"You're so soft," I said, my voice sounding rough and needy.

She gave me that shy smile again, and I was hard in an instant. I pulled her to her feet and bent to kiss her. She seemed completely open to it, so I gave it all I had. Sliding my hand behind her head, I kept her in place while I explored her mouth. I trailed kisses along her jaw to beneath her ear and sucked her sweet skin until she moaned.

When I stood to my full height again, she looked up at me with glassy eyes.

"You don't have to stop."

"Well, I have to keep checking myself here, or I'm going to break a promise I made, and I don't want to do that," I admitted.

Shepperd stood and slid her arms around my waist. "What promise was that?"

"To take things slow. I don't want to pressure you or risk triggering you. That first night when you left so abruptly..." I shook my head, remembering that night. "That was hard on me. Harder than I expected."

She just held eye contact without saying anything.

"I was really worried I fucked things up with you and didn't like it," I continued. "Can I be honest with you?"

She nodded but stayed silent.

"I really like you. I don't know what's going on here, but

I mean, I *really* like you." I laughed a little hearing my words. "Even saying that"—I gave my head a little shake—"it's so out of character for me, but you make me feel things, want things. I don't know. I'm definitely in uncharted waters right now."

"You said you dated someone for over a year in high school," she reminded me. "Didn't you really like her? I mean, that *definitely* counts as a girlfriend."

"No. Not really," I answered immediately. "To be honest, I've never had these kinds of feelings before."

"Not that I'm assuming that's what you want with me, to be your girlfriend. I'm just asking—"

"It is what I want. If you do, I mean. Or at least I'd like to try to see how things go between us." Christ, this all sounded so ridiculous.

Her full, genuine smile was back, and it nearly knocked me off my feet. The woman was so gorgeous when she was open and not guarding her reactions.

"You're so beautiful," I admitted and moved in for a long kiss. I couldn't stop myself from tasting her again.

With our lips pressed together, she murmured a quiet, "Thank you." We kissed there in the kitchen for a few minutes, but I could've gotten lost with her for the rest of time.

Shepperd broke our connection and asked, "Should we go to bed? I think this day has officially kicked my ass. I want to lay my head down and forget it ever happened," she confessed while I turned out the kitchen lights.

We moved through the living room, and I clicked the lights off there too. At the doorway of the master suite, I realized we never talked about sleeping arrangements. Should I assume she wanted to sleep in my bed with me? That's what my heart wanted. It was definitely what my dick would choose.

Shepperd looked at me quizzically when I stalled in the doorway, so I just broached the subject with no finesse. "Where do you want to sleep?"

She tilted her head to one side.

"Well, I didn't want to just assume you'd be comfortable in the same bed. Which I totally vote for. But if you want your own space, there's a guest room right here." I motioned to the door across the hall. "You could set up shop in there if you'd rather."

"Would you mind sharing your bed?" she asked timidly.

"Not at all. Honestly, I've fantasized about you sleeping with me," I admitted, shocking myself that the words flowed so easily.

Her grin was as breathtaking as her genuine smile. Seeing this woman happy and content was quickly becoming my obsession.

"Good, I'd like that too. But now..." she trailed off as we entered my bedroom, "I really want to hear more about these fantasies of yours."

I grabbed her around the waist and pulled her against me. I couldn't resist burying my face in the crook of her neck, making her burst with a delightful, playful squeal.

"No way," I chuckled into her skin. "Those are mine to keep to myself. Don't want to scare you off just when I got you here."

She pulled back with a devious look. "Oh, I have my ways of making you talk, Mr. Masterson."

"Yeah?" I said with a hundred hopeful ideas running through my mind. "I'd like to see you try."

"Challenge accepted!" she announced excitedly and marched off toward the bathroom. A low light came on at the vanity when the sun went down, so she easily navigated through the unfamiliar space.

But she pulled to an abrupt stop in front of the mirror. I was hot on her heels, so I almost crashed into the back of her when she stopped so suddenly. The look on her face took my mood from playful to concerned in an instant.

"What's wrong?"

"I don't have anything. I keep forgetting I literally have nothing with me other than the clothes on my back. I can't even brush my teeth. Or my hair, for that matter." She dropped her face into her hands and let out a deep breath. "This was so stupid," she grumbled into her palms.

"Hey, listen," I said, wrapping my arms around her tiny frame from behind.

She didn't look up, not even to meet my gaze in the mirror.

"Shep, look at me." I shocked myself with the tone of my voice. It was low and deep and completely in charge. I didn't want to rewind to the unsure, insecure and emotional girl that I found at my door earlier. I also knew her temperament could change radically in very little time, and I just didn't want to go back to that place right before bed.

She lifted her gaze to meet mine in our reflection. "I have everything you'll need for tonight. Tomorrow we can go to your parents' house after work and pick up more stuff if you decide you want to stay, okay? Don't stress about it. We'll work it out."

"Are you sure? I just need a toothbrush and some toothpaste. I can sleep in my underwear."

A groan escaped my lips. Christ, just picturing her in nothing but her bra and panties while I held her body to mine made my blood pressure spike. The sound made her smile, even though she tried to hide it the second she realized it was happening.

"You like that idea, I see," she said and pressed back into my thickening crotch.

"Behave yourself, young lady. I'm trying to be a good guy here, and if you do that again, I'm not sure I can keep the promise I made to myself."

So she blatantly reached behind and rubbed over the bulge in my pants with her small hands. We both let out a sound that time, and I dropped my head back on my shoulders.

Promise or not, when a hot girl rubs your cock, there wasn't a man alive who wouldn't enjoy it. It's plain biology at work. Add the science of how much I wanted to fuck her, and I burned beneath her touch.

"What promise was that? To fuck me better than anyone has ever fucked me before?" she asked in a low, sultry voice.

I actually choked on the air I sucked in when I processed her suggestion. If I didn't get a grip on the situation—and fast—there would be no turning back. So I put more distance between our hips.

"I don't want to feel like I took advantage of you in a vulnerable state. You came here tonight pretty distraught, and I don't want to be a jerk and jump your bones when you're looking for comfort."

She spun in my arms to face me, and I was looking at a much more confident woman suddenly. "What if that's what I want too?"

"Mmmm," I replied while trying to get my head on straight. My dick was going rogue at that point and straining toward her from behind the fabric of my pants. It was hard to think when she stared at me like that. All the blood in my body was rushing below my belt.

"You're a little temptress, aren't you?" I warned and asked at the same time. She openly raked my body with a hungry stare. The air in the bathroom grew thick and heavy, and our bodies weren't even touching. Memories of the way we would eye-fuck across the gym filled my mind, and a slow smile spread over my entire face.

"What's this smile?" she asked and reached a hand toward my chest.

I gently caught her by the wrist before she hit her target, though, and she made the most adorable pouty face I'd ever seen.

"I was thinking about the way we used to flirt at the gym. God, I had to beat off three times one day because I was so worked up by the time I left." I laughed at her wide-eyed reaction and moved past her in the small space to get her some toiletries.

"Hey," she called after me. "Where are you going?"

"To get you a toothbrush. I keep extra things here in this linen closet in the hall. Help yourself if you need something and I'm not around for whatever reason. There's just bathroom stuff in here. Towels, wash cloths, things for the shower." I figured a little impromptu tour wouldn't hurt if she was going to be staying.

"Oh, okay. Thank you," she said so quietly I almost didn't hear her. But the way she followed my every move with hungry eyes proved the heat between us didn't dissipate.

About thirty minutes later, we climbed beneath the covers. Shepperd finally accepted one of my T-shirts to sleep in even though the thing hung close to her knees. She snuggled against my side and rested her head on my bicep, and we both let the troubles of the day evaporate into the still air.

"Good night, darling," I said with a slow kiss to the top of her head. I felt so calm and content. Sleep would claim me in minutes because my normally busy mind was at peace.

She let out a tortured sigh and replied, "Good night, Law."

I pulled my face back and tried to find her stare in the dark room. "What was that sigh? I feel so peaceful here with you beside me, and you just sounded like it was your turn in the dentist's chair."

"Don't get me wrong. I love being right here with you, too. But this *take it slow* thing you've imposed upon us is frustrating. I thought your resolve would've faltered by now if I'm honest."

"Oh, trust me." I paused there to make sure I said the right words with the right tone behind them. "I would love to be with you right now. But I want to do this right, you know? I don't want to mess this up."

"Have you had bad breakups in the past? I've heard you say that a few times just tonight. That you're afraid of messing this up. I'm wondering what has you so worried."

The silence between us ballooned while I debated how much sharing was too much. I didn't want to scare her off, and I didn't want to taint our budding relationship with shit from the past.

Finally, I said, "No, I haven't had a lot of bad breakups, per se. Mostly, I never really commit in the first place. But in my own defense—"

"Please don't feel like you have to defend yourself. I'm way too familiar with being put in that position and would never intentionally do that to someone else. It's shitty."

"I agree. And to be fair, my feelings are my own. You haven't done or said anything to make me feel one way or another."

"Spoken like a man who has been to therapy," she teased with an air of confidence. When I didn't respond right away, she propped up on a bent elbow to look down at me. "Am I wrong?"

"No, you're right. We all went when my niece was having..." I paused there, never really knowing how to label Stella's experience. But I had told Shepperd the entire, awful story before, so when I faltered, she nodded and gently placed her other hand on my chest.

"I'm sorry," she whispered into the darkness.

I covered her hand with mine. "Don't be. You haven't done anything wrong."

"I brought up something that took the smile I love so much right off your face. That's enough to owe the world an apology," she said softly.

Damn, that one hit me right in the feels. I crunched up to reach her mouth and gave her a quick peck. "Thank you. That was a lovely thing to say."

"It's the truth. You have that kind of smile that literally lights up the whole room you're in." She grinned wider as I studied her features. "And I'm not just saying that because I want to jump you right now."

"Girl. You're not going to quit until I'm inside you, are you?"

She shrugged. "A girl's gotta do what a girl's gotta do. Am I right?"

"In all seriousness, though, yes, I've seen a therapist."

"At this age, and especially by *your* age, everyone has been a few times."

I poked her ribs before playfully threatening, "You're going to get it." Immediately I remembered how tickling her triggered a panic attack and silently prayed I didn't just repeat the offense.

Thankfully, she let out a delightful squeal and rallied back. "I'm not afraid of you."

This time she was the one to initiate our kiss, and by the time we were both breathing like we'd run a marathon, Shepperd was straddling my hips and rocking on my stiff cock.

"You're a troublemaker," I said with lips pressed to hers. "I can't take much more of this and not fuck you."

"Please don't let me stop you," she said breathlessly.

"We're going slow, remember?" I said, completely baffled where the resolve was coming from. "Plus, it's very late, and we both have to work in a few hours. When I do finally get inside you, I'm going to take my time and fuck you all night long."

Of course, those words just made the flames in her eyes glow brighter. It wasn't a lie, though. It was almost two in the morning, and I was exhausted. We were both jacked up on lust, but once we settled down, I was sure we'd pass out. Or I knew I would, at least.

I kissed the tip of her nose and easily moved her off me. "Now be a good girl and get some sleep. I don't want a grumpy bear in my kitchen in a few hours."

"Do I seem like the grumpy bear type?" she asked, trying to hold a pout but grinning instead.

"Totally." We snuggled together again like when we had first lain down. "Good night, darling. Sleep well," I whispered. "I'm so glad you're here."

"Me too."

And we both fell into deep sleep.

CHAPTER NINE

SHEPPERD

Disoriented, I jerked up in bed and looked around the room. Then it all came back to me. I was with Law and had just logged more sleep than I could ever remember. And yes, it was very late when we finally gave in to sleep, but after glancing at the clock beside the bed and doing some quick math, I knew five hours was more than I'd had in a long time.

My eyes dropped to the empty bed beside me. I ran my hand over the sheet where the indent of his body was still fresh. I needed to get up and on my way home—or to my parent's home, at least—so I wouldn't be late for work. But Law wasn't in the adjoining bathroom either, so I pulled on my jeans and threw on my top right over his T-shirt. Scooping up my shoes on the way out of the bedroom, I padded down the hall in socks to the open, brightly lit kitchen.

"Good morning," he said in a low, rumbly voice that made the hair on my forearms stand on end. His warm smile coaxed out my own, and he slid a mug of coffee across the island toward me.

"Not sure if you take cream and sugar, but I guessed yes based on the drinks I've seen you with at the coffee shop."

"Mmm, thank you. Mind if I take this with me, though? I think I'm pushing my luck with time here, and I still have to get to my parents and get cleaned up."

"Yeah, no worries. I have a travel mug that should fit in your car," he said, already rummaging through his cabinet, looking for the cup. He had an adorably victorious look on his face when he found it and turned back to where I was admiring his ass.

He set the mug on the counter while keeping me captivated with his stare and prowled toward me. I sucked in a breath and felt heat flooding my face. This man had the most intoxicating effect on my body. Just looking at him was like taking a potent drug. He pulled me into his embrace and gave me a slow, intense kiss.

I stared up at him when we parted and couldn't come up with a single thing to say. My brain was completely scrambled, and my body wanted things we couldn't accomplish if we were going to make it to work on time.

"Jesus Christ," I muttered, and his smile grew wider.

"What?" he asked before taking another sip of his own coffee.

"You scare me a little bit. Not going to lie."

"Scare you?" He looked panicked.

I rushed to explain. "Actually, what scares me are the feelings you stir inside here." I pressed my hand to my sternum where I could feel my heart hammering like an engine. "But seriously, I need to take off or I'm going to be late."

"I'll walk you out to your car," he said as we made our way to the door.

"I'm right out front, you don't have to. I don't want you to be late either."

But he continued walking beside me down his driveway to where my car was parked. "I don't want to say goodbye yet.

Today is going to be the longest day ever."

There were so many things about this guy that I liked. And so many more that surprised me. When I used to stare at him from across the gym, I had a picture of who he was painted in my mind, and it was completely wrong. He was more than a gorgeous face and incredible body. So much more. I wished in that moment that my twin and I weren't on the outs, because I really wanted to gush to someone about this guy.

By the time I was headed toward my parent's neighborhood, all the joy and peace from the time I spent with Law started leaking out of my good nature. It felt like a puncture in a car tire, hissing and whining until I felt flat and depleted.

The driveway to my parent's house was longer than the others in the neighborhood. They said they had a flagpole lot, meaning the footprint at the street was narrow and long and the expanse of the pad was farther back.

I pulled in alongside my dad's car and inwardly cringed that he hadn't already gone to the office for the day. I wasn't in the mood for a confrontation this morning, and I gripped on to whatever was left of my cheerful mood after being with Law.

Inside the front door, I made a beeline for my room and right into my closet to grab some clothes for work. I hurried back down the hall and into the bathroom to take the world's fastest shower. If I wore my hair up, I wouldn't have to wash it, so I planned on a quick, low bun. If I felt like makeup later, I could apply some at my desk while on break. Most of the time, I didn't mind just having a natural look, but if I was going to see Law after I got off, I wanted to look better than what I stared at in the mirror now.

I gave a quick shrug. "Oh, well. Good enough." I was clean,

in clean clothes, had an incredible night's sleep, and I even had some caffeine surging through my system. It was a better start than I usually got, no doubt. The smile on my face said it all.

I was happy.

For the first time in a very long time, I was happy. With my hand on the front door handle, I heard my dad call from the kitchen.

"Shep? Is that you?" His voice easily carried through the entire house, so there would be no pretending I didn't hear him.

"Yeah, it's me. But I'm running late, so I've gotta go." I pulled the door open and was blinded by the sun peaking over the neighbor's tree line. Just as I closed the front door behind me, it opened back up, and my father's imposing figure filled the frame.

I hurried to my car and fumbled with the key fob to open the doors. The battery in the device was getting weak, so I had to hit it a few times before it worked. Hopefully today would not be the day the engine decided to give up because I'd been ignoring a handful of warning lights on the dash and didn't have time to deal with that today.

I wasn't sure if thinking those thoughts manifested my shitty morning luck, but when I tried to start the car, it made some sort of terrible grinding noise and completely shut off.

My dad stood with his car door open, watching the nightmare unfold.

I banged my head on the steering wheel a couple of times and looked to find him staring at me. "Goddammit. Not now," I mumbled and thought of trying to start it one last time.

But my dad shouted my way before I went for it. "Just let it be, Shep. You might do more damage trying to start it again."

I got out of the car and slammed the door way harder than necessary. It was my own fault. Those warning lights had been on for weeks, and I just kept ignoring them. Kept promising myself I'd get it taken care of but never did. Not to mention, I didn't have the money for car service at the moment, and the last thing I wanted to do was ask my folks to help me out. As a rule, I'd rather figure out my own solution than ask for help.

I whipped out my phone and pulled up the rideshare app. I'd be late for work, but I could call my boss on the way and explain that my car broke down. I mean, showing up late had to be better than not showing up at all, right?

"Do you need a ride to work?" my dad called over the roof of his car. He had one leg inside the car and his body half-twisted to slide in behind the wheel.

"It's in the opposite direction of your office. You'll be late too."

"Come on, hop in. I don't mind giving you a lift, and no one will care if I'm a little late. It's not like it happens often, so really, it's no trouble."

Honestly, I didn't have money for a ride. As much as I didn't want to be confined inside a car with the man, it was my best option. I could suffer through fifteen minutes with him and maybe still be on time. So I ran around to grab my purse off the passenger's seat, slammed the door shut on my piece of shit car, and slid into the pristine luxury of his.

Quietly, I said, "Thank you for helping me," once I was settled in my seat.

"What are parents for?" he asked lightly, and I resisted the deadpan look I wanted to shoot him. Instead, I just gave a little shrug, forced a smile his way, and busied myself with the seat belt so he'd just start driving.

My dad tried starting several conversations while we drove, but I just stuck to as few words exchanged as possible. I tried really hard not to be rude, though, because he was saving my ass when all was said and done.

"I may have to have that thing towed to the shop from the way it sounded. Have there been warning lights on when you've started it?" he asked after a few minutes of silence.

Oh great, here we go.

"Hmmm," I drew out, trying desperately to sound innocent. I had to be careful not to lay it on too thick, though, because my dad could be as cynical as me when he put some effort into it. He knew when we were lying almost every time.

"Is that a yes or no?" he asked, darting his eyes between the road and me. "Where is your work?"

How it just dawned on him at that moment to ask where I worked, I couldn't say. And if he didn't know where I worked, why was he heading in the right direction?

"Do you know and are trying to force me to incriminate myself? Or do you really not know?" I accused, feeling my mood slowly transform the longer I had to chat with him.

When I was young, like most little girls, my daddy was the apple of my eye. After the molestation started at school, I began to withdraw from everyone. But especially him. I had a hard time trusting grown men and was convinced they were all the same. Evil, cruel, conniving, and not to be trusted. So our relationship suffered as badly as mine and Hannah's did.

"Shepperd," he said in that tone that ground on my nerves. Like he was on his very last bit of patience with me. Like I was a big inconvenience.

I refused to fight with him before walking into my job, though, so I took a deep breath and banished the negativity. I gave him the address, and he nodded.

After a few minutes, he asked, "Where are you working exactly? The name of the business, I mean. Because I thought you were working at a hair salon, and I know there isn't one in the middle of that business park. I'm pretty sure that address you just gave me is a bunch of offices."

Well, wasn't he just the super sleuth of the morning. I choked back the acidic remark and nodded. "Yeah, it's an office."

In a much gentler voice, he asked, "Well, what do you do?" Maybe he wasn't in the mood to start his day by going a few rounds with me either. We were only a few miles away. If we hit the green lights on most of the blocks, I had a good chance of making it right on time.

"Just paperwork stuff. It's just to pay bills and have pocket money. It's not a career choice," I rushed out. Next would come the lecture about not using my full potential or not choosing a job in my chosen major.

Thoughtfully, he nodded at my reply. "What kind of paperwork? That's a pretty vague job description."

I let my tense shoulders drop down to their rightful position and blew out a breath. "I process medical billing stuff. Payments, monthly account statements, stuff like that. A lot of data entry. It's all very boring."

"So what happened at the hair salon? Weren't you working at one at the beginning of the summer?"

"It didn't work out. The owner was an asshole, and our personalities clashed. It only lasted about two weeks," I summarized while staring out my window. I couldn't take his disapproving scowl this early in the morning.

But to my surprise, he just said, "That's too bad. It seemed like you were enjoying it."

"Not really," I said with little emotion. "It was money. That was about it."

"Are you enjoying the office setting more?" he fired right away.

I swung my head toward him and just stared while he negotiated his fancy car through traffic. Finally, when he could take his eyes off the road, he met my stare.

"What?" he asked calmly.

"What's with the third degree?" I snapped.

"Shepperd," he sighed. "It's not the third degree. It's called making conversation."

A few moments passed, and I considered flipping on the stereo but then he continued.

"Do you think your mother and I like arguing with you all the time?" He asked the question and then answered it too. "We don't. I just thought we could catch up a little while we ride in to work this morning. I realize I've lost track of what you've been up to, and that's on me."

Instantly, I felt suspicious. Where was all this loving, doting parent crap coming from? I hadn't felt nurtured or even interested in for years. The only child that existed in our house for the majority of my life was my sister, Hannah. Another reason I resented her so much.

Drifting away from the conversation in the car, I gave that fact a little more thought. Was it really Hannah's fault that our parents favored her? Rationally, I knew all the reasons why. I knew she was a victim. It's not like she wanted to have two random strangers try to abduct her one day while shopping with our mother at Target. They chose her. She was an innocent, six-year-old girl just minding her own business.

It was the fallout from that fateful day that caused all the problems in our house. And true, I had no idea how I would have reacted if I had been a parent in their situation. For all these years, it had been easier to just blame my parents for my misery than look inside and see where it was really coming from.

Shit.

Where the hell did all of that just come from? And why now? Why this morning, of all mornings, did I have to go down this path in my brain. I was having such a great morning after leaving Law's house. But this bullshit lived right at the surface of everything I did. Every relationship I had—and destroyed. Every conversation I took part in. Every interaction with family, friends, and especially strangers. Being bitter toward, frankly, everyone and everything became my best defense mechanism. It was easier to push people away than let anyone get close and have them discover how fucked up I really was.

Until I met Law.

With that realization, the car came to a stop, jarring me from my thoughts. When I looked out the window, I realized we were in front of my workplace, and I couldn't get out of the car fast enough.

"Hey, Shep, wait a sec," my dad called while leaning across the center console so he could maintain eye contact with me.

"Dad, I'm going to be late," I said but mentally reminded myself that he really had saved my ass this morning. "Thanks for the ride," I forced out past a lump of emotion I resented for rising in my throat.

"No worries," he said with a kind smile. "Do you need a ride home? I can swing by and pick you up. What time are you off?"

Was that hope in his expression?

"No, don't worry about it. I'll catch a ride." I tried to wave him off, but he persisted.

"With who? Really, it would be no bother."

"My boyfriend is picking me up. We have plans," I lied. Twice, really. First, who said Law Masterson was my boyfriend? Second, I had no idea what his day looked like or if he'd be able to give me a ride. Truth be told, I probably wouldn't even ask him.

"See you later, Dad," I said in hopes he'd drive away.

"Okay, let me know if your plans change. Love you, kiddo," he called, and all I could do was lift my hand to about hip level and give a pathetic wave.

I hadn't uttered those words to anyone in years. I had no intention this morning to overturn any other apple carts in my mind. I already had enough to think about after that uninvited self-introspection.

On my lunch break, I dug my phone out of the bottom of my bag and realized I'd never turned the ringer back on from last night. I had a handful of texts from Maye and Law and couldn't deny the way my entire body reacted when I saw he reached out.

The first message came earlier that morning.

Hey you. How's your day going? Hope
you made it on time. XO

A second message came about an hour after the first. As I read the text, a grin spread across my whole face. I took a surreptitious look around the lunchroom to see if anyone saw the way I was fawning over my phone's screen. Thankfully, the two other people in the room were involved in their own conversation and likely didn't realize I was in the room with how rapt they were paying attention to each other.

Interesting. I wondered if there was something going on between them based on their body language. I'd have to check out that theory with Joy when I got back to my desk to see if she picked up the same vibe.

Hope you're okay. I thought I'd hear back from you, but you must be busy. What time are you off today? Still want to go to your parents' to pick up some of your stuff?

Shit. I forgot we had that loose plan in the works, and I wasn't sure if I could take more interaction with the folks today. I shot a message back to Law and figured we could just see how the evening played out.

Hey yourself. Sorry I missed your messages. Forgot to turn the ringer on this morning. Made it on time but not sure about tonight. My car died in the driveway this morning, so I'm kind of stuck.

I absolutely hated having to admit that to him for more reasons than I could list. If I knew this guy as well as I felt I did, the next message would be some version of him coming to my rescue. I never wanted to appear needy or dependent. On anyone. Especially not a man, and especially not a man I cared about. And there was no doubt after last night, I cared about this one possibly more than I'd ever cared before. But I didn't need a savior, and I didn't want to seem incapable of fixing my own shit.

What time are you off? I can swing by and pick you up?

You don't have to do that. I'll figure something out.

It's settled. What time should I come by? The sooner I get to see you, the happier I'll be, so we both win.

Very clever.

You know it! Time?

I'm done at 3:30. If you work later than that, I can find a ride. Seriously.

See you at 3:30. Shoot me the address, please, or drop a pin when you have a chance.

You're too sweet. You know that?

Not always. It would seem you bring out the best in me. See you soon. XO

These little x's and o's were starting to do funny things to my stomach. How could two letters in the alphabet make my body react this way?

CHAPTER TEN

LAW

The afternoon dragged on after I got in touch with my girl. Yes, I was calling her mine. I chuckled. It was so unusual for me to feel the need to claim a woman. And I could just imagine my little independent warrior's reaction to my desire to own her. But I was confident it was something we both wanted.

I saw her reactions when I did things that showed I cared for her. She lit up from inside like there was a fire burning deep in her heart that had been neglected for so long it was almost snuffed out. When I added some fuel to it though, she absolutely glowed. And if I thought she was gorgeous before? When I stoked that flame with kindness and genuine caring she was absolutely stunning.

That settled it. My new mission in life was to watch Shepperd Farsay radiate happiness and confidence as her norm. From the little I knew about her past, I didn't think it was actual neglect on her parents' part, but the woman herself pushing everyone away to avoid getting betrayed. I still had a lot to learn about her though.

My car's engine purred in neutral outside the address she sent me this afternoon. It was a nondescript office space in the middle of a complex of similar buildings. Just before I opened my text thread with her to check the address again, I saw her walking toward my car. The smile on my face was involuntary and all-consuming. I jumped out and dashed around to the passenger side to open the door for her. I also couldn't miss the chance to greet her properly with a slow, tempting kiss.

"Hi," she said in a voice so sultry and inviting, my own mouth instantly dried up.

After swallowing hard, I said hello back and snuck another peck before she got settled in the car.

Once I was behind the wheel, Shepperd said, "This car is amazing. What happened to the one from the gym?"

I had completely forgotten I had driven my SUV that day. "I usually drive that one when I have errands and stuff to do on the weekend. I like this one for the daily commute, though. More comfortable, and I don't need all that cargo space."

She just nodded and grinned. "Makes sense, I guess."

"What do you mean, you guess?" I asked as I left the lot of her business park. "And where are we headed? My place or yours?"

"I don't know." She gave a quick shrug and looked out the window.

"Talk to me."

"I don't know," she said again. "I just feel like a loser. The one car I have is a broken-down piece of shit, and you're over here with a different one for every day of the week."

"You're not a loser. Not even close. Don't forget, I've got a few years on you, for one thing. And my family has more money than they know what to do with. So their providing me with a work car isn't about me as much as it is about a business write-off for them."

Hearing her talk negatively about herself cut right through me. It wasn't something I'd tolerate, either. The last thing I wanted to come between us was money, so I really hoped this wasn't going to turn into an issue. There were some things in life you couldn't change. Having a lot of money was just a part of the family I was born into. It wasn't like I could really share in the claim of amassing any of it. I was just fortunate enough to now have it.

"Maybe I should get a job where you work, then. I have a bad feeling about that car of mine. I think the only place worthy of it now is the junk yard."

"Do you have any idea what's wrong with it? Was there a warning light or anything?" I asked while I drove toward Brentwood.

"Dude," she said flatly.

I reached for her hand across the center console and entwined our fingers while I drove.

"There were like four different lights on the dash this morning when I left your place. I know one was gas. The tank was super low. But I have no idea what the others were. When I went to start it to come to work..."

I snuck a glance over to her.

She gave a mournful shake of her head. "Yeah, it wasn't good. But enough about that. I can't do anything about it. How was your day?"

"Fine. I mean, I guess it was fine. I had a hard time concentrating." I stopped short there because I was in danger of saying something that might make her uncomfortable. But I wanted her to know how into her I was and that she was all I could think about. What was the point of hiding it? I was pretty sure we were on the same page with how we felt.

"Oh, yeah? What's going on?" she asked, not knowing she was setting up the perfect opportunity to say what I'd been choking back.

"Well," I started with a huge grin. While I drove, I could see from the corner of my eye how intently she was listening. "I met this girl."

Shepperd looked panicked. She quickly masked her expression and tried to engage in the conversation.

"Oh? A new coworker?" she asked in a tone pitched much higher than her natural voice.

Slowly, I shook my head, smiling even bigger. "Nah, I met her at the gym, believe it or not. Months ago."

"At the gym? That's interesting. Were you checking her out while she did her workout? That's kind of pervy, no?" she asked, now wearing a smile to match my own.

"At first it felt a little scandalous, but I would catch her staring at me too, so I was pretty confident it was a mutual attraction."

"Okay, so then what? You just stare at the girl and haven't talked to her?"

"No, I've talked to her. And you know what?" I paused there, letting the seriousness fill the quiet cabin of the car. "She's amazing. Smart and really funny now that she has relaxed enough to be herself around me."

"Hmmm," was all she said, and my nerves spiked.

Was this too much? Too soon? Well, too bad. I was committed to the cause. I wanted her to know how I felt. If she wasn't there with me, I'd rather find out now before I got in even deeper.

While we were stopped at a traffic light, I shot my glance her way to find her staring right back at me.

"What?" I asked with a nervous smile.

She swallowed so hard I could see her throat constrict.

"You think she's amazing?" she asked in the most insecure voice I'd heard from her.

Normally she was a confident, no-holds-barred warrior. But receiving a compliment reduced her to a shy little girl.

I nodded enthusiastically. "I do. One hundred percent. But that's just the start of the list of incredible things about her. Honestly..." I inhaled, now as nervous as she seemed. My voice had started excited and confident and was now quiet and serious when I said, "I'm head over heels for her. I want her to be my girlfriend, but I don't know how to ask. I'm afraid I'll scare her off."

"Why would that scare her off?"

With an awkward laugh, I said, "I'm not sure. What if she doesn't feel the same, you know? What if it's too soon for her, and I get turned down?"

She shook her head and smiled. "Don't be afraid. I bet she's feeling the exact same way. Right down to the part about being nervous to be upfront about her feelings."

"Yeah?" I was incapable of hiding the excitement I felt. Then I gave a resolute nod, as if cementing my plan. "Okay, I'll talk to her. Thanks for the advice." I gave her hand a squeeze.

Silence bloomed between us after that. We were both grinning but lost in our own thoughts until I pulled into my driveway. I hustled around the front of the car to open Shepperd's door. When she stood from the passenger seat, I pulled her into my arms. She felt especially small today in my embrace, and I buried my face in her neck.

"Hello, girlfriend," I murmured through a ridiculous smile. I felt her cheek bunch against my own and knew she was smiling too.

"Why does that sound so good when you say it?" she

asked when we parted enough to see each other's faces.

"Because it feels right. Sounds right. I have to be completely honest with you, though..."

After she gave me a nod of encouragement, I explained, "I have literally no experience in being someone's boyfriend. I have ideas of what it might look like? But I'm pretty sure there will be times I screw things up."

"Law, listen." She cupped my cheek with her small palm. "There are no rules for this kind of thing. Well, other than I won't put up with you going out with other girls if you want me to be your girlfriend. That means we're exclusive."

I nodded. "No question. I need the same." Maybe if we just worked the details out like that—one at a time—we could find our way.

"Let's just take it one day at a time. I'm not super experienced with any of this either, but there is one thing I do know."

While she paused, I turned my face into her palm and kissed. "What is that?"

"We have to be honest with each other. All the time." Her tone was serious and sultry, and despite the importance of what she was saying, my dick picked that moment to wake up and take notice of the sexy goddess in my arms.

"You have my word," I promised and closed the small space between us for a deep kiss.

We were both breathless when we parted, and I wanted to throw her over my shoulder and stalk straight to my bedroom and claim her fully. I was blinded by need and desire, and when she let out a low, throaty chuckle, I gave my head a little shake to try and clear the fog.

"Christ, woman."

She tilted her head to the side in question.

"I want to fuck you more than I want to breathe right now." I wasn't interested in beating around the bush anymore. Hell, if we were officially exclusive, shouldn't we at least celebrate? Judging by the way she was staring at me, she was thinking the same thing.

"Mmmm," she hummed. "I approve of that message." She gave me a slow nod, and I battled just pushing her back into the car and taking care of things right where we were.

As exciting and appealing as that thought was, the more rational side of me knew she deserved better than a quickie in the bucket seat of a car. I wanted to spend my time worshipping her body. Take an entire evening to explore every inch of her delicate skin.

"Let's go inside," I said on a sigh. "I'll get changed and maybe grab something quick to eat, and then we can head over to your place and start moving your stuff."

As we walked up my front walk, she said, "No, seriously. You don't have to help me do that. I can work on it while you're at the office tomorrow." She quickly added, "I don't have work tomorrow."

If we hadn't been going single file to the front door, I would've studied her face. Something about the rapidness and insistence of her response was throwing me off.

So I whirled around and pulled her against my body by her belt loops. I held her there until she lifted her face to meet my gaze.

"Tell me what's going on," I said with my lips pressed to hers.

She struggled a tiny bit to pull away, so I held on just a bit tighter.

"Uh-uh. Don't run from me, darling. Tell me what's going on in that beautiful mind of yours. Something just shifted, and I want to be here for you."

I could feel her discomfort building in the air between us. Didn't we just promise to be honest with each other? I'd remind her of that if I had to. Her entire body deflated in my arms as she prepared herself for what I was guessing would be a vulnerable moment.

"I want to keep you for myself," she rushed out and then studied the ground as though she were counting blades of grass in the small patch of lawn along the sidewalk.

"I'm all yours. I promise. But can you explain what you mean?"

"This is going to sound so bad..." she said and rubbed her furrowed brow.

Pulling her hand down from shielding her face, I said, "Let me be the judge. Give me a chance here." I ensured my voice was gentle and supportive rather than stern or authoritative. I wanted Shepperd to know how committed I was to being partners in this.

"Can we go inside? I promise I'll keep talking, but I feel like your neighbors are going to think we're arguing out here." She looked up and down the block and then to me. "I don't like that."

"Sure, whatever you need."

And I meant that, but I would definitely hold her feet to the fire on this, because I could feel how tense she had become just at the thought of returning to her parents' house. How bad were things between her and her folks?

Inside the door, we both set our things down on the entryway table. I had keys and my laptop bag. Shepperd just had her handbag.

"I want to change out of this suit. Will you talk to me while I do that?"

"Sure."

As we made our way down the hallway, I loosened my tie and released the top button of my shirt. God, instant relief from the formality of the attire. I slid the jacket off and hung it up in my closet while Shepperd sat at the foot of the bed.

"Okay, talk to me. I know we just agreed that honesty is a must for a relationship to work, and I want you to know this is a safe space to say whatever's going through your mind," I said from the depth of my closet, where I tossed my shirt into the laundry basket. "I'm not going to judge you or chastise you."

"Thank you. It's been a very long time since I've been comfortable talking to anyone honestly, other than my twin. And even with Maye, I haven't always told her everything. Too many bad experiences with having what I've said used against me later."

From the doorway of my closet, I waited while she organized her thoughts. I pulled a casual shirt over my head and didn't miss the way her eyes raked over my body while I dressed.

With a playful smirk, I asked, "Like what you see?"

"Indeed I do," she replied with a grin. "I'd much rather be getting some of that than having this shitty conversation."

"I know, baby, but this is important." I refused to let her distract me even though we both wanted the same thing. I dropped to my knees in front of where she was perched on the edge of my bed.

"Okay." She inhaled deeply. "I'm just going to say all of this, and it probably won't make sense at first, but I'm going to try to not censor myself. Again, it's been a really long time since I've told anyone what I'm truly thinking, so I'm praying you don't go running out that door." She motioned to the tall wooden panel with a wave of her hand.

"I'm all ears."

"I don't like that house. The one I grew up in. Just walking in the door does things to my head." She tapped her temple and then slid her flat palm down her throat and clutched her fingers around her neck. "I can't breathe in there."

Treading carefully, I said, "Can I ask you something?"

She nodded while looking up at me with unshed tears in her eyes.

"Have you seen a therapist? For your PTSD?"

"PTSD?" she croaked, and one fat tear rolled down her cheek.

I rushed to sit on the bed beside her and hiked up a knee so I could angle my body toward her and wiped her flushed cheek. "I'm no expert, but it seems like that might be what's going on."

She shook her head.

"Based on what I've seen with Stella—that's my niece—and what you're describing, I think that some counseling might do you a world of good. How do you feel about that?"

"I don't need a shrink to tell me how fucked up I am, Law. I mean, come on..." She shot to her feet and began pacing back and forth. "Look at me."

I stood too, intercepted her on the next lap, and pulled her against my body. "Baby, sshhh."

She was trembling from head to toe.

I swayed back and forth with her pressed to my chest, hoping to comfort her. "That's not the point of a therapist."

She plopped down on the bed again and rubbed her

forehead. "It's a really sore subject."

Sitting beside her, I took her hand in mine. "I think a lot of people have the same misconceptions you do. At least before giving it a go."

"Remember the other day when I showed up on your doorstep? My God, was that just this week?" she asked with the most bewildered expression. "My parents threatened they were going to check me into some rehab place if I didn't do something on my own. So, therapy, or help in any form, has always been wielded as a threat or way to control me when they feel like they have no other tricks left. It's never, not once, been suggested in a spirit of help or healing."

"Rehab?" I asked, trying desperately to keep the anxiety out of my tone.

I didn't think I was equipped to deal with substance abuse after the past few years I'd just lived. Being a hypocrite didn't sit well with me. Lecturing someone else about the perils of partying too hard or too often would be a soapbox I'd fall right through if I tried to step up on it.

"For eating disorders," she croaked, and the tears were back again. "They're all so fucking blind, they can't even see what the real problem is. Or they see it and refuse to deal with it. They wouldn't want to shatter their perfect little lives."

"Okay. Can I ask you something else?"

She gave a curt nod while swiping tears away.

"Do you think you have an eating disorder?" The moment the words came out, I wanted an instant do-over.

Shepperd shook her head. "No. I don't think I do. Do I neglect myself when it comes to nutrition? Yes. Could I stand to gain a few pounds? Maybe. But I'm not sticking my fingers down my throat or working out like a maniac."

We both knew the truth about that last one, but I let her work through her emotions and self-correct.

"The gym is one of the few places I can go to escape. It probably seems like I go excessively, but again, people have no idea what I'm really dealing with in here," she explained with another gesture to her head.

"Forgive me if this is a dumb question... Have you thought about telling them about the janitor?"

"Are you kidding? I've thought about telling them a hundred different times." She hung her head until her chin nearly rested on her chest.

I hooked my index finger beneath it and lifted her face back to look at me.

"I'm sorry," she whispered. "That came out ugly."

"You don't have to apologize. I can only imagine the different emotions this brings up. I really appreciate you talking with me so openly about it." I leaned closer and watched for a sign that she wouldn't like me to kiss her in the middle of all this.

She closed the last bit of space, and our lips pressed together gently.

I held her in my arms for a few minutes and gathered my thoughts. Finally, when I felt like I had something productive to offer, I put some space between our bodies so we could talk. My brain refused to work right with her in my arms. All I could think about was what it would feel like to be inside her.

"I have an idea," I began. "Hear me out, okay?"

She just nodded and looked up at me with an impossibly blue stare. Her tears had made the depth of the color of her irises so intense, it was like staring into the Pacific.

"If you're open to it, I can schedule an appointment

for you with my therapist. It would be easier than going to a stranger, and she specializes in trauma, PTSD, and personal crimes. Or whatever that's called. Rape, abuse, molestation. Things done without consent to one person's body by another person. I can go with you," I offered, but that last part instantly had her shaking her head.

"I meant drive you there and home so you don't have to worry about navigating around downtown. I honestly didn't mean sit in the session with you. Actually, I don't think Tiffany would go for that anyway. At least not until she knew you and if we needed to address anything that is affecting us."

"That seems like a huge imposition, Law. I don't know." She smoothed the bed's coverlet over and over. "I really don't want to go at all."

"I hear what you're saying, and it makes sense that you'd be unsure about it. But I'm thinking if you get some sessions under your belt, she could help you navigate talking with your parents about what happened. It could be the first step in healing your relationship with them."

She tilted her head to study me closely. "This might sound shitty when it comes out, so just a heads-up. I don't always tip toe around stuff, so know that I mean no offense here. Why do you even care? It's not like you know them. Why does it matter to you what kind of relationship I have with my mom and dad?"

"It's not the relationship with your family I'm invested in, Shep." I paused and waited for her to look up again. "It's you. I want to see you heal and move on from having that kind of reaction." I pointed toward the front of my house where this whole conversation began. "If you end up having a healthier relationship with your folks because of it, that's just icing on the cake."

"I don't know..."

"Will you at least think about it? Just consider it. I truly believe you will be glad you did it in the long run."

"Okay, fine," she huffed, not completely happy with me pressing her for a commitment. "I'll think about it."

I pecked her lips again and stood. "In the meantime, we have to get some of your stuff. I'll be with you the entire time. How likely are they to bring up anything too touchy in front of a stranger?"

"Oh, you'd be shocked. Sometimes I think that's his favorite time to corner me. He loves looking like the big bad alpha guy in front of people. And she just stands there." She clasped her hands beneath her chin and looked up toward the ceiling with an exaggerated dreamy stare, "Crushing on him like he's the star of the football team, prom king, and porn star all wrapped into one."

I burst out laughing. "That's quite the picture you've created."

"I wish I were joking," she lamented.

"Well, you're going to need clothes at the very least. The only other option would be to buy you all new stuff." The idea was originally to persuade her to go back to her family home, but now that I introduced the concept, I would totally enjoy buying her stuff.

"No way in hell. Hell no."

"That wasn't meant to be an ultimatum. Just an option. I'd be happy to do either," I vowed.

My new girlfriend stepped close to me and wrapped her arms around my waist and wrested her cheek on my sternum. "I don't know what I've done to deserve you, Mr. Masterson, but I'm sure glad I did it. Whatever it was."

I held her closer and kissed the top of her head. Taking care of this woman was going to be the best experience ever. The rough road we had ahead with her coming to terms with her abuse would be eclipsed by the love and compassion I planned to shower her with.

CHAPTER ELEVEN

SHEPPERD

"Ready to go? Are you hungry?" Law asked as we headed toward the front door to leave. "We could always hit a drive-through on our way back. Or the way there. You pick."

I felt like I was headed to the gas chamber the way my body was physically reacting to taking this perfect man to that fucked-up house.

I shook my head. "I'm not really hungry right now. My stomach is all in knots, to be honest. But if you want to get some food, I'm cool with that." I gave a quick shrug, trying to don the cloak of little concern I wore around my family like a shield. If I didn't let them get to me, I could manage the pain.

"Will they be home from work at this time? Maybe we can get in and out and not have to see them. Though you're going to have to deal with all this stuff eventually, babe." He paused at the door, and I wanted to just push past him and hightail it out of there.

Instead, I looked up at my handsome boyfriend and sighed. "Yes, I know. I can only take small doses and remain sane, though. And to be honest, my cup is pretty full here, so if we could move on to a different topic now, I'll be in a better headspace when we get there so we can just get this over with."

I silently threw up a prayer that he would drop it. So much

had been said between us since he picked me up from work. Normally, I'd prefer to sit quietly with my thoughts and review all that had been discussed. I mean, we'd just committed to being exclusive! That was huge!

The next best coping mechanism I had in a heavy situation was to just shut down. I couldn't process any more deep conversation, so I hoped like hell my parents, or at least my dad, wouldn't be home.

It was a short drive to my parents' house, and that was probably a good thing. I didn't have a lot of time to get worked up more than I already was. We turned down the long driveway, and my body temperature rose. Both of their cars were parked close to the house.

I groaned. "They're both here," I mumbled into my hands.

Law parked behind my dad's sedan and scurried around to open my door. I would've thought this kind of treatment from a guy would annoy me, but I loved it. Every gesture, touch, or look reinforced how much he cared about me. Constantly being reassured that way gave me confidence I was so desperately lacking. The weirdest part about all of it was that I didn't realize what I was missing until being around him.

God, don't let me fuck this up and scare him off.

"They're either going to be obnoxiously fake and friendly or just open fire on me. You should probably not say much either way," I advised.

He just returned a blank stare, and I didn't know what to make of it. Did saying that hurt his feelings? Maybe I was too blunt? In my own twisted mind, I was trying to protect him. It was too late to explain, though, because the front door whooshed open with a flurry, and my mom stood beaming in the entry.

"Hey there!" she said brightly. "I thought I heard car doors."

Total lies. My dad always blasted the volume on the television so loud that you couldn't hear a conversation you were having in the same room. She watched out the window as a hobby. That's why she knew we were here.

Whatever. It wasn't worth pointing out the truth.

"Hey," I mumbled.

"And who's your friend, Shep?" she asked, wiping her hands on the dish towel she was holding, preparing to offer one in greeting.

"Oh, right. Mom, this is Law, my...ummm, boyfriend." I looked at him with an uncomfortable shrug. I wanted to run and hide more than anything.

Luckily, Law took over and approached my mom. "Hello. Nice to meet you," he said in his deep, sexy, and oh-so-confident tone.

Christ, just the sound of his voice sent shivers through my entire body.

"Hello. I'm Lisa, Shepperd's mom," Mom said as they shook hands. She made a big show of looking behind her to the empty space and then back to Law. "My husband, Dave, is around here somewhere."

"It's nice to be here. Shepperd's told me so much about her family," he said. It wasn't the whole truth, but it wasn't a lie, either—just the basic pleasantries someone said when meeting someone new.

"I'm just making dinner. Are you two staying?" she asked toward me with a hopeful expression. Was this really the same woman who threatened to commit me to an inpatient treatment facility just a few days ago?

"No," I rushed out before Law got us into something that would surely be the death of me. "Just picking up some stuff. I'm going to be staying at his place."

"Oh?" my mom asked in surprise.

I hurried past her and beelined toward my bedroom, towing Law behind me. The moment we were behind the closed door, I leaned against the thing and let out a huge gust of air. He watched me as if I had been a grenade with its pin pulled, not sure if he should take cover or dive on top and try to smother the pending explosion.

"I'll just grab whatever I can. I knew I should've done this alone. This was a huge mistake," I grumbled while frantically moving around my room. I was spinning myself up into a frenzy and getting nothing accomplished because of it.

Law stepped in front of me on one of the pointless laps I made around the room and wrapped me in his arms. He kissed the top of my head and held me close. "Calm down, darling. It's fine."

I scoffed. "You have no idea how fine it's not. He's going to be at that door any moment now. Once he has me cornered in here, things will get ugly. I'm not in the mood for this tonight. I knew we shouldn't have come here."

"Baby, listen to me," he said, putting an arm's length between us. "It's fine. I'm not going to let anything happen to you, okay?"

Knowing I didn't want to get into this with him again, I just sighed. "Let me just get some clothes and we can go." I swung my head from side to side with no clue how to make that happen. My brain was locked up, and I was moments from a breakdown.

"Do you have a suitcase? A duffle bag or something?" Law

suggested, clearly sensing I was coming unglued.

"Yeah, good idea." I gave him a half-hearted smile. "Thank you."

"I'm here to help you. Where should I start? Where are your pajamas and underwear?"

"You want to pack my panties and bras?" I smiled genuinely, letting some of the tension slip away.

"It will be a tough assignment, but I'm up for the challenge," he said with a wink.

I dragged a suitcase and a couple of other bags out from beneath my bed and tossed the totes on top. Rolling the suitcase on its rickety wheels, I headed to my closet. There, I dropped to my knees and opened the case like a giant clam shell and scurried deeper into my closet to pull out some work clothes.

In no time we had three bags packed and the suitcase I stuffed beyond capacity. Law leaned on the top while I secured the zipper. He had to stand the thing upright because it was way too heavy for me to manage, and it hit me like a bucket of cold water.

"Dude," I said and let my shoulders fall.

"What?"

"Is this going to fit in your car? Does it even have a trunk?" I smacked my forehead, and the sound echoed around my room.

"Please don't do that," he said quietly and kissed where I just cracked myself.

"Sounded way worse," I muttered but continued staring up at him.

"Yes, this will fit in my car. Surprisingly, the trunk is pretty big. What about toiletries? Makeup or any of that stuff?"

I hadn't even given those things consideration, and since we were on borrowed time, I shook my head. "No let's just go. What I need and you don't have, I can just replace. I'll get back over here while they're at work and pick up the things I can't part with."

With two bags in hand and one slung across his body, Law reached to open the door.

I was right behind him, struggling with the suitcase when the dreaded *knock-knock-knock* came on my door. I knew just by the sound that it was my dad. Law shot his stare over his shoulder to me and then back to the door. Then back to me again with a silent question.

"What?" I shouted and winced at how ugly it sounded. No wonder people turned and went the other direction when they saw me coming. If I knew someone like me, I'd do the same thing.

"Shep? Can I come in?"

With a gentle hand to Law's abdomen, I moved him out of the way so I could lead our escape. I whipped the door open and clearly caught my dad off guard as he stepped back in surprise.

"Hey, Dad. We're in a hurry here, so...yeah..." I rushed out and pushed past him with my suitcase.

"Here, honey, let me help," my dad offered and tried to take the case from my hand.

"It's fine, Dad. We've got it."

That seemed to be the first moment he realized I wasn't alone. Did my mom really not tell him I had a man in my room with me? A man I introduced as my boyfriend? Once again, proof that they didn't listen to me when I spoke. Either that or they didn't really care enough to process the information and react like a parent should.

"Hello," my dad directed to Law. He wasn't friendly, necessarily, but he wasn't rude either.

"Hello, sir. Law Masterson. Nice to meet you." Law thrust his hand forward, and my dad gave it a solid shake.

With a raised brow, he asked, "Masterson? The business mogul Masterson?"

"Yes, sir. My father and his father before him have been involved in many businesses in the city for decades."

God how I wished I possessed a fraction of this man's composure.

"What's going on here, Shepperd? What's with all the bags?" my dad asked as he took inventory of all we were lugging through the doorway.

"I'm going to stay with Law," I said defiantly. He put me in this predicament. I was serious as a heart attack when I told them I wouldn't be going to a treatment program I didn't need.

"I see," he said thoughtfully.

Before he could organize an attack, I tilted the suitcase back on its wheels and hurried down the hall. I prayed Law would just fall in step behind me but didn't look back to ensure it.

At the front door, I slowed enough to open the thing but hustled right through the second it was open wide enough to fit.

Law held the panel open so I could wrestle the suitcase over the threshold, and I mumbled a quick, "Thanks."

I rounded the back of his car and finally inhaled fresh air deep into my lungs. It felt like I was about to pass out from all the adrenaline, and so far, there really hadn't been an altercation. But that's when I saw my dad following right behind Law to the back of his car.

"Nice car, young man," he said with a nod toward Law's pretty sports car.

"Thank you, sir. I really enjoy it," he answered politely. I had to hand it to him. He was handling the situation like a pro.

"Please, call me Dave," my dad said with a friendly smile.

What the hell was he playing at?

I narrowed my eyes with serious suspicion. A few possibilities danced around in my head while Law loaded my bags into the trunk. Either my folks were really glad to see me go, or my dad was smitten with the idea of who I was leaving with. My father knew who was who in the Los Angeles business scene and had once told me to never burn a bridge you might need to cross one day. Was he trying to get in good graces with the Mastersons? I didn't really know how successful or powerful Law's family was, but I didn't miss the way my dad's facial expression changed the moment that last name was spoken.

Each thought made me as sick as the other. Was getting ahead at work more important than, say...my safety? He didn't know this big man I just announced I'd be living with, yet he was fawning over him like he wanted to claim dibs on an invitation to the bachelor party.

Law shot a quick glance my way while slamming the trunk closed. "Looks like we're set here."

"See you later, Dad," I said as Law opened my door for me to slide in.

"Shep? Not a hug or anything?" my dad asked, looking like he just lost his puppy.

What a bunch of bullshit. And now what was I going to do, ignore his request? In any other circumstance, I probably would. But with this whole nightmare taking place that Law was witnessing, I wanted to be a better human.

I climbed back out of the car and stepped up to my father. He gave me a tight squeeze, and my entire body trembled.

"We'll see you soon," my dad said and kissed the top of my head. The gesture instantly reminded me of Law, and I wanted to kick my dad in the shin for tainting one of my favorite things in my new relationship.

"Take care of my baby," my dad said to my boyfriend, and the two shook hands.

"I'll do my very best," he replied then stepped back. "She means the world to me."

I mean the world to him?

Tears immediately filled my eyes. Between that incredibly sweet comment and the stress of the past half hour, a meltdown was approaching. We had to get out of here. Now.

Law slid behind the wheel and pressed the ignition. The engine roared to life and settled into a throaty purr.

My dad looked on with a beaming smile. The man had always loved cars, and this one was right up his alley. At least they'd have that in common if we ever happened to be stuck in the same room with them again.

Rest assured, I'd do everything in my power to keep that from happening.

CHAPTER TWELVE

LAW

We drove a few blocks in tense silence before I pulled into a shopping center. After maneuvering into a parking space, I killed the engine. Shepperd scanned the storefronts then looked over at me with confusion.

I just held her gaze for a few beats then scooped her small hands into mine. "How are you doing?"

She relaxed by a degree or two. "A lot better now. I don't know if I should thank you or apologize to you first. Though I did tell you I would've done that alone."

I sat quietly at first and then very calmly said, "I'm not sure how long it's going to take for you to understand this, but lucky for you I'm a very patient man. You don't have to do the hard stuff alone anymore, Shepperd. I want to be there for you. Help you. Hold you when things are shitty, celebrate with you when things are great."

She stared at me until a slow grin spread across her lips. "What on earth have I done?" she muttered while shaking her head back and forth.

"What?" I asked.

"What have I done to deserve you? I'm so scared I'm going to fuck this up. That or you're going to come to your senses and run away terrified."

"After you meet my family, this will make more sense, but believe me when I say that was nothing."

She raised a brow with doubt.

"Seriously. My father is a formidable man. He makes other grown men cry on a weekly basis. Your dad's game is child's play comparatively, darling."

She chuckled at my word choice. "I don't know whether that's a good thing or bad thing."

"Well, it depends on what side of the conversation you're on at any given moment. He spares no one when he thinks he's right. He's put me in my place enough times so I know not to challenge him. And he doesn't care who's around to bear witness."

"Why do parents always think they know what's best for you?" she asked, but I wasn't sure if she really wanted an answer or was just thinking out loud.

So I took a chance and offered my opinion. "For my parents, I can honestly say I think they act the way they do—do the things they do—believing it's in our best interest. Whether to teach us a lesson or stop us from making what they perceive to be a mistake, I really think they come from a good place."

I thought about those words for a few seconds and added, "That doesn't mean it's always what I want to hear. Or in my dad's case, the delivery couldn't use some polishing."

"Yeah, that must be a dad thing," she said wistfully. We were both lost in our thoughts, probably each about our own relationships with our parents.

I loved my family. They'd given me a very comfortable life and every opportunity to succeed as an adult. Sure, there will always be things we'd like to change about those closest to us, but in the end, I was grateful to have the parents I had.

"Ready to head home?" I asked. The biggest grin spread over my lips, and when I looked at Shepperd, she was smiling too.

She took my breath away. I didn't get to enjoy her genuine smile as often as I would like, but my God, when the woman smiled and truly meant the feelings behind it, she lit up the entire room.

"You are so beautiful," I murmured and closed the space between our bucket seats. I kissed her slowly at first, always careful not to spook her. I followed her cues, though, and the kiss became passionate and hot. Abruptly I pulled away and stared at her. Her eyes were shiny new nickels, and I struggled to get enough oxygen.

"Why did you stop?" she whimpered and gently touched her bottom lip right where I had sunk my teeth moments before.

"Because I don't want to fuck you in my car, and if that went any further, that's exactly what would've happened." I started the engine and backed out of the parking spot before looking at Shep.

Our eyes met briefly as I put the car in gear.

"Danger," she muttered and shook her head slowly.

"Darling, you don't even know."

"But I really want to find out, Law."

That was all I needed to hear. When we got to my place... well, our place now...I was leading her directly to bed. I needed to be inside this woman more than anything.

I don't know how we got home, I was in such a lust haze from that kiss and thoughts of fucking her. If someone had me draw a map of the route I took to get back home, I'd be lost. She had me that ramped up. I probably couldn't have spelled my last name if someone had asked me to.

"You've gotten quiet," she said into the thick air.

"Lost in thoughts."

"Yeah? About what?" she asked innocently, and I wondered if I should censor myself here or be open about how long I've been wanting to claim her.

"Truth?"

"Always. We promised, remember?"

"Oh, I remember. I'm just not sure if this is in the category of TMI or not."

"I'm pretty tough to shock," she boasted. "Let's hear it."

"All I can think about is fucking you. I've been daydreaming and wet dreaming about it since the first day I laid eyes on you."

"Oh, my. See why I call you Danger?"

"I don't want to scare you. You wanted the truth." I shrugged, making no apologies. "And if you're not ready, I can wait. I may need another cold shower, but I'll wait."

There. That should make up for any part of that truth spill that sounded boorish.

"No, that's not it," she rasped and slid her tiny hand up my thigh while I drove. "You're dangerous because I want the same thing. If we're both feeling a bit desperate, who will keep the sensible head?"

My voice dropped at least one octave when I admitted, "I don't care much about sensibility right now, Miss Farsay."

When traffic permitted, I snuck a glance in her direction. She still had giant, curious eyes on me, so I gave her a little wink.

"Can I ask you something?" I prayed I wasn't about to destroy the mood brewing between us. No matter how nervous I was about that happening, this conversation needed to be had.

"Yes, of course. Open book right here," she answered, pointing back toward her sternum.

"I want to be careful not to have a repeat of that first night you were over." After she gave a quick nod, I continued. "If you have known triggers, can we talk about them now rather than after I hit one?"

Shepperd didn't answer right away and seemed more interested in looking out her window than having this discussion.

Shit. Did I blow my chance with her now?

While still gazing at the passing scenery, she finally began talking. "I'm so embarrassed that happened," she said quietly, and this time I was the one to reach across and put my hand on her thigh.

"Don't be. Please. But I don't want to have a repeat of that scene, because I felt awful for days. I want our intimate time to be amazing and fun."

"Amazing, huh?" she teased with a grin.

I screwed up my face as if she were insane. "Hell yes, amazing."

"Okay." She nodded. "I'm about due for some amazing in my life."

"Soooo?" I drew out the transition. "Triggers?"

"Ummm, well...I seem to freak out when someone tries to pin me down. That's what happened that first time. I know certain smells do it too, but I doubt I will encounter those in your bedroom, you know? Gasoline, motor oil, decaying-grass clippings." She still hadn't turned to face me, and I figured it was easier for her to have this talk without direct eye contact.

So I nodded, more interested in listening and learning

about her than adding my own comments. Of course I wanted details. That was the way my brain worked. Of course I wanted to find the monster who molested a little girl and tear his dick off and stuff it down his throat. But those were thoughts to keep to myself right now. I was smart enough to know that, at least.

She shrugged like this was just another everyday conversation. You know, how was your day? Crazy weather we're having, right? What triggers do you have from being sexually abused? Yep! Just another ho-hum conversation between friends.

"I'm not sure I like the way you're looking at me right now," she said after studying me for a few seconds.

"I'm sorry, baby. Really, I am. I'm just marveling at how strong and resilient you are."

She burst out with a laugh. "Oh, I'm the furthest from either of those things, Law."

"I don't think you give yourself enough credit. That's what I see when I look at you. I'm not sure what my expression was that made you uncomfortable, but that's really what I was thinking."

She reached over and cupped my cheek as I turned onto my street. "You're an incredible man," she said quietly. "I'm not sure how I got so lucky, but I'm going to do everything I can not to fuck this up."

I swung my car into the driveway and put the car in park. We both inhaled loudly and looked at each other. The anticipation was back between us, and my heartbeat became a jackhammer in my chest. I couldn't remember the last time a woman made me feel that way.

"Let's go inside," I said and gave her a quick peck. "We have the rest of the night, and I want to take my time."

She sucked in another breath, and I smiled. She was right where I wanted her mentally—here with me, in the present. I would do everything in my power to erase all the bad memories she had. By the time I was finished loving this girl, she wouldn't be able to remember a time she wasn't mine.

★ ★ ★

In the low light of my bedroom, I lifted her shirt over her head and let it drop from my fingers to the floor. I knew she had a slight build from watching her so often at the gym, but seeing her without clothes was a different experience.

I didn't mind thin girls. In fact, I preferred it. But Shepperd was on the dangerous side of too thin, and I filed the impression away in the recesses of my mind to address it with her when the time was right.

This was not that time. Right now, I stood before the incredible creature and carefully studied her reactions. Breaths were even if a bit shallow. If she wasn't truly calm, she was forcing herself to appear that way.

Even after I promised, "Baby, I'm going to make you feel so good," while snaking my arms behind her to release the clasp of her lacy bra, she held my gaze with attentive eyes. I slid the light blue straps down her arms with sure fingers and let the sexy little thing fall to the ground between our feet.

"My God," I whispered into her ear while kissing and licking her there. "You are stunning, Shepperd."

"Thank you," she said between the little mewls and sighs she treated me with. "That feels so good."

"Tell me what you like," I growled. My blood was thrumming in my veins, and my dick was harder than it had ever been.

I just wanted to worship her. I wanted to show her how amazing I would make her feel every time we were together. From a very young age, I became fascinated by women's bodies. Not that I sexualized every female I saw, but I admired the differences between the way men and women were built. The way a woman's waist nipped in on the sides and created that alluring hourglass silhouette. Or the way a woman's neck was long and graceful compared to a man's muscular, thick one that was designed to carry heavy burdens.

She put a little space between our bodies, but I didn't approve of that. At all. I gripped her waist in both hands and pulled her right back against my body.

"Where do you think you're going?" I teased before planting a long, deep kiss on her mouth.

The way this woman kissed was driving me crazy. First, she teased a little with her lips on mine, the top and then the bottom, before she plunged into the experience with so much passion it felt like our lips would fuse.

"I was trying to see your face better. I couldn't tell if you were serious or just saying sexy things." Her voice had become low and husky and, if possible, even sexier than it normally was.

"Christ, even your voice is sexy." I gave her a playfully menacing look. "You're going to be the death of me."

"Well, that wouldn't be much fun, would it?" she replied, and we both smiled. "Especially before I get some of this." She reached for the obvious erection pressing on the fabric of my pants, but I intercepted her dainty hand before she made contact.

"No. Not yet," I directed and quickly reminded myself to

dial it back a little. I maneuvered her to my bed and instructed, "Lie back, baby. I want you completely naked." I gently pushed her by the shoulders after she sat on the edge of the mattress, then crawled over her and took a few seconds to admire her beauty again. I shook my head a little trying hard to figure out what it was about this woman that had me so tied up in knots.

Throughout the years, I'd had plenty of women in my bed. Maybe by some standards, more than my fair share. But I never felt this all-consuming need to possess a woman like the way I was feeling in that moment. Something about this blond bombshell laid out before me was doing things I couldn't make sense of.

Keeping my head on straight and playing it cool became my biggest challenge. I continually reminded myself to go slow to not freak her out. Once we had more time as a couple beneath our belts, I would talk to her about the side of me that was more dominant than I had been letting her see. I knew a lot of trauma survivors responded well to particular aspects of the BDSM lifestyle, so it could turn out to fit very well in our relationship.

Relationship...

Crazy to think that's what we were building here. This was our very first night together, and it had to be perfect. I was so out of my element with this. I kept getting lost in my own thoughts. I didn't typically entertain doubt while fucking a woman, but the stakes had never been this high. I really wanted this to work out.

"Law?" Shepperd's voice brought me back to the here and now. "You okay?"

"Yeah, baby." I nodded. "I'm so good I'm having trouble wrapping my head around it."

Shepperd made the cutest gesture by lifting her arms to me, inviting me closer to her on the bed.

So, with a satisfied smile on my face, I covered her body with my own. I was careful not to crush her beneath my much larger frame and studied her expression.

"Is this okay?" I asked while kissing along her neck.

"Mmm, yes. More than okay." She put her hands on my shoulders and pushed me back a fraction of an inch. "You're not going to set me off, Law. I'm here. I'm present. I promise." She gave me that shy smile that melted my heart and made my stomach flip at the same time. My smile matched hers before I pressed my lips to hers once more.

"Tonight we'll go nice and slow. Get to know each other's do's and don'ts," I explained while kissing a path toward her breasts.

She arched into my affection, and I latched on to her dusty pink nipple. The stiff bud felt so perfect in my mouth, I had to pause and suck—and then suck harder. She moaned a low, throaty sound so I did it again. I used my tongue to draw a slick path from her nipple to the sensitive underside of her breast.

Her vocal approval gave me the green light to continue my exploration. Her tits weren't big, but they were surprisingly ample for how thin her frame was. If she were older, I might have suspected she had implants, but based on the feel of her flesh when I kneaded and squeezed her mounds, she was as real as they came.

"Ohhh," she sighed as I moved down her body.

"Feel good, baby?"

"So good," she whispered. "I suspect you don't really need my praise to know that, though."

That was the first slightly insecure comment she'd made,

so I locked eyes with her from where I was licking and nibbling the skin on her flat belly. Instead of getting defensive from my stern look, she melted me with a little smile, so I went back to enjoying my mission.

Her pants had to go. Immediately. I felt possessed by the need to see her completely bare. I sat back on my heels and unfastened the button and zipper at her waist. Using my flat palms, I spread the fabric open on each side, exposing delicate light-blue panties that matched the bra she had been wearing. I might have actually whimpered when I discovered they were my favorite thong style.

"You're so fucking sexy, girl. I'm going insane here." I had to palm my cock through my pants to gain some sort of control. I felt like a high school boy, I was so excited. Like this would be the first pussy I'd ever touched or tasted.

Peeling the lacy material down her thighs, I imagined all the ways I'd like to bind her with the lingerie. I knew we had to work up to that, though, so I pushed the idea to the back of my mind for now. The differences between the way I handled this girl versus the normal dirty fucks I'd enjoyed in the very same bed were startling and, strangely, not at all disappointing. I felt compelled to burn the damn mattress I'd had other partners on and have a new one brought in just for her.

The panties were tossed to the floor with the bra and pants. I took a moment to appreciate her from head to toe. Shepperd's long blond hair fanned out behind her head on the pillow. I instantly thought of old religious paintings where the artist depicted a person's holiness with a glowing yellow circle behind their head. I could picture the stained-glass windows in my childhood church that were all done that way. This girl could easily be an angel or saint. Something so pure and good, and so incredibly beautiful.

"Spread your legs for me." My voice sounded more like a growl, and she did what I'd asked. I inhaled the air and prayed I'd catch her scent. Yes, I was one of those men who loved that womanly scent. Nothing came close to matching it, and my cock somehow grew thicker knowing that soon I'd have her deliciousness all over my lips and tongue.

I ran my hands from her knees up to her pussy and framed the treasure between my thumbs and index fingers, and added a few more strokes in the same manner while I appreciated how silky and smooth she was. Her fair skin glowed in the dim light like a pale moon in an overcast night sky.

"You're so damn beautiful, lady. I can't stop looking at you." I shook my head, wondering how I got so lucky to have this woman here with me. The thoughts had my heart thumping in an unfamiliar way and a lump building in my throat.

True emotion, I decided. Not just lust or physical attraction. I genuinely cared about Shepperd, and it fortified my need to show her how good I could make her feel. When I ran my palms up her legs one more time, she let out a frustrated whimper when I reached the junction of her thighs.

"What is it, baby?" I asked, knowing damn well what the answer would be.

"You're driving me crazy with the teasing," she whispered into the barely lit room.

"Tell me what you want."

"Touch me. Please, just do it already."

"I don't want to rush this," I confessed.

She relaxed deeper into the bedding while I exhaled. The more comfortable she was with me touching her, the less likely she would be to freak out. Or at least that seemed like the way it should go. I reminded myself to keep the slow pace regardless.

Finally, I positioned myself between her spread legs and licked a path toward her pussy. I wanted it more than air. Shepperd widened her legs, and my cock swelled beneath me.

I ground my hips into the mattress for some relief. At this rate, I'd last two minutes inside her. I'd been anticipating this moment for so long, but the reality was beyond anything I'd imagined.

Her silky skin smelled like a day at the beach. Coconut and sea breeze filled my nose with an alluring scent as I nuzzled my way to the treasure between her legs. Once there, I took my time exploring her body with my fingers and tongue until she was moaning into the still room. Her feminine musk was deep in my senses, and I kept the pace until she exploded beneath my ministrations.

"Fuck yes. Come for me, baby," I coaxed as the first tremors of her orgasm tensed her muscles. I lapped at her folds and drug out the pleasure until she squeezed her slender thighs against my face, urging me to back off.

"You taste so good, I don't want to stop."

She gasped. "So...sensitive," she said between quakes of her legs and stomach. "Jesus Christ, Law."

My male pride swelled along with my dick. Nothing in the world was better than giving a woman pleasure that way. I'd spent years figuring out the secret little ways most women reached climax, and my attention to detail paid off once again. Though I had to admit—to myself at least—that this particular woman was nothing like any other I'd known.

A strange thought kept pushing its way to the forefront of my mind. The intensity of the feelings I was experiencing should alarm me. Yet I couldn't wipe the smile from my face.

Something about her here with me felt just—right. Perfect, really. So again, I pushed the worry away and stayed in the moment. I wanted to absorb it all. Catalog every detail and tuck them all away for safekeeping. I didn't want to share any part of her with anyone else, and that ownership vibe should've scared me too.

But instead, I just wanted to claim her completely and make sure she never wanted to leave.

Ever.

CHAPTER THIRTEEN

SHEPPERD

With my arousal coating his lips, Law moved back up my body and planted an open-mouthed kiss on me. He demanded entrance with firm pressure from his lips and then tongue. I moaned when the taste of my own pleasure hit my tastebuds. Why was that so erotic? Especially while he pushed his way closer to settle between my thighs. In this position, I could feel his firm cock against my already throbbing pussy, and it was ecstasy.

I was so used to unsatisfying encounters with men. This guy was scrambling my brain, and all I could think was *more*. More lips. More tongue. More cock. More everything. And right goddamn now.

I clutched his toned shoulders while he kissed me and felt so secure and at peace. With him, with what we were doing—it all felt so right. Confidence oozed from every slide of his tongue, caress of his fingers, groan from deep in his chest, and it lit me up from within—like the brightest sunny day. I felt happy and excited for the first time in so long, tears pricked the backs of my eyes and threatened to ruin it all.

To hide my emotions, I buried my face in the crook of his neck and sucked in greedy gasps while I wound down from my climax. But with his dick rubbing persistently against my sex, I was finding it difficult to get to that serene place where I normally settled after coming.

I just wanted more. Trying to put a sliver of space between our faces, I whimpered, "Law...please."

"What, baby? Please what?" he asked and actually looked concerned.

"I need you," I said and felt slickness flood my pussy. Mentally I was ready. Physically I was ready. If he didn't fuck me soon, I'd take matters into my own hands and guide his cock to the spot where I needed him.

When I first started having casual sex, I was always the aggressor. I felt safer being the one directing the action and making the choices. Being in charge assured me nothing would happen that I didn't want to happen. At my core, I was still a red-blooded woman. I wanted to be satisfied and loved regardless of the fact that some slimeball loser took advantage of me as a child.

As soon as a shard of a memory about my experience stabbed into my mind, I banished it. That fucker wouldn't rob me of this chance at happiness. So many other opportunities had been passed over in my life out of fear, thoughts of unworthiness, and anger. He wouldn't win this time.

Law pulled back to get a good look at my expression. "Still doing okay?"

Gulping the resolve down deep, I said, "Yeah. Yeah, I'm good."

I couldn't be sure if I sold my reassurance based on the way he continued to watch me. I realized I had scared the guy good the first time we fooled around, but I couldn't do this twenty-questions bit every time I needed to get laid. I would not have pegged Law to be the doting, careful guy he was in bed.

The sexy, hungry way he used to watch me in the gym always unspooled fantasies of rough, dirty, carnal sex. Typically, reserved and measured guys turned me off. I just wanted to break his resolve and see what he was hiding beneath this shell of restraint.

Might as well just jump to the point. "Do you have condoms? I probably do if you don't."

He kissed the tip of my nose before teasing, "Getting impatient?"

"Hell yes, I am. I couldn't be more desperate right now. Please." I added that last word to the end because I didn't miss the naughty glimmer in his eyes the other times I'd said it.

This time was no different, and it finally spurred him into action. He sat back on his heels for a moment and gave my body a long, wolfish look. To push him more, I snaked my hand down my abdomen and gave my clit a slow circle.

"Oh, fuck me, Shepperd." He moaned with his eyes fixed on my busy fingers.

"That's what I've been begging you for, man. We want the exact same thing."

Law scurried off the bed and bent over the nightstand to riffle through the top drawer. He shuffled its contents from side to side before identifying the blue square box. Two condoms were tossed onto the bed beside me, and he was back. I watched him roll on the protection and reposition himself between my legs.

"You good like this? To start at least?" he asked with a mischievous grin.

"I'll take it however you want to give it to me," I rasped. His cock was going to hurt a bit, but nothing that would be unbearable. I would definitely enjoy the little aches and pains tomorrow that would remind me of how we spent our night.

"Fuck, you're so wet," he commented as he guided his dick through my folds to my entrance.

I brought my knees closer to my chest and squeezed my thighs against his rib cage while we kissed. He slid in slowly, drawing out the exquisite feeling of that first thrust.

There was no containing my vocal thrill, and the sounds I made seemed to encourage him to go deeper, and then deeper still. By the time his pelvis was against mine, the moaning and whimpering had turned into nonsensical babble. I repeated the words "Yes, please" and "Oh my God" over and over until his thrusts came at the perfect pace to rob my breath. He had wedged one forearm beneath the slope of my back and lifted my hips to crash with his. Wet, sexy sounds of our bodies joining filled the room in chorus with our voices, and before I knew it, I teetered on the edge of another orgasm.

"Shit, Law. My God, I'm going to come. Don't stop, please."

"That's my girl. Shatter for me, baby. Let me feel your cunt flutter all around me," my gorgeous lover demanded, and I was more than happy to comply.

I tilted my head back in hopes he'd lean over and kiss me while my pussy spasmed around his cock, but instead, he sucked one of my nipples into his desperate mouth and bit me. The sharp pain kicked off another tremor through my nervous system that somehow turned into a mini orgasm as Law's dick swelled and then erupted into the condom.

After a few slower pumps of his hips, he collapsed to the side of me and quickly gathered my body in his arms and pulled me against his hot, slick chest.

He smelled so damn good, I wanted to inhale the deep,

rich scent over and over. His arms remained banded in a snug, secure embrace so tight that I felt his heart thundering against my spine.

"Thank you," I murmured with my lips pressed against his bicep. I don't think I'd ever thanked someone for fucking me, but the words tumbled out before I could barricade them in.

Law had his face buried in my hair, rubbing his nose and lips along my nape. The motion, coupled with his warm breath, ramped me up all over again.

"It was my absolute pleasure. Thank you."

He added the second part after a beat, and I wondered if he said it because I had.

I chuckled at my busy brain's nonsense. "What are you thanking me for? You did all the work, man."

"Turn over and face me," he issued in a demanding but kind tone. I was doing it before I could shoot my mouth off to defend myself. It was a knee-jerk reaction I took whenever I felt cornered. If I could shock someone with a rude remark, it usually threw them off my scent so I didn't have to deal with messy feelings.

No words were available, but I held his stare in the dark room.

Law cupped my cheek in his large palm and finally spoke. "Thank you, beautiful girl, for trusting me with your body. Thank you for staying present with me here in this room, and most of all"—he smirked in a boyish way—"thank you for agreeing to stay here with me. I hope this is the first of many, many, hot, dirty nights in this very bed."

So, it wasn't exactly what I was expecting, but not too far off either. I was definitely caught off guard when he admitted he was glad I moved in. His words helped ease the anxiety mounting over being a charity case.

I decided to reuse his words and replied, “It’s my absolute pleasure too.”

CHAPTER FOURTEEN

LAW

Later that night, we sat in the living room, sprawled out in front of the television. Shepperd lay in front of me on the sofa, and I had a heavy arm draped over her hip. I couldn't tell you what we watched because I was lost in thought and distracted by her warm body.

My dick wouldn't settle down for more than five minutes, even though we fucked in the shower after the first time in my bed and again when we took up this entwined spot on the sofa. I still wanted more.

"You're like a drug, I swear," I breathed into her hair.

"Law," she whimpered, her voice sexy and raspy from all the activity. "I don't think I can go again. I'm not sure I can even walk at this point."

"Sshh, baby, I know. My body is running on its own agenda right now. I don't think I could either." It only took a second to reassess that dumb comment, and I laughed aloud. "Okay, that's not true, but I understand what you're saying. I'm obsessed, not cruel."

"Obsessed? Really?"

"Oh...one hundred percent."

"Does that concern you?" she asked but continued staring at the television screen where two girls took turns gossiping about each other.

I answered honestly. "No, not really. Feels damn good, actually." But then I realized maybe the words made her uncomfortable, so I asked, "Does it worry you?" Oxygen was in short supply while I waited for her to reply.

Her body didn't tense, though, and she only took a few seconds to reply. "Nah, I'm not worried either. This has been one of the best days I can remember."

I wanted to turn her to face me but thought it might be easier for her to talk openly without the scrutiny of my direct stare.

"Hey, listen, while I'm thinking of it," I began, and she looked at me over her shoulder. "It's nothing bad, I just keep forgetting to ask you."

"Okaaaay," she dragged out skeptically. "What's up?"

"My niece's birthday is this weekend, and my brother and his woman are throwing a party for her. I was hoping you'd be my date." Why the hell did I feel so nervous asking her to go with me? Probably because she'd meet a lot of my family members there and damn straight I'd be introducing her to everyone as my girlfriend.

"Sure, I guess. What day? Saturday or Sunday?"

"Pretty sure it's Saturday. Do you have to work?" I asked, hoping she didn't have a readymade excuse not to go.

"Nope. That's the best thing about an office job. Monday through Friday," she said and sat up so we could chat. "Have you gotten a gift already?"

"Shit, no. Well, looks like I'll need to do that before the party. I swear I'm the worst gift giver on the planet."

But the little angel sitting in front of me lit up like a Christmas tree. "You're in luck! I love picking out presents for other people. Maybe more than receiving gifts myself."

"Would you mind going with me to pick something up?"

"I was hoping you'd ask. I'd be happy to go with you." She looked at the dainty watch on her wrist and wrinkled her nose. "Probably too late to go now, so we'll have to go tomorrow. How old is she?"

I thought for a second and remembered Jacob telling me that his daughter Vela and our niece Stella were in the same class at school. "She's the same age as my niece, so...nine. In fact, I'm sure Stella will be at the party too, so you'll get to meet some of my family."

"Oh, wait a second," she said, and her entire demeanor shifted—from excited and enthusiastic to trepidatious in the blink of an eye.

"What's wrong?" I asked and took her hands in mine, ready to reassure her.

"I wonder if my sister will be there. Maybe I shouldn't go. I don't want to cause any drama." She bit into her bottom lip with worry.

"Darling, why would that cause drama?" I asked innocently. I knew there was some tension between Shepperd and her family members, but I didn't realize it was intense enough to make her miss out on something she just seemed excited about.

She stood and began pacing around the room. "I probably used the wrong word. Not drama necessarily. Just awkwardness. Plus, maybe she won't be there. Her baby is still pretty young. I don't know if they're taking her places just yet."

"I guess I didn't realize you didn't get along," I said, and she stopped pacing long enough to give me a look I hadn't seen before. Something along the lines of Be serious, you moron, and I didn't like it very much.

"Explain this look you're giving me."

"What look?" she snapped back. Man, this girl's moods flipped like a switch.

"This look." I stepped up to block her pacing, and she looked up the length of my body until she met my eyes.

"Sorry," she murmured. And just like that, the defensiveness was gone, and she was small and contrite in the space she took up in front of me.

"You don't have to apologize, Shep. Just help me understand. What's the beef between you and your sister? Sorry, I can't remember her name even though I'm sure you've told me before."

"Hannah," she said with a grimace toward the floor.

"That's right. Hannah. She's the one married to Elijah Banks, right?"

"She is. And they just had a little baby girl a few weeks ago." She thought for a moment and then corrected herself. "Shit, it's been almost two months already." She cradled her face in her hands and mumbled, "Another reason for everyone to be pissed at me."

I tugged her hands down and wrapped them in my own. They were cold in my warm grip, and I waited patiently for her to look at me. "What's going on?" I asked when she finally lifted her chin. "Even your hands are cold now." In the back of my mind, I suspected she was working up to an anxiety attack but didn't want to suggest it out loud.

"They all hate me," she said in a small voice. "Everything I do is wrong. I don't want to ruin your niece's party, Law. Maybe I shouldn't go."

And we circled the wagon completely. "Okay, please

settle down." I winced the moment the words came out of my mouth. I knew the first thing not to say to someone having an anxiety attack was *calm down.* I'd been through this before with another girl I dated and learned some crucial lessons the hard way.

"Sorry," I apologized instantly. "I know that doesn't help. Can we sit down and talk about this?"

It was a true testament to how much I cared about this girl. Normally, I didn't have an ounce of patience for stuff like this. It felt manipulative and a tad childish if I were being bluntly honest. But having that thought just made me frustrated with myself.

Obviously, she was having a barrage of issues crowding her brain. She deserved patience and kindness while she worked through it all.

I wanted to be the one to show her that grace.

Carefully, she lowered to the couch as though it caused her physical pain. I took the cushion beside her and angled my body toward hers. I wanted to blurt out question after question but knew she needed time to organize her thoughts. So I waited for her to start the conversation.

Finally, she said, "I'm sorry."

"What are you apologizing for? You've done nothing wrong."

Waving her hand in the air in front of us, she said, "This. All this. It's ridiculous." She shook her head a couple of times before dropping her face into her open palms.

"It's not. Talk to me. Walk me through where that came from so I can understand," I requested as gently as possible.

"It's my family. It's just so much crap between us all that has never been dealt with. So it just builds and builds and builds, and now we have this enormous pile of crap between us and not one shovel to be found."

I hoped I wasn't stepping over the line but asked, "Have you ever tried talking to them? Like not in the heat of an argument but when everyone is calm and thinking open-mindedly?"

"I'm sure over the years I've tried. And for whatever reason, nothing was resolved. Things have just gotten worse and worse over time. I'm not sure if I told you this before... I don't think I have..." She paused and took a deep breath as though whatever she was about to say was so heavy she needed to gather strength to say it. "My sister Hannah was nearly abducted when she was six years old. Maye and I were just babies. My mom had all of us in Target by herself, and two people cornered my sister and dragged her to the restroom."

"Oh no..."

Judging by the look on her face, there was still more to the story.

"They drugged her, cut her hair, changed her into little boy's clothes, and then tried to leave the store with her as their own child. The management locked down the entire store, and my mom recognized her in their arms as they tried to leave. So they were caught, prosecuted, and sent to jail."

Strangely, she recited the facts like the anchor on the evening news. Detached and unfeeling, even though she was talking about her own family.

Still, I said, "Oh, baby, I'm so sorry. Your mother must have been terrified." It seemed like an appropriate response to that bomb drop.

She shrugged. "I'm sure she was. Hannah has had nightmares her whole life about it even though her actual memory is spotty about it happening. I'm sure it's been just as hard on her," she added, and I thought it might have been the first kind, understanding thing I'd heard her say about one of her siblings.

So why all the bitterness and resentment? I wanted to ask the question but didn't want to interrupt her now that she was sharing.

So she continued. "But here's the thing. We have all relived that day over and over again. Whether it was through my parents' paranoia that something was going to happen if we were out of their sight for even a minute or my sister always being handled with kid gloves. Like she was their only child, you know? While the rest of us needed our parents just as much and were often left to fend for ourselves. Over the years, especially now that I'm older, I think they've done more damage in the way they've dealt with the experience than the experience did itself."

I scooped her hands into mine and lifted her knuckles to my lips. After placing gentle kisses on both hands, I looked at her for a long moment. I was angry for her. I was sad for her. But most of all, I wanted to be here for her. In all the times her parents and sisters failed to support her, I wanted her to know she could count on me. Her trust issues made a lot more sense now.

I decided to take a risk and draw a line connecting what she had just told me to the original situation she'd shared. God save me if I set her off.

"It makes sense why you never trusted your parents enough to tell them about the abuse at school. You probably thought either they wouldn't believe you or didn't have the time for you because they seemed to be more focused on

Hannah all the time."

While I spoke, she nodded in agreement. And then another thought was born from the previous. I could definitely be connecting dots that had no business being connected, but it seemed pretty obvious to me. Maybe talking about it with me would give her the courage to finally address this topic with her family.

"You've said before that you suspected the same janitor molested your sister. Knowing about her history now, I would think she made a pretty ripe target for the bastard. Do you ever think about talking to her about what happened?"

"I mean, I've fantasized about it, you know? Like what would that be like to have something we could bond over? And what an awful thing to bond over, right?" She forced out a laugh, but we both knew it wasn't close to being funny.

Christ, this was a fucked-up situation. But these women deserved peace and security in their lives. The strength they could get from each other could help them navigate daily life after being taken advantage of so cruelly.

Suddenly, Shepperd inhaled deeply through her nose and sat up taller. "Okay," she said. "That's enough of that bullshit for one night. Please let's change the subject."

I was baffled by her declaration and didn't know how to react. How did she just turn it off like that? I couldn't figure out the how, but I was sure about the why. This was her unhealthy way of coping. Still, words escaped me completely.

Shepperd shot to her feet, pivoted to face me and planted her hands on her hips. "Why are you just staring at me now?"

"Sit down," I said in a quiet but direct tone.

Out of instinct, she followed my instruction and sat back down on the cushion beside me.

Keeping my voice calm, I said, "If you could be fair here, you could admit that was a lot for anyone to digest. I'm trying to process everything you've told me and at the same time be careful in how I respond. I realize that attitude is your normal go-to with people, but I don't think I deserve to be spoken to like that. I wasn't staring at you in any way other than complete admiration."

She made a disagreeing sound and crossed her arms over her chest. Tempting me—more than she realized—to sling her across my lap and spank her ass for the bratty behavior. But I knew I couldn't use that approach with her just yet.

"How could you possibly admire me, Law? Be serious. I just admitted to all that shit, and you want me to believe that? Come on..."

"Shepperd, listen to me. The stuff that has happened in your life? Those things don't define you. You were the victim. You didn't choose those things." I waited until she locked her deep blue eyes on mine and then continued. "The way you've handled these experiences is what makes you who you are. For the most part, I'd say you've been incredibly brave and strong to have risen above it all and make the best out of your life. Is there still work to be done? Of course, there is. We are all a work in progress, don't you think? I mean, really, until the day we die, we work on being better versions of ourselves. The only thing that would make me look at you in any other way than awe would be if you just gave up on yourself and didn't continue to persevere."

I realized that was a bit of a lecture, but she needed to hear positive things about herself. The number she was doing on her own self-esteem was hard to battle. And she had years of a head start.

She studied her folded hands in her lap after I let all that fly out. The silence in the room was bigger than either one of us. When she finally looked up to meet my waiting gaze again, she had tears in her eyes.

"Oh, baby..." I started and opened my arms in time to catch her slim body coming my way. She hurled herself into my embrace, and I pulled her into my lap. With my arms banded snuggly around her, I gently rocked her back and forth for a long time. I kissed the top of her head and murmured sweet, reassuring things into the still room. Every once and awhile she'd let out a sniffle or a gulp of air, but mostly we sat there in silence.

"I love holding you like this," I admitted with my nose buried in her long hair. "You feel so perfect in my arms, I could stay like this forever."

"Don't you think they'd miss you at work?" she teased into my neck, and I grinned behind her head.

"Thank you for sharing all of that with me. I'm honored that you feel safe enough with me to tell me about your past," I said against her crown, and she clutched my body tighter.

"I'm so scared," she mumbled.

If the room hadn't been so still, I would've thought I'd misunderstood what she'd said.

"Why? I'm right here, baby. No one is going to hurt you as long as I'm around," I vowed. And those words came out on their own will. It was like my mind and body just reacted to this woman on a wavelength that didn't involve conscious decision.

"No, that's not what I mean. I'm terrified you're going to run in the other direction. I know I have a lot of baggage, Law. I do. It's been a really long time..." she paused there and slowly shook her head back and forth as if disagreeing with herself.

"Okay, that's not true. I've never actually felt strong enough to deal with it all myself, let alone share it with someone who matters to me."

I separated our bodies so I could see her face. I couldn't help the grin I was sporting and knew she would get defensive if I didn't quickly explain the expression.

"So I matter to you?" I asked, somewhat teasing, somewhat thrilled she admitted her feelings for me.

She tilted her head to the side. "Yeah. More than I'd care to admit, actually."

"What do you mean?" I asked and tried to keep any hurt I might have been feeling out of my tone.

"I don't want to get hurt, you know?"

"I'm not going to hurt you, Shepperd. Or rather, I can promise to do everything I can so that doesn't happen."

"Thank you. I can't really ask for more than that, can I?"

"Oh, darling, you can ask for anything your heart desires, and I will be thrilled to give it to you," I said with a playful wink. It was time to lighten up the conversation a bit.

"Hmmm," she said with her finger to her chin. "In that case, I'd really like some ice cream."

"Done!" I said and stood with her still in my arms, laughing as I kissed the tip of her nose. "Let's go see what we have in the freezer."

CHAPTER FIFTEEN

SHEPPERD

By the time the weekend rolled around, I had myself convinced that going to this family birthday party would be a monumental mistake. I never did well in social gatherings, whether it was with family or friends. The noise level alone typically got me so edgy, I ended up biting off someone's head for the most minor of infractions.

Getting out of it didn't seem like an option, though. As the week progressed, Law became more and more excited that I'd be meeting his closest brother, oldest sister, and her little girl. Adding to my tension, we were able to confirm that my sister Hannah and her husband, Elijah, would also be at the party.

The one bright spot in all of it was that I'd get to see my brand-new niece. I loved little babies and couldn't wait to hold her. It would be neat to see Law around his niece, too. From the way he talked about her, she was the apple of the family's eye. Already, I knew there would be a lot of choked-down emotions, and I needed to bring my best game face so I didn't embarrass myself.

Then there was the food situation at gatherings like this. It was hard to say what I dreaded more—copious amounts of food and drink or general people-ing. Eating in crowds made me terribly uncomfortable. When you're the "too thin" girl in the room, everyone nonchalantly keeps track of your caloric intake and does a shitty job at hiding their concern.

Which brought me to the current dilemma as I stood wrapped in a bath towel trying to find something to wear. I didn't have an expansive wardrobe to begin with, and about half of what I did own was still at my parents' house. That left me with the handful of outfits I rotated through for work and a few things that registered higher on the scale of acceptable for public viewing. The rest were oversized sweats or workout clothes.

Warm arms circled my waist, coaxing me to lean back into Law's embrace.

"Mmmm," he groaned and trailed kisses across my shoulder and up the length of my neck. "You smell good enough to eat," he growled before sinking his teeth into my skin.

I smacked the top of his head playfully and warned, "Don't you dare leave a mark on me." When in truth, I'd love nothing more than exactly that. But not right before meeting his family for the first time.

We just had amazing sex before I got in the shower, but the man's libido was in high drive all the time. Not that you'd hear me complaining. He was an incredibly generous lover. He spent hours lavishing my body with his attention, and I was utterly addicted. I'd never had a boyfriend like this man before, and I reminded myself constantly not to fuck it up.

"What are you going to wear?" he asked when he finally peeled his face from my body.

I dropped my shoulders low. "That's exactly what I'm trying to figure out. I had this one dress in mind, but I don't see it here. It must still be at my parents' house."

"Do you have a lot more stuff there? And what did you

decide to do about the car? Last we talked, your dad was going to have it looked at..."

Something in my expression pulled him up short, and he stood there nervously waiting for me to either reply like a normal person or permit the explosion of frustration I felt regarding the situation in general.

Not his fault. Not his fault.

I reminded myself not to snap at him with a sassy answer.

It was almost unnerving how well he already knew me. As quickly as my anger flared to life, it ebbed as he shifted from foot to foot. A grin spread across my lips as I watched his confusion blossom at my mood swing. So I reached out to reassure him I wasn't about to blow.

"I'm fine, man. I swear. I'm getting better at the whole"—I made air quotes—"*control the rage* routine." I wrapped my arms around his fit waist and hugged him. "I can't tell you how grateful I am to have found you, Mr. Masterson."

He looked down at me with one brow raised high. "I think I was the one who found you, no?"

"Oh, no way. I saw you first."

"No way."

"Seriously. I watched you do squats one day for thirty minutes, and you never even knew I was there." I rolled my eyes back and fluttered my eyelashes. "It was a glorious show, let me tell you."

Law pulled me into his arms again as we both laughed.

Undoubtedly, I had laughed more in the past few weeks with this man in my life than I had in multiple previous years combined. It felt so good. Laughing with Law felt like I had sunshine sparkling in my veins. He made me feel like I effervesced from deep inside, and it was a heady feeling. I wanted more and more days like these.

Was I falling in love with him? Was it too soon?

When we were little girls, our mom would tell us stories about meeting a man, falling in love, and one day, getting married. Since it was the highlight of her life, she made it sound like it was all a girl could hope for. Even as a child, I was skeptical. But she painted such a magical picture, we would listen with starry eyes and bated breath.

She insisted she fell in love with our dad in a matter of days, and if asked, he would say the same. So that became exactly what we all wanted. After I was molested, though, I completely lost faith in humanity, and any dream of getting out from under that dark, oppressive experience seemed hopeless. In my bitter world, there was no way in hell the end of the rainbow would be at a man's feet.

Growing serious, I stared into Law's deep, rich chocolate eyes. He stilled as the words danced on the tip of my tongue. No way would I say them first and drive him screaming from the room. No way...

"You've been the greatest gift the universe has ever given me," I told him instead. And I meant every word of that statement. It just seemed like the safer of the two overwhelming feelings to share.

"Thank you, darling. That's a lovely thing to say."

So I expounded on the thought. He deserved to hear the effect he was having on me. Normally, I wasn't that brave. If I had strong emotions, especially positive ones, I kept them to myself. If I didn't put them out into the world, they couldn't be taken away or destroyed.

"I think I had given up hope that I'd ever be happy. It just didn't seem like it was in the cards for me, you know? One by one, my sisters have met their forever guys. In the meantime, I've been sitting on the sidelines convinced it would never be my turn at love. Or happiness."

Oh shit.

Maybe I shouldn't have used the L-word in any context. At least I added happiness on there at the end. A quick scan of his reaction showed no signs of discomfort or panic.

He slowly closed the space between us and kissed me. Like every other time, he took my breath away. He had soft but demanding full lips. The kind of lips women look at with envy. The kind of lips you daydream about feeling all over your body.

When we parted, he gave me the slow, sexy smile I loved the most. "And we're just getting started, baby."

My brain stalled in the fog of bliss he created. I just stared at him, unable to respond intelligently.

"Now let's get ready or we're going to be late. Want to pregame a little bit? I'll open a bottle of wine or something."

Damn. Why hadn't I thought of that? Perfect way to take the edge off the nerves that skyrocketed again the moment he reminded me of our afternoon adventure ahead.

"That sounds perfect." I smiled over my shoulder as I turned back toward the closet. Law walked off to the kitchen, and I rummaged through my pitiful clothes and tried to put an outfit together.

Ninety minutes and two glasses of wine later, I looked at myself in the mirror and felt pretty good about the results. I ended up going with a denim-on-denim look, some chunky heels that brought me a little closer to Law's height, and fresh make-up that had my skin all dewy and glowing. I looked and felt fuller of life than I had in years and took a moment to absorb it all.

"Fuck me, woman," Law groaned low when I entered the kitchen. He was ready long ago and busied himself on his laptop while perched at the island. "Maybe we should stay in," he said in that husky voice that made goosebumps pop out all over my body.

He pulled me between his spread thighs as he sat on the counter stool, and I clasped my hands behind his neck.

"I don't think I can take you out in public like this," he said, shaking his head. "I'm going to end up in a fistfight."

Heat crawled up my chest and neck while I burrowed my face into his chest. He had a way of making me feel so good yet so awkward at the same time. I wanted to be fierce and confident like everyone thought I was, even though I knew the truth was so much different.

I had become a master at covering all the fucked-up things inside with a brave, no-nonsense mask on the outside. Whether people were intimidated because they thought I was truly that confident or put off because I seemed that brash, it didn't matter. It just meant I didn't have to engage with people I didn't know well. It was my way of mediating risk. If I didn't get close to anyone, I couldn't be hurt.

Law eventually put some space between our bodies. "Ready to go?"

"Mmmm, I was warming up to the idea of staying home," I said through a smile. A girl could dream, right?

"It's going to be fine," he reassured as he stood and closed his laptop. "Everyone will be focused on the birthday girl and not even notice us there."

"See? We could skip it, and no one would know the difference," I teased but followed him to the front door. I stood to the side while he set the security alarm and locked the front door.

He clasped my hand, and we walked to his parked car on the driveway.

"Wait!" I realized just as he opened my door. "We never got a gift!"

"In the back already," he answered coolly. "I had my assistant deal with it yesterday. Wrapped and everything."

I narrowed my eyes his way.

"What?" He chuckled. "That's what I pay the guy for."

Internally I let out a sigh of relief, thankful that he had a male assistant and not some little hottie I had to worry about on top of everything else that poisoned my mind. People had no idea about the war going on inside my brain. Every little thing was examined and reexamined for signs of truth or dishonesty, for hidden motives versus pure altruism.

We spent the drive to Law's brother's house chatting about the movie we watched the night before and planned what shows we wanted to binge the next time we had an entire day to ourselves.

Before I knew it, we were creeping along a residential street looking for an open parking spot. My nerves were fine until I saw the chaotic activity on the street clearly centered around this birthday party. Parents towed little ones dressed in their party finest along the sidewalks. Some staggered with the burden of large, wrapped gifts while others jogged frantically behind their offspring as they hurried to the front door of the shindig.

"Oh my God," I muttered and peeked beneath the edge of the sun visor to absorb what I saw.

"How many people are going to be here?" I asked, afraid I might vomit when I heard the answer. Judging on the parking situation alone, this was going to be an epic blowout.

"I'm not sure, but if I know my brother, they went all out. This is the first birthday he gets to celebrate with his daughter, so I'm sure he's making up for all the years he missed," Law explained as he expertly maneuvered his car into a spot about a block away from the house.

"Wait...what?" I asked as the words he so casually uttered sank in.

"What?" he asked with his face adorably screwed up in confusion. My God, could this guy get any hotter? I stole a kiss with a big smile on my face, and he looked even more confused when I pulled back afterward.

"What do you mean this is his first birthday with her?" I finally asked rather than justify my goofy reaction.

As we walked through the lovely neighborhood, he explained that the mother of his brother's child hid the fact that she gave birth for eight years.

"Oh my God, you're kidding," was the nicest thing I could come up with. What kind of woman does something like that? Then I reminded myself to keep an open mind. You never really knew what drove a person to the decisions they made. It wasn't my place to judge her any more than it was someone's place to judge me and my choices.

"Crazy, right? They were college sweethearts," he continued. "Well, really more than that. Jake never got over this woman. She did a real number on him when he moved away."

"Wait a second," I interrupted. "He moved away, yet she was the one that did a number on him? That doesn't make sense. I mean, if he left her..."

"No, it wasn't like that. He got an incredible internship in

Barcelona fresh out of school. She encouraged him to go, and they planned to stay together. Do the long-distance thing. But she got pregnant and didn't know until after he was already gone. So she ghosted him and planned to raise the baby herself. She knew if he was aware of the pregnancy, he would've come back to the States to be with her. And that's exactly what he would've done because he's that kind of guy. She said she was saving him from making the wrong decision regarding his career, but still..."

"Wow, what a tough situation to be in. Can you imagine?" I asked, trying in fairness to put myself in that mother's shoes. Or his, for that matter. It was bad timing, for one thing. But so much more the longer I thought about it.

"Yeah, no, I can't. It's hard to say what was right or wrong in their situation, you know?" Law looked my way to see me nodding. "Some shoes are way too hard to imagine walking in when you haven't actually done it."

And with all that backstory fresh on the brain, we rang the doorbell at his brother's house. You could hear the ruckus from inside while standing on the front porch.

"Do you think they can even hear the doorbell?" I asked when Law pushed the button a second time.

"You're probably right. Let's see if it's open." He tried the handle on the cobalt blue door, and it opened freely. He gave me a quick wink and said, "You're so smart."

I just grinned because I knew he was teasing, and honestly, it seemed like I just couldn't stop smiling with the guy around. When I let myself really process how great my life had been lately, I was immediately filled with fear.

Nothing good ever lasted. Not in my life anyway. The trick was to enjoy it while things were good and not spend too much time worrying about picking up the pieces when it all went to hell again. Because it would. It always did.

We wandered through the busy house, Law towing me behind him by one hand. I held on tighter as the crowd thickened in the kitchen and someone informed him his brother was out in the backyard. I tried to smile at the people I made eye contact with but was more worried about running into my sister.

The backyard was an entertaining paradise. The pool took up most of the lot, but the outdoor patio and kitchen area had enough space for plenty of tables and chairs for the partygoers. Music thumped through the whole place and kids ran wildly from one end to the other. Parents chatted in groupings while several dads anchored a serious game of volleyball in the swimming pool.

That's where I spotted my brother-in-law. He was on the far side of the floating net, whooping it up with his buddy, Sebastian Shark. Their team must have just scored because the men were celebrating with high-fives.

Breathe.

It's all I could repeat to myself as I scanned the crowd again for my sister. She had to be here somewhere, and likely not far from her man. They were sickening like that—always connected at the hip. Though I couldn't really tell if it was her neediness or his controlling tendencies that fed the behavior.

Law must have felt me tense beside him because he steered us to the edge of the crowd and tipped his head down beside my ear. "You okay, baby? I know there's a lot going on here, might be a little overwhelming."

Bless the man for understanding what a scene like this might do to me. The smile I offered was genuine. His caring enough to check in with me when he noticed my demeanor shift was so touching and thoughtful. From across the gym, I had found the perfect man and didn't even know it at the time. Now that I had him, I wanted to keep him.

"Yeah," I squeaked. If he heard me above the cacophony of this soirée, I'd be shocked. Louder, I repeated, "Yeah, I'm good. It's just a lot, you know?"

He nodded while I spoke, basically agreeing about the decibel level. Even outside.

"You know, this is kind of birth control in a way," I joked, regarding the hordes of children in that backyard.

Law looked at me with almost a hint of sadness in his expression before he covered it up with a forced laugh.

Time to backpedal. And quick.

"I mean, I want kids, someday, but yowzah, this is a lot." I squeezed the hand he had slipped into mine and studied his face to see if my damage control was enough.

"Definitely overwhelming." He nodded. "Especially if you aren't used to being around little ones. Oh, there's Stella and my sister. Come on, I want to introduce you," he said excitedly and began towing me across the patio to a beautiful woman and the most adorable little redhead standing before her.

The child was pleading her case for another soda when we approached. Her mother expertly handled the situation, though, and agreed to another sugar-filled drink if she first had an entire bottle of water. She just happened to have a water to offer, and the little girl took it and was off.

"Cecile, how are you today? Looking gorgeous as always," Law said to his sister as they embraced. If he hadn't told me this was his sister, I would never have guessed they were related. They looked nothing alike, which seemed odd to me.

Given my sisters and I were all spitting images of each other, I guess I expected they would've looked at least a bit alike.

"Oh, you're so full of it, Lawrence. It's nice to see you out and about, though." She kept her eyes on me while they hugged, and Law quickly turned in my direction. Hearing his older sister teasingly use his proper name had me smiling.

"I have someone I'd like you to meet. Cecile, this is my girlfriend, Shepperd Farsay. Shep, my oldest sister, Cecile." He made the introductions with that infectious smile that calmed my anxiety no matter when he bestowed it upon me.

The fact that he just introduced me to a family member as his girlfriend didn't go unnoticed. I'd have to give that one some brain time later when I reexamined the day. On first impression, I loved everything about it.

"Hello, very nice to meet you," I said and extended my hand. She shook it and smiled. Ahh, there was the resemblance. The two had the exact same warm, genuine smile.

Playfully, she gave her brother a sideways look. "Law, you've been holding out on me. I didn't know you had someone steady, or that she was this gorgeous." She lightly punched his shoulder, and like a good brother, he pretended it hurt.

"No need to hit me over it," he laughed and rubbed his upper arm.

The woman turned in a circle before saying, "Your niece is around here somewhere. She's in heaven with all her classmates here to play with."

"She's adorable," I said. "We saw you talking to her when we were crossing the lawn."

"Oh, you witnessed that, did you?" she asked with an eye roll. "Everything is a negotiation these days."

"She's just gearing you up for the teen years."

Cecile dropped her face into her hands and shook her head back and forth. "I'm not ready," she teasingly wailed, and we all chuckled.

"Have you seen Jacob?" Law asked.

"I think he and Pia are inside. He mentioned something about the magician they hired cancelling this morning. I think they're scrambling for a replacement."

"Oh, that stinks," I added. "It will probably be hard to find someone last minute."

"Well between the two of them, they have a lot of connections," she replied. "So if anyone can make it happen, it will be that power couple."

"Do you want to go see if we can find them inside?" Law asked me.

"Lead the way," I said as cheerfully as possible. Honestly, negotiating our way back through the crowd sounded awful, but staying here alone with his sister while he went himself would've been worse. I don't mind chatting with people once I know them, but this whole day was going to be filled with awkward introductions and niceties.

We snaked our way through the throng of kids and parents, pausing occasionally to chat with someone Law knew. His niece skipped by at one point, and he caught her with his long arm around her waist and hoisted her right up off her feet. The squealing laughter bubbling out of the child warmed my heart, and by the time she took off with her friends again, I thought my ovaries were going to explode.

Watching my man with the child was enlightening. He was going to make an amazing father someday. I had to keep my head out of the clouds for the moment, though, or I could get lost in serious daydreams about being the mother in that scenario.

Once inside, it was marginally quieter, but not much. There were people milling around, whether changing into bathing suits or play clothes after already dipping in the pool. We found Law's brother in the kitchen with his wife, or girlfriend—I wasn't completely sure what their status was.

"There he is!" Law said and strode excitedly toward the other man. I knew from other conversations we had had that this was the sibling he was closest to. Even if I didn't have that knowledge, you could feel how close they were just from their joy when seeing each other.

"You guys made it," Jake said while the brothers embraced. The beautiful brunette smiled at the men's affection, and Law gave her a big hug too.

"Hey, Pia, how are you? This is one hell of a party you guys put together," Law said after kissing the woman's cheek in greeting.

"Hey, Law, thank you. And thank you for coming," she said while his brother's gaze was laser focused on me.

"This must be Shepperd," he said, wrapping me in an unexpected hug. Normally I had real issues with strangers touching me, even in a friendly greeting. But these people were so non-threatening, I didn't mind. Not one shiver or inkling of panic after his exuberant hello.

Law's eyes were on me the entire time, watching to make sure I didn't come unglued. From personal experience, he knew how easily triggered I could be. He intercepted me from his brother's hug before the woman thought to do the same.

"Yes, this is Shepperd. Babe, this is my brother Jacob and his partner, Pia Shark."

Oh, we were really rolling with some local celebs at this

get together. And these were the people my sister routinely hung out with. It was astonishing, really. She had as many social anxieties as I did, so I wondered how she dealt with this all the time. Unless she had worked through her shit by now. I knew so little about her life anymore.

"Nice to meet you," Pia said and offered her hand.

"Same." I smiled. "Thank you for having us. Cecile said you're out a magician. Any luck finding a replacement?" I asked, hoping we wouldn't get into the six degrees of separation we all had. The longer I could keep Hannah out of a conversation, the better.

She sagged in defeat. "We've called all the people we can think of, trying to cash in any favor owed, but no luck. There are a few calls that haven't been returned yet, so there's a sliver of a chance. But what can you do? Everyone seems to be having a good time, so it should be fine."

But her man seemed to be the most stressed about the missing entertainment. She gave his hand a little pat and smiled up at him. Their height difference was at least a foot, so she had to tilt her head way back to meet his worried gaze.

"Chill, Jake. Seriously, those kids"—Law thumbed over his shoulder toward the backyard—"are having the time of their lives."

"I know," Jacob said. "I just wanted everything to be perfect for Vela today. She's been through so much this year, I just wanted the entire day to go off without a hitch."

"Well," Pia replied, "we've done all we can do. She'll have to understand."

"Have you tried blasting it on social media?" I suggested.

Pia snapped her head my way. "That's a great idea! Let me get my phone and make a few posts. Then we officially have done all we can, Jacob."

"All right. And I know you're right."

"Ahh, spoken like a kept man," Law teased his brother.

Jacob pointedly looked at me, then to Law, and raised one eyebrow.

Law shrugged with his arms extended as though he was admitting guilt to the same thing. The whole wordless exchange was so endearing, I found myself grinning along with everyone else.

CHAPTER SIXTEEN

LAW

The day was going great. Kids and parents were having tons of fun, and my brother and his woman were in their element as hosts. Being a father really suited him, and the love he had for those two ladies was evident to everyone there. It was time to sing and blow out the candles, and the crowd was finally subdued while Pia walked across the lawn with a blazing cake the size of a boogie board.

While she covered the distance between the house and the birthday girl, a deafening sound echoed through the party. It sounded eerily like a gunshot, but that was doubtful in the upscale neighborhood. There were a few older boys at the party, and my bet was that one of them pulled a prank. Some sort of harmless firecracker, most likely. But the pandemonium that ensued was catastrophic. Especially for all the attendees suffering from anxiety of one type or another.

A neighbor had brought their dog with them, and up until that gunshot-sounding bang, the animal was having the time of its life playing with all the kids. But when that shot rang through the air, the poor animal went apeshit. It took off running, dragging the leash its owner had dutifully held on to the entire afternoon.

But the sound startled everyone, and the leash was

dropped, allowing the dog to take off through the crowd. The animal's panic-driven path crossed right in front of the cake-carrying hostess, tripping her in the process. Several people dove to help break her fall but were seconds too late.

The cake hit the ground, and the blazing candles came too close to the dyed fabric and circus-themed streamers of the party decorations. Before anyone could stop it, half the backyard was engulfed in flames. People panicked and ran for safety, dragging their little ones by the hand or under arm. Half the people ran for the house while the others beelined for the gate that led to the front yard and driveway. People were knocked down and stepped on, and where the air was filled with laughter and cheers just minutes ago, it was now a haunting symphony of screams and wailing.

The birthday girl watched in horror as her magical day went up in flames. Vela was rooted to the spot at the head of the table, and even though the fire came dangerously close to her, she was frozen in place.

My brother finally realized what was happening and physically removed her from the dangerous path. My other niece was in a similar state, though not in the path of oncoming flames. My sister shouted her name several times, and it was like she was in a trance. She didn't flinch or twitch or seem to hear the shouts to get to safety. She stood like one of the majestic King Palms dotting the landscape.

Like my brother, I ended up scooping her up in my arms and hustling her inside where my sister received her catatonic child.

Where was Shepperd?

In the melee, we were separated, and now that I'd seen both Vela and Stella freeze in panic, I feared the worst. Was she somewhere dangerous in a similar state? I raced back out to the pool area and looked frantically to the left and to the right.

"Shepperd!" I shouted, but between the sounds of fire blazing and children crying, I doubted she heard me.

Just out front of the house, car door after car door slammed in succession as parents stuffed kids into car seats and got the hell out of harm's way. Who could blame them? Farther in the distance, the wail of sirens could be heard. Thank God someone had the sense to call the fire department.

Where was Shepperd?

I had to find her. The flames were tearing through the backyard, not sparing landscape or furniture in their wake. Fuel was abundant from the party decorations. The flames leaped from one section of the property to another. The gentle afternoon breeze became a vortex of fear as the fire became its own storm.

Finally, I spotted her. She and another woman were huddled close to the ground trying to shield themselves from the heat and debris whipping around the yard.

Elijah Banks burst through the sliding door that led from the house to the backyard with the same panicked look on his face that I suspected I wore.

"Hannah!" he bellowed and looked from side to side.

"I think they're over there, by the playset," I shouted, and we both took off in the same direction.

"Hannah!"

"Shepperd!" We took turns shouting the women's names.

"Help!" one of them finally yelled back. "We're over here!"

There was a barricade of fire between us and them. Something was fully engulfed in flames about twenty feet from where the sisters crouched and held each other. From what was left and recognizable, it looked like a picnic table.

"Get a hose!" Banks shouted, and I took off toward the house. I searched along the stucco, trying to find a hose reel or faucet. Luckily at the far side of the wall, a green garden hose sat coiled in a big clay pot. By some miracle, it was already hooked to a faucet coming out of the house. I grabbed the business end and sprinted back toward the girls, handed Elijah the nozzle, and had to double back to turn the fucking thing on. In my panic, I didn't think of that, and now I was wasting precious time having to go back.

"Stay there until this is out," he was shouting when I returned.

The women were watching with wide, horrified eyes as Elijah doused the flames between us and them. As soon as they were low enough to leap over, I took the chance. I landed on the other side of the fire and hit the ground with a thud. The tuck and roll I attempted did little to absorb the shock to my body, but I wasn't feeling pain at the moment.

"It's okay!" I shouted to the women. "He'll have it out in a second, and we'll run out of here. Okay?" I looked from one to the other, but they were both unmoving with fear.

"Shep! Answer me! We're heading to the front of the house. Are you ready?" I shouted but still, nothing. I'd throw her over my shoulder if I had to, but our opportunity was coming up, and we had to be ready.

Elijah positioned the hose on the ground at the base of the fire and joined me and the girls.

"Beauty!" he called as he grabbed his wife. He wasn't wasting time with negotiations, and it seemed like the smartest route for me to take as well. He hefted his wife into his arms and frantically looked from side to side.

"Just pick her up, man. We have to get out of here before that tree falls," he said and motioned to a huge pepper tree behind me with his chin.

I hadn't noticed the state of the old tree until he pointed it out, but he wasn't exaggerating. The trunk of the thing had been badly compromised, and it looked like it was moments from toppling over.

I leaned into Shepperd and told her, "I'm picking you up, baby. We have to get out of here."

She gave a slight nod, or at least I thought she had, but I couldn't wait for her agreement. I just prayed my seizing her body didn't freak her out more.

When I scooped her up, I was thankful she wrapped her arms around my neck and pressed her face into my shoulder.

We hustled across the lawn toward the house as the old tree creaked one last time and fell to the ground in a shower of sparks and ash. Half the leaves landed in the pool with a loud hiss as the flames were extinguished.

Firefighters passed us as we reached the sliding glass door and one yelled in our direction, "Get inside. Is anyone else out here?"

"Not that I know of. I wasn't looking past these two, though," Elijah responded.

"EMTs are on their way. If the women need to be looked at, just let someone know," he advised and then dashed off to join his team fight the blaze on the lawn.

Inside the house, far fewer people lingered than I expected. Families probably wanted to get out of harm's way and left for home. Who could blame them?

"Holy shit, Law," my brother gasped as he approached,

"Are you two okay?"

"Yeah, man, I think so. Physically at least," I replied with a pointed look at the woman tucked under my arm beside me on the sofa. "How's your crew?"

"Pia's with Cecile and the girls in Vela's room. They needed a quiet space to calm down," he answered while scanning the backyard disaster from the sliding glass door. "Christ, this is like a bad YouTube prank," he muttered to no one in particular.

I turned my attention to Shepperd. Her entire body was shaking, and holding her close wasn't fixing it. I pressed a kiss into the side of her head. The poor thing's beautiful hair smelled of smoke, and her palms were scraped with dried blood. I took her lifeless hand in mine and turned it over to inspect if she needed medical attention. They needed to be cleaned, but none of the cuts were deep enough to need stitches.

"Do you want to get out of here?" I asked gently.

She didn't react in any way. She just kept staring at the ground and trembling.

"Jake?" I said a bit louder to get my brother's attention. "Do you have a blanket?"

He turned from watching the fire department make quick work of extinguishing the blaze. "Huh?"

"Blanket? I think she's in shock," I said as calmly as possible.

"Oh, yeah, one sec," he said and dashed off toward the bedrooms. He was back with two fuzzy blankets—one with cartoon unicorns and the other striped in rainbow colors. He helped drape them over Shepperd's shoulders while I cradled her on my lap.

"Where did Elijah go with her sister?" I asked my brother. "Did you see?"

"Yeah, they're in our room at the end of the hall. She looks a lot like this." He motioned to Shepperd with his chin while standing over us. "What the hell happened to them?"

"They were trapped on the other side of the playset. They both had childhood trauma, so they completely locked up in the face of danger. Elijah and I used the garden hose to cut the flames down low enough to get them to safety. Where the hell are the EMTs? The one firefighter said they were on their way, and that was at least ten minutes ago."

"I'm sure they'll be here any minute," my sibling reassured. "Let's lay her down and raise her feet. That should help blood flow get back to normal."

I eased my body away from Shep and spoke quietly to her. "Baby, can you lie down here on the sofa? I'll stay right here, but I think your body is in shock."

She allowed me to maneuver her into a supine position. Jacob stuffed a throw pillow under her legs while I covered her with both blankets.

When she was settled, I asked my brother, "When did you become the house doctor?"

"Dude, we've been through so much shit since Vela was abducted. On top of that, my soon-to-be-wife is diabetic. It made sense for me to learn some basic first aid." He shrugged like these were common problems in every household.

"Man." I shook my head. "I'm so sorry."

"For what?" he snapped.

"You've been through so much, obviously still going through so much shit, and I've been so wrapped up in myself and my own life, I didn't even know. I'm shit for a brother." I studied the ground, feeling ashamed of how little I'd been there to support my brother while he no doubt needed it.

"Law, shut up. There's no way you would've known unless I told you. And I didn't. On top of all that, there's not much anyone can do to help us anyway. We just get through one day at a time."

"Are you guys going to therapy at least?" I asked. I might have been prying into his home life too deeply, but I was genuinely concerned.

"Oh, hell yes we are. We all go separately, as a family, and as a couple. I think I pay more to that damn office each month than our mortgage payment," he said with a laugh.

It reassured me that he was being so open about the care they were getting and was still grounded enough to joke about it.

"Well, if you ever need anything, just say the word," I offered, not really knowing what more to say.

Finally, a guest ushered the paramedics through the house, and Jake flagged one down. "We've got two little ones with PTSD in a bedroom in the back and two females in the same condition. This young lady here, who I'm pretty sure is in shock, and her sister in another bedroom who is presenting much the same way right now."

"Okay, thanks. You are?" the first responder questioned.

"Jacob Cole. Masterson." He added our family name almost as an afterthought, but we'd all experienced the power of being from a prominent family. There were times you just used it to your advantage.

"My name is Logan, and I'm the scene captain. I need to sweep the property and see if there are any other injuries. Since these ladies are stable and in safe conditions, I need to triage all identified patients and then we'll decide to treat here or transport. Sound good?"

"Sure," Jake answered. "Let me show you the little ones and the other woman before you head outside." My brother didn't wait for Logan to agree. He just started off toward the bedrooms, and the EMT followed.

I knelt on the floor beside her and stroked the sooty hair back from her face. "How are you doing?" I asked gently.

The vacant stare I got in response should've alarmed me but didn't. This was the first time she turned in my direction—however slight it might have been—when I spoke to her. She didn't say anything, though. Just blankly fixed on some point on my face. Still, it was better than no response at all.

"Are you warming up? Looks like the tremors have eased up a bit," I said and kissed her forehead. "The paramedic is checking the kids first, then is going to have a look at you. Your hands are pretty torn up," I rambled, hoping she was hearing me despite the empty gaze I was getting in return.

She was scaring the shit out of me, but I tried to stay calm. There was a voice in the back of my mind sounding a lot like what I assumed a past version of me sounded like. Asking questions I didn't want to examine at the moment but could still hear them.

Is this what life would always be like with this woman? Will she always be one step away from a breakdown? Is a relationship with her worth all the drama?

Present day me was annoyed with that voice. Was I really that shallow before meeting Shepperd? Or was I that selfish? Just because a person struggled with some mental health issues didn't make them unworthy of love and companionship. There were a lot of personal growth points in there to dig deeper into, but this wasn't the time or place.

There were things I was sure about. If I wasn't before this

afternoon's pandemonium, I certainly was now. Not being able to find Shepperd when the fire broke out terrified me. In those few short moments that she was missing, a sense of fear and panic completely took over. I didn't want to lose her. I was sure of that.

Seeing her frozen in panic broke my heart. She ended up in a much more dangerous situation because she lacked the ability to function in crisis because of what some asshole predator did to her when she was a girl.

She deserved to live a safer, happier life than that. And I wanted to be a part of that life. I was completely sure of that too.

CHAPTER SEVENTEEN

SHEPPERD

As my senses began to come back online, I felt a chaotic mix of emotions. While going through the comedown, the last place I wanted to be was at a stranger's house. I still wasn't one hundred percent clear on what happened, but based on the aftermath around me, it was bad. Really, really bad.

All I could think above anything else was, "Please don't let it turn out to be my fault." And maybe that was selfish given the amount of upheaval I could plainly see around me, but, there you have it. I thought I had been holding up really well given the situation. And by that, I meant a party largely made up of people I didn't know. The few I did know before today I wasn't particularly fond of.

But then I found myself lying on the sofa in Law's brother's home with every pair of eyes on me as people milled in and out through the back door. I couldn't bring myself to speak just yet or ask what happened in detail.

Before this fiasco—whether it seemed like a big accomplishment or not—I'd never set anything on fire to deal with my pain. But now, based on the way my hair smelled more like Santa's Christmas Eve red-and-white-fur getup, that might no longer be the case.

Law was perched on the edge of the sofa in front of me

but had his body twisted to keep a watchful eye. My first instinct was to shove him away—put space between our bodies physically. At the exact same time, I wanted to crawl into his lap and let him comfort me. It didn't make a lot of sense, but at the moment, there wasn't much around me that did.

"Hey, gorgeous," he said in a low, husky voice.

I gave him the best version of a smile and knew it was a pitiful attempt. If I looked anything like I smelled, he was crazier than me to have said that.

"How are you feeling?" He stroked some low-hanging hair off my forehead, leaned in slowly, and planted a soft kiss on the skin he just exposed.

He sat tall again, and I couldn't imagine where to begin. Apologizing would probably be a solid start, so I inhaled and gave it my best shot.

"I'm so sorry," I began but stopped abruptly in reaction to the alarm on his face.

"What are you apologizing for?" he asked immediately. He wasn't angry, necessarily. Maybe frustrated, though.

"Did anyone get hurt?" I asked instead of answering his question.

"Looks like you and your sister got the worst of it. Vela and Stella are pretty upset too, but I just checked on them, and they're doing okay."

"My sister?" I stuck on that part at first, but concern for the children ramped up my anxiety once more. When I tried to sit up, the bossy guy put a firm palm on my shoulder and eased me right back down.

"Yes, but she's fine other than a bit shaken. Elijah's lying with her in one of the bedrooms. Looks like he's a pro at managing this kind of thing," he said with what seemed like a bit of awe at what he saw in that bedroom.

So why did that rub me so raw? Probably because everything always turned up roses for the perfect Hannah, didn't it? Of course she found a man who would jump right in and rescue her from the demons of her past. Of course her man was quietly lying with her in private while she pulled herself together while I was out here on display on a stranger's fucking living room sofa.

If one more person walked by and gave me that morbidly curious side eye, thinking they were being super clever about it but really weren't, I might just blow my top.

So I croaked, "Can we get out of here?" I tried to sit up again, but he stopped me. This time I let my instincts win and pushed his thick arm out of the way. "I'm serious. I'm fine. Everyone's staring at me, and I don't like it, Law." I muttered that last part for his ears only, and something finally registered on his face.

He leaned in close so our conversation remained private. "As soon as the EMTs check you over, we'll go. I promise. They already know you need some attention, so they'll be here shortly."

"You don't know that. Law, there were so many kids here. They should worry about them, not me. I probably just had an anxiety attack. Happens all the time." I didn't miss the way he winced when I let that little nugget fly.

"Okay, let me say it this way, then. I'll feel better after they check you out, okay? That was way more than an anxiety attack, Shep. I think I've seen enough of those now between my niece and you. You could've died out there today."

"Well, I didn't," I snapped and instantly knew it was shitty. He didn't deserve to be talked to that way. But why wouldn't he hear my words? Can't I even be trusted to know when I need help and when I don't?

And that fucking annoying voice in the back of my head gave me a fast answer to that one. Tears filled my eyes, stinging and blurring the image of the handsome man hovering over me.

"Oh, baby," he hushed. "Don't cry. You're safe now. I'm not going to let anything happen to you." He issued the promise right before hugging me. I held him so tight and so close. I didn't want to let go.

"I'm sorry," I said again, and he pulled back to give me a stern look.

"Stop apologizing. You didn't do anything wrong, darling. I'm just worried," he said, but it felt like he stopped himself there. I kept my eyes fixed to his, waiting for him to say whatever was on his mind.

"Finish," I encouraged but wondered if I really wanted to hear the rest.

"No, it's nothing. I was just so scared. When I couldn't find you, and then when I did and you were trapped, damn..." He gulped down heavy emotion and scrubbed a hand down his face. He was dirty from smoke and soot and smeared the dirt with his palm.

"Trapped?" What the hell was he talking about? This was always the worst part of these episodes. It could be days until I recalled what really happened. I don't know why my brain locks up, but it's frustrating and embarrassing. I just wanted to get out of here.

Just as I mounted the energy to ask him to take me home again, an EMT squatted down in front of me.

"How are you feeling?" the young guy asked.

I couldn't help but fixate on how clean and neatly groomed he was. Law and I both looked like we had been in battle, and this dude had every hair on his perfectly styled head tamed into compliance with some divine-smelling product. The comparison between us and him was so stark, a bizarre giggle bubbled out of my throat and mortified me when it burst free.

"Oh my God," I said and buried my face in my palms. Such a freaking idiot. Like I never talked to a good-looking guy before. I mean, Christ, look at the man standing here by my side.

"Sorry," I muttered. "I'm fine, honestly," I said with the last bit of energy I had in me. "I think we're about to get out of here."

"Well, let's have a quick look and make sure we haven't missed anything, okay? Wouldn't be doing my job otherwise." He opened the bag at his feet and pulled out a blood pressure cuff and stethoscope.

He performed his exam and did a lot of note-taking throughout. When he was finished and zipping up his bag he said, "Clearly you were in shock when we first got here. I saw you the moment I walked through the room. Your blood pressure and heart rate are still a bit low, but nothing to be concerned about. Are you feeling tired?"

Yes! Here was my ticket out of here. "Oh, yeah, exhausted."

"Also very typical from shock," he said as he stood. He directed my home care instructions to Law. "Get her to bed, and she'll probably sleep a good amount over the next twenty-four hours. That's just what her body needs. Bring her to the ER if symptoms come back like confusion, chills, sweats, anything similar to what you just saw."

"I'll be fine," I insisted. "I just need to sleep it off. That was a lot of excitement for everyone," I said casually, hoping everyone else would adopt my carefree attitude about what had just happened. I hated when people made a fuss over me.

The look on Law's face said he wasn't buying my bullshit for a second. He looked as exhausted as I felt. A pang of guilt nearly knocked the wind out of me. He turned his attention to the EMT, thanked him for his help, and then the guy joined the rest of his team talking to Law's brother, Jake.

"See? Told you that wasn't necessary," I said and instantly felt like a bratty child for it.

"I feel better knowing you're okay. Physically. I'm not a doctor, Shepperd. If something happened when we got home because I rushed you out of here, I would never forgive myself." His tone was weary, and I promised myself to cut the guy a break. I wasn't used to people caring about me and needed to be more grateful that he insisted I was checked out.

"You're right. I'm sorry," I said and stood up abruptly. The room betrayed me instantly with a spin and tilt combo that nearly knocked me right back down.

Law steadied me with strong hands on my hips and ducked down to be at eye level.

"You okay?"

"Yep." I nodded and tried to pull away. As I turned, he sighed loud enough for me to hear his frustration.

Be nice, Shepperd.

I faced him and put my hand on his cheek. He leaned into my palm for a brief moment while I sincerely said, "Thank you." I gave him a gentle smile, and he smiled back, took my hand from his face, and gave it a quick peck.

"Let's go home," he said but stopped before we made it even halfway to the front door. "I want to tell my sister I'm leaving. Be right back." He handed me the keys, but I decided to wait in the foyer while he said goodbye to his family.

He was back in no time and supported me around the waist as we made our way to his car. The distance we parked away from the party house seemed three times longer now that I was so exhausted.

Sleep claimed me before we even left the neighborhood.

★ ★ ★

I didn't wake up until the following morning. Law was nowhere to be found as I wandered through the quiet house, ending up in the kitchen with designs on something to fill my aching stomach.

After foraging through the refrigerator, I decided on scrambled eggs and toast. I was just transferring the steaming, fluffy protein to a plate when I heard the keys rattling in the front door.

Where the hell had he gone so early in the morning? But when I glanced at the time on the stove, it was after ten. Not so early after all.

Law came into the kitchen and tossed his keys on the counter. He looked stressed and tired, and of course, I instantly felt guilty about it. Just assuming yesterday had taken a toll on him, the first thing I wanted to do was apologize.

"Hey, gorgeous," he said, rerouting my thoughts to a more content space. He took me in his arms, and I wanted to spend the rest of the day like that. He always smelled so good and felt so safe. I was getting spoiled and maybe too comfortable because good things like this never lasted for me.

I pulled back a bit to get a good look at his face. "Hello

yourself." I smiled. "Where have you been already?" I asked and cringed with worry that I was coming across as too controlling or clingy. "I mean, if you want to tell me."

"Just went for coffee," he said nonchalantly, but something about his tone sounded forced. Was he being evasive? Was I just being paranoid?

"Oh, are we out? I'll put that on my shopping list."

"No, I think we have some here. Just wanted to get out. Clear my head a bit."

Okay, fair enough. Yesterday was a lot to deal with, no matter who you were or what part in the whole fiasco you played. Guilt piled on guilt, though, because it was my natural inclination to blame myself for all things that went wrong.

"I'm so sorry," I began, and he instantly bristled. I put my hand on his arm to stop him from telling me not to apologize. "Really," I said. "It was a lot to deal with."

He listened and then just nodded.

After a weird silence stretched between us, he said, "I'm going to take a shower. Unless you were planning on getting in..."

I just stared at him for a few seconds. He was definitely holding something back, but I wouldn't badger him. I had to trust that he would talk to me when he was ready.

Fear sparked through my bloodstream. Maybe the events of yesterday were too much for Law to handle. Maybe he got a little too much exposure to my brand of turmoil. It was something I worried about since the day I moved in. Something would inevitably happen to make him run for the hills. Had we already reached that junction?

"No, go ahead," I said, and before the words were completely out of my mouth, he turned and headed down the hallway toward the master bedroom.

I watched him until he disappeared through the door and wondered if that was a preview of when he would walk away from me and not come back.

CHAPTER EIGHTEEN

LAW

After I carried her in from the car last night and tucked her into the bed we now shared, Shepperd slept better than I'd seen her do—ever. The paramedics told us to expect her to be tired, but the twelve plus hours of sleep she logged gave me a lot of thinking time. I went over and over every detail I could remember about the party and felt like more questions arose than were answered.

So I did something I could end up regretting, but only time would tell. My heart was in the right place, I knew that for certain. I cared about Shepperd more every day. And what I witnessed at the birthday party rocked me to the bone.

I reached out to Elijah Banks and asked him to meet me for a cup of coffee and some honest conversation. He was definitely curious, if nothing else, and agreed to sit down with me. We met at a downtown coffee shop since he had to drive in from Malibu.

When I arrived, I scanned the café and saw that he had already secured a table and had a steaming cup of something in front of him. A quick look at my watch ensured I wasn't late, so I assumed he was met with lighter traffic than he expected.

"Hey, how's it going?" I asked and offered my hand in greeting.

He gave me a shake and fist bump combination, and I took the seat across from him. "I appreciate you meeting me."

"Yeah, no worries. Hannah's family means everything to her, so when you said you wanted to talk about her sister, I made the time."

"I have to be honest, I'm a little worried this might cause trouble between Shepperd and me because she doesn't know I'm here. As a general practice, I don't like doing things behind people's backs, you know?"

"Then why are you?" he asked bluntly, and it threw me off. I was already on the edge about being there and hoped he would at least pretend what I was doing wasn't as shitty as it felt.

"Because I care about her," I blurted. And it was the truth. It was more than just caring about her at this point, but I wasn't here to confess my feelings to the guy. I needed answers. I needed advice.

He tilted his head to one side, calling me on my shit, and his beachy casual hair flopped over one eye before he pushed it back from his face.

"Yesterday at the birthday party," I began but pulled up short. How did I even dive into all of this without exposing the information Shepperd confided in me. "What happened to the girls," I continued while turning my cup in a full circle as though I preferred to drink from the other side. Honestly I was stalling while I figured out what to say and just needed to keep my hands busy.

"Look, man," he said, and I stilled instantly. His green eyes were piercing as he studied me from across the table. "I've been involved with Hannah for a while now. I have to assume I have a lot more backstory from her than you do from Shepperd at this point, right? You guys haven't been dating that long, have you? Like a month or two?"

"Yeah. I mean, we've been talking longer than that. We met at the gym we both go to, but things just got serious when her parents kicked her out. She showed up at my door one night, basically without any other option of where to stay. I was stoked she did, but yeah, it hasn't been that long."

"The parents what?" he asked incredulously.

I shrugged. "All I know is her side of the story. But yeah, that's what it boiled down to. I guess they were threatening to send her away to rehab for eating disorders."

"Would that have been a bad thing?"

I felt defensive immediately but took a minute to relax and not bite the guy's head off. There were a lot of things I could appreciate about his directness.

"Yes and no. I don't really think she needs intervention at that level. From what I've seen, anyway. Yes, she's very thin, but I also know she has an incredible appetite when she allows herself to enjoy a meal instead of worrying she'll be critiqued about it." Those occasions seemed to be increasing in number, but I kept that detail to myself. "But her eating habits aren't what I wanted to talk to you about."

"Okay, fair enough. What is it, then?" he asked, but seriously...after yesterday, he had to know where this conversation was going.

"I really care about her, you know? I want to understand what she has going on up here." I tapped my temple a couple of times. "Why did they both panic and freeze like that yesterday? You can't tell me that's a normal reaction. Everyone else except Stella and Vela, of course, ran for safety. Those four froze like statues and put themselves at greater risk by doing so."

He tilted his head to the side again. "Think about it, dude. What do those four have in common? Isn't it obvious?"

I sat silent for a moment and gave it some thought. It wasn't the first time I'd tried to draw some parallel between them after seeing them all react so oddly but similarly to each other.

"I think it has something to do with trauma, right? All this is new to me, so I'm trying to understand."

Elijah nodded. "You're on the right track. I've done a lot of reading about trauma, PTSD, panic, anxiety, and so on. When Hannah and I first got together, I didn't know shit about mental health outside of what I deal with myself. But I knew it would be best to figure it out. Our therapist has helped a lot too."

I nodded as he spoke.

"Does Shepperd have a therapist?" he asked.

"Mmm, not that I know of. I mean maybe at some point she has gone, but she isn't actively seeing someone right now. At least not that I know about."

"Well, she should be. That's obvious, right? You both should go, really," he said with authority, and I couldn't help but agree. This was way more complicated than I had the tools for.

"She seems resistant to it, so I'm not sure if she'll do it."

"There's no way I believe that she wants to live the way she has been. She seems so angry and in pain. She isolates herself from the family, no matter who tries to reach out. Other than her twin, Maye, I'm not sure she even has any friends."

I hadn't even thought of that before, but he was right. The only other person I'd heard her talk about besides her sisters was the one girl she worked with. Joy. But Christ, one thing at a time. This was overwhelming.

"She's a good person. Funny and smart. She's the kind of girl that usually has hordes of friends," I said in my girlfriend's defense.

"Well, not when she pushes everyone away. Either because she's embarrassed about what she's dealing with or she's scared someone will figure her out and insist she do better for herself."

"Do you really think that's what's going on?"

He gave one solid dip of his chin. "I do."

"Why did they freeze like that? When everyone else was getting out of harm's way, they froze. I don't understand."

"Our therapist has explained it like this... When a child experiences trauma, especially deep emotional or physical trauma, they freeze in time emotionally. They mature physically and intellectually, but emotionally they stay rooted at the age the traumatic event occurred. So, the girls never developed coping skills past a young age. I'm not sure what Shepperd went through exactly, but I do know about Hannah's experiences. For the most part."

"The most part?" I asked.

"Yeah, just being real, man. And not because I think she's keeping anything from me. She just hasn't been able to get her brain to let down its guard to remember what happened. I'm kind of surprised it still hasn't happened after everything else she's been through."

"You're talking about the kidnapping attempt?"

"Well, yes and no. I think that's where she got stuck emotionally, but based on some dream regression therapy she's done, we're pretty sure something else happened. We just haven't unlocked what that was yet."

Of course I had some potential backstory here but didn't feel like it was my place to expose the fact that Shepperd suspected the same school janitor who abused her also abused Hannah.

"Wow. That's intense. But so much of what you're saying makes sense. I mean with the way Shep behaves in situations. And don't get me started on the sleep habits. Oh my God, I've never seen someone exist on so few hours of sleep."

Elijah laughed. "Dude, I remember those days all too well. Thankfully, she worked hard on that problem early on. Now that the baby is here, she's back to very little sleep and not liking it one bit."

His face changed completely when he spoke about having a child, and I knew then—if I were at all uncertain before—getting my girl squared away was the most important thing in our lives now. She deserved a happy, healthy, fulfilling life, and I wanted to be right in the center of all of it.

I had one more comment floating around in front of my other thoughts, and this was the guy who would understand best. "Can I ask you one more thing? I've probably taken up more of your time than you can afford, so if you have to go, I get it." At least he had an out if he was done talking about the Farsay girls.

Elijah waved his hand between us. "Yeah, go for it."

"What's up with the parents? How the hell do they not see what's going on? Or do they just not care?" That sounded harsher coming out than it did in my head. I winced apologetically, but he didn't seem to be bothered by the questions.

"You know, I'm not really sure. On the surface, they seem like good people. Good parents, you know?" Then, with a forced laugh he said, "Though my own were such shit, what do I know?"

I didn't think I wanted to touch that comment with a ten-foot pole. Luckily he went on.

"They seem to clue in on the things that other people might notice. But then they don't want to ask themselves why the shit is happening. It's also possible they're just not capable of asking themselves why these things are happening to their kids. Does that make sense?"

"It does because I can apply that directly to Shepperd. They can see she's starving herself but aren't asking themselves why. What happened to her that she's choosing to do that to herself."

"Exactly," he agreed. "I'm not sure if they are more worried about appearances or just don't have the tools to dig deeper."

I thought about that for a couple of minutes and concluded I just didn't know the people well enough to have a solid answer. We both finished our coffees and stood to leave. I was glad we had this conversation. Whether it gave me a better direction regarding handling my home life, I wasn't sure. So much of where we went from here would depend on Shepperd.

When I got home, Shepperd was awake. I realized I was hoping she would still be sleeping when I felt like I was sneaking through the house trying to be quiet as a mouse. If she was still sleeping, I wouldn't have to explain where I'd been, but I wasn't that lucky.

Her go-to inclination was to doubt those around her, and I just set myself up to be lumped into that camp. The sooner I came clean, the less damage I'd do. I knew all this, but instead of having the conversation we needed to have, I ran off to the shower the second I could get out of the chit-chat she tried to initiate.

I did some deep soul-searching while the hot water pelted my skin. Was building a life with this woman worth the obvious hard work ahead? My head and heart agreed... Absolutely.

With that established, I had to give myself a hearty pep talk about telling her about meeting with her brother-in-law. The trickiest detail would be making my intentions clear. I wasn't trying to sneak around behind her back or betray her in any way. I was hoping to understand what she was going through, what she dealt with on a daily basis. I just had to be honest with her about my motives and feelings and hope she understood and believed me.

I put on some fresh clothes, dealt with my hair, and then went to find my girl. My heart was thundering in my ears, and I had to force myself to take some calming breaths so I didn't look guilty before I even began talking.

Based on our conversation when I first got home, she already suspected I wasn't being honest with her. It was all over her body language. I just hoped she hadn't worked herself up even more while I was getting my thoughts together.

"Shep?" I called out when I didn't find her in the kitchen. Her purse and keys were still on the table by the front door, so she couldn't have gone too far.

"Out here," I heard her muffled voice call from the patio. I had a very small backyard. Really, it was criminal to even call the postage-stamp sized bit of grass a yard, but it was pretty typical for southern California condos.

I found my beautiful woman lounging in the sun with black, oversized sunglasses perched on top of her blond hair. The sun had already kissed the apples of her cheeks, and she looked livelier than I'd seen her look in the past month.

"Wow," I muttered.

She smiled up at me. "What?"

"The sun looks amazing on you. Do you like going to the beach?" There was so much we didn't know about each other.

"I used to when I was a kid. I haven't been in a really long time. I guess that's kind of lame when you think about it, huh?"

"What do you mean?" I lowered to sit on the end of her chair beside her feet. Kindly, she moved over a bit to make more room for me.

She shrugged. "People come from all over the country to visit our beaches, and we live here and just take it for granted."

"True. But we also live here and have to make our livings here. We aren't on vacation every day. Sometimes life gets in the way of the fun stuff."

"Absolutely. But maybe we just need to make a bigger effort to enjoy what's right here in our backyard."

"Good point. Would you like to go to the beach? Maybe next weekend?" The more I thought about it, the more fun it sounded.

"I think I'd love that," she said with a sweet smile. "How was the shower? You must have been solving world hunger in there."

"Yeah, I definitely do serious thinking in the shower. You too?"

"Oh, absolutely. Although, growing up in a house with so many other people, someone else always wanted in the bathroom while I was in the shower, so I couldn't really take my time."

This conversation was sweet and normal, and I dreaded the fact that the one I had to initiate next had the potential to wreck the whole day. Shit, maybe worse than that.

"What's up?" she asked after studying me for a few seconds.

"What do you mean?" I asked but also marveled at how astute she was.

"You've got something on your mind, I can tell. You have since you came home. Do you want to talk about it?"

I took a deep breath and slowly exhaled. "You're very smart, Ms. Farsay. You know that?" I said with a heartfelt smile. I truly adored this girl and didn't want to hurt her. In any way.

She looked down at the book she was holding and shyly said, "Thank you."

I put my hand on her leg and enjoyed how warm the sun had made her skin. "I'm afraid you might be upset with me, and I don't want to make you mad."

"Ohhh kaaaay," she dragged out with worry clouding her features in an instant.

"I'm sorry," I said at once. "That's not a great opener, is it?"

"Nope. Not really," she said, still concerned about what was coming.

Might as well rip the Band-Aid off. "I had coffee with Elijah this morning."

"Elijah Banks?" she quickly filled in, her voice immediately gaining volume and fear.

I just nodded and stroked her leg. At least she didn't pull away.

"Why? Did he call you?" she asked, and I couldn't figure why that mattered—who called who.

"No. I reached out to him and asked him if we could talk. He said he was free this morning, so I took the opening. He's one busy guy. Did you know he also has a private company in addition to working for Sebastian Shark?" I was totally rambling.

She just slowly shook her head while keeping her eyes glued on mine. Suspicion was all over her body like an ill-fitting, uncomfortable suit.

"Look, Law. I don't want you to feel like you have to account for every minute of your day. I don't want to be *that* girl, you know? Is it a bit concerning that you met with my brother-in-law? I can't lie and say it's not. But only tell me about the conversation if you want to. I don't want you to feel like you have to."

That all came at me in one long run-on sentence. I could tell she was trying to be mature and brave about the situation, but it wasn't her natural inclination.

"I appreciate you saying all of that. I just didn't want to feel like I did something behind your back, knowing you don't get along with your sister, aka his wife."

"Well, that's exactly what you did. But like I said, you don't have to account to me how you spend your time."

"But I want to be respectful, Shepperd. I don't want you to feel betrayed. Ever."

"Betrayed? What the hell did the two of you talk about that the word betrayed would even pop into your head? God, the more you talk right now, the more concerned I'm feeling. Maybe we should just call it here." She stood abruptly from the lounge chair.

I intercepted her escape and wrapped my arms around her. I wanted her to calm down so she would just listen. I was fucking this up by tiptoeing around the issue even though I had been very careful not to expose any details that she wouldn't want her family to know.

"There's nothing to be concerned about, baby. We just talked about what happened yesterday. I thought he might be a good person to shed some light on what we're dealing with, you know?"

She planted her fists on her hips and glared at me. "And what exactly are we dealing with, Law?"

"I shouldn't have said it like that. That came out wrong," I tried to amend, but she was already madder than a nest of hornets. "Please," I begged and tried to tug her hands away from her hips and hold them in mine.

She was having none of the touchy-feely stuff, and I didn't blame her. She yanked her hands from mine and put some distance between us.

I sank back down on the end of the lounge chair and buried my face in my hands. This was turning into a train wreck, and we'd barely gotten into the heart of the conversation.

"Oh, don't look so defeated," she bit.

"I just don't want to screw this up. Pissing you off was the last thing I wanted."

"Well, I can't imagine what you did want, going behind my back to have a little pow-wow with my family. What next, Law? You'll be on their side and ship me off to rehab?"

Okay, this was getting out of hand. I shot to my feet and crowded into her personal space. "That's not fair, and you know it," I told her in a low voice. My neighbors didn't need to hear every word between us.

I took a deep breath, hoping to calm down before trying one more time to get her to actually hear what I was saying instead of letting her insecurities run away with the conversation.

"I'm worried about you. That experience yesterday scared the shit out of me, and if there's something I can do to help you never go through something like that again, then I want to do it. I'm just so far outside my wheelhouse on all of this. So I reached out to someone I thought might be able to shed some light on the topic. Why is that such a bad thing?"

Why was she freaking out? When I explained my thought process, it sounded perfectly reasonable.

"Because no matter what you said to him, what you told him, it will all get back to my sister. And then the rest of my family. Do you really not see that?" she asked, her voice even louder than before.

"Please calm down," I said. "The entire neighborhood doesn't need to hear our disagreement."

As her eyes bulged out of her head, I knew that was the wrong choice of words. Again.

Damn it. I couldn't win here.

"So appearances are more important than my feelings? You're just like my parents!"

"No. That's not true at all. And stop putting words in my mouth. The only motivation behind the get-together was wanting to understand your PTSD better. Do you not realize how much I care about you? How watching that episode yesterday turned my heart inside out, Shepperd? I want to help you. However I can...I just want to help."

"My PTSD? What are you talking about?"

We stared at each other for a while before either one of us said anything else. The tears in her big blue eyes gutted me. I didn't want to hurt her. At all. Everything I was afraid of happening was happening. No matter what I said, she was masterfully twisting around to align with her perception.

What a clusterfuck.

"Shepperd," I began, but she held her flat hand up to my face.

"Just stop. I don't know how much more of this I can take. Especially after everything yesterday." Her tone was acidic and nasty, and I didn't particularly care to be spoken to that way. I didn't do anything wrong.

"Shepperd," I tried again, but she had apparently reached her limit. She was fully crying as she glared at me and took off through the house with me hot on her heels.

"Baby, let's talk this out. I'm not trying to upset you. It's the last thing I wanted," I said to her back as I followed her through the kitchen and down the hall to the bedroom.

"Just leave me alone," she said through her tears that had ramped up to full sobs. She was the first one through the bedroom door and tried to slam the heavy thing in my face. Luckily–and that was probably the only time I would say that—her tiny body was no match for the thick, oak slab, so it closed with much less force and speed than she wanted.

I easily caught the door before it closed and barged right into the room behind her.

She basically trapped herself by storming in here, but maybe with her cornered she would hear me out.

Instead, she started yanking her things out of the closet and tossing them in a heap on the floor.

"What are you doing?" I asked, watching her move back and forth between the closet and the pile.

"What does it look like? Leaving. Then you won't have to be burdened with the likes of me," she said in uneven gasps.

I stepped forward and caged her entire torso in my arms. "Stop this."

“I don’t want to be here with you,” she whimpered while struggling to get away.

Not going to lie. That one hurt.

“I know you’re angry, but don’t say things you don’t mean or can’t take back when this blows over.” It was solid advice from years of maturity on her young twenty-two. “You can’t run away every time we don’t agree on something.”

“Watch me,” she seethed and tried to pull out of my arms again.

So I waited her out. Let her wear herself down struggling in my embrace until she finally collapsed against my chest and cried. I stroked my hand over her head and down the length of her silky hair. The whole time I stayed silent except for lots of shhhhh and random kisses to the top of her head.

“I’m so mad,” she finally croaked from against my body.

“I know, baby. And I’m sorry for that. The last thing I meant was for you to be mad or hurt,” I replied but didn’t move. I was afraid if I let go, she’d take off again.

“Why does everyone think they know what’s best for me? I’m not a child.”

“Having that conversation this morning with Elijah wasn’t because I think I know what you need. In fact, it was the exact opposite of that. I don’t know what you need, and I thought he would have some insight.”

She didn’t respond, but she finally hugged me back as we stood in the middle of the bedroom.

“You don’t have to fix me, Law. I mean, I get that I’m totally fucked up, but just once in my life, can’t someone love me for the person I am? Not the person they wish I were?”

“First of all, that’s not what I said.” I pulled back and ducked down a bit to meet her teary stare. “I said I want to help you. I never said fix you. You have to stop twisting my words around to fit your narrative here."

Again, she said nothing. I badly wanted her to take responsibility for that habit. It needed to stop, but if she wouldn't admit to doing it, we were further from that happening than I'd hoped.

But I wasn't done responding to her last comment. Hopefully, I wasn't about to make things worse.

"I do love you for the person you are, and I think you're perfect just the way you are. I don't have some manufactured version of you I'm trying to mold you into. I love this version of you right here." I cradled her face in my palms and swiped her tear-streaked cheeks with my thumbs.

"You love me?" she whispered.

I smiled. "It's definitely feeling that way," I responded after taking in the features of her angelic face.

Even though she'd been crying, I'd never seen a more beautiful woman. Her eyes were big and bright with unshed tears. The glassy sheen made the blue so much deeper, so much more intense. Her long lashes were stuck together in pointed clusters that framed her eyes like my sister's childhood dolls. She looked innocent and fragile, and every manly instinct in my body roared to life. I wanted to take care of her and protect her in a way I'd never felt before. If that wasn't how it felt to love someone, I had no hope of ever feeling it.

"What did you tell him? I have to know what damage control I'm looking at."

"Damage control?" I asked, frustrated that we were going right back to this. "I told you I didn't say anything that would betray the confidence you've given me. I wouldn't do that to you." What I didn't admit out loud was how much her distrust stung. It really seemed like I was paying for crimes I didn't commit, and she wasn't capable of seeing how unfair that was.

But I was exhausted. This whole situation was exhausting, and it was at the point that felt like we were chasing our tails.

Her silence wasn't helping but I didn't want to fight anymore. I wasn't used to this kind of interaction with a woman. Typically, my relationships were very surface level and light spirited. I never got involved deeply enough to involve feelings past passion and, before Shepperd, didn't care to.

I needed to get my head on straight. I knew that much. If we kept at this right now, I feared things would be said that weren't meant just because I was frustrated.

So, I pulled her close again and said, "Let's stop, please. I'm so tired and, to be honest, confused on what else I can say to you right now."

"That's fine," she mumbled, and I couldn't tell if she was placating me or not.

"Wanna watch TV or something?" I asked. Lying with her in my arms sounded like the perfect way to spend the entire day.

"I think I'm going to go out for a bit," she said, and I felt like I'd been punched in the windpipe.

"Where are you going?" I asked, worried it sounded a bit too demanding.

Her return stare held a ton of warning, confirming what I'd feared. But I didn't want to apologize or backpedal. Was it wrong to let your partner know where you were going when you left the house? I didn't think so. Not in theory, at least.

The tone was what needed work, and I understood that the minute the question flew out of my mouth.

"Like I said, out," she volleyed back.

I nodded a couple of times and kissed the top of her head. “Please be careful. You can take the SUV if you want. I don’t think there’s been a change in your car’s status.”

Okay, was that a shitty tactic? Maybe. I didn’t want her to feel indebted to me because I would loan her my vehicle. But it also wouldn’t hurt her to be a bit nicer when I’d been nothing but the best version of myself I was capable of in a very unfamiliar situation.

CHAPTER NINETEEN

SHEPPERD

This man was so much more than I deserved. If it wasn't my solid opinion before, it was after today. As I drove aimlessly along the busy freeway, my mind jumped from subject to subject. Every conclusion I came to—even the small inconsequential ones—pointed me in the same direction. This was years in the making, and finally, I needed to have a long, hard conversation with my sister, Hannah.

So I found myself winding through the tight streets of the beach town of Malibu, trying to find her address. I had been to the house once or twice before, but now that I was behind the wheel and responsible for navigation, all the properties looked the same.

I drove past her street twice and had to loop around the neighborhood before I made the turn in time and searched for her house number. As luck would have it, there was a great parking spot less than a block away, so I maneuvered Law's SUV into the spot and made sure to get as close to the curb as possible.

While I waited at her gate, I took a deep breath and blew it out, almost choking on the exhale when Elijah's voice came through the speaker.

"Not interested in buying anything," he said in a clipped

tone.

"Hey, Elijah," I said, and my voice came out way huskier than I expected. Not a surprise, though, from the amount of crying I'd done today. I cleared my throat. "It's me, Shepperd. Is my sister home?"

Silence seemed to stretch for an hour when it was probably only ten seconds. Even so, why didn't he answer right away? Were they conspiring inside their huge castle to not let the commoner in? A low buzz sounded, and then there was a metallic click.

I gave the tall gate a push and found he had released the lock to allow me to enter.

My nerves jackhammered through my whole body. By the time I made my way up the pathway to the front door, a light sheen of sweat chilled my skin.

Hannah, in all her maternal glory, opened the front door. She had a sweet little baby bundled in a yellow gauzy blanket cradled in her arms. She spoke quietly so the infant continued to sleep and invited me inside.

"Thank you for seeing me," I said before anything else.

She wrinkled her nose. "Shepperd, you're my sister. You're welcome at my home anytime."

And that was my oldest sister for you. She always took the high road, no matter how shitty a person was to her. She was always right there to offer the benefit of the doubt. And why was that? How did we turn out so completely different when I was pretty sure we had more in common than I did with my twin—at least with respect to the crap we'd been through in life.

"Thank you," I muttered as we walked into their home. I couldn't take my eyes off the sweet little bean in her arms, and she noticed my attention.

"Do you want to hold her?" She smiled kindly and started to hand the baby off to me.

"Are you sure?" I asked and met her eyes for the first time.

"I would love for you to know her. She's the sweetest baby, I swear. Of course, not at three in the morning when all she wants is to nurse."

I took the swaddle as carefully as possible and moved the blanket away from her angelic face. She was absolutely perfect and made a little squeaky sound as I readjusted her in my arms.

"She looks so much like Elijah, huh?" Hannah asked.

"Definitely. But I see a lot of you in her too. What color are her eyes?" I asked since the baby was sleeping.

"Well, they're still blue. We'll have to wait to see what happens there, but I'm secretly hoping she got his."

Her husband had piercing ice-green eyes that were so unusual and striking, it was the first thing you noticed about the man. And that was saying a lot since the guy was as beautiful as a human could be.

"Her name is Elissa."

"So pretty," I commented, not really knowing what else to say.

We sat down on a moss-green velvet sofa that was so plush and comfortable, I wanted to curl up with this little baby and nap alongside her.

Hannah was explaining the origin of the child's name while we got situated.

"It's a combo, really, of Elijah's name and Mom's. I always liked the name, so it just worked out." She shrugged with a little smile.

We were just making small talk, and we both knew it.

So I mustered the courage to talk about what had been on my mind. "I wanted to talk about what happened yesterday." I waited for her to say something, but she was quiet. "Would that be okay?"

She nodded but still didn't speak. This woman had as many triggers as I did and was probably steeling herself for a tough conversation.

Finally, Hannah asked, "Do you remember what happened?" She waited for me to slowly shake my head and said, "Yeah, me neither."

I fussed with the baby's blanket again.

"Elijah told me what he knows, but I can't really piece much together," she said. "Something happens when I'm in bad situations like that, and I completely shut down. He has theories." She chuckled. "But he basically has theories about everything."

Her words were filled with so much love and adoration, and it made me think I wanted to look like that to the outside world when I talked about Law. Maybe not with the intensity I saw in her features, because she and her man had been together a lot longer, but I wanted what she had in her relationship.

And what a revelation that was. I spent most of my life being jealous and resentful of Hannah. She got all our parents' attention. She was the one the entire family would uproot plans for. She was the sister all the girls wanted to be friends with and all the boys wanted to date. I lived a lifetime of the world according to Hannah.

Now, here I was, still wanting what she had, but for the first time being ecstatic about it. I saw her life and her relationship as goal-worthy, not a cause for jealousy. Damn...it felt so good to see the difference for the first time.

Little Elissa stretched and made the cutest face. Unfortunately, there came a deafening wail hot on the heels of the cuteness overdose, so I quickly handed her off to my sister. She maneuvered the baby and her top like she'd been doing it her whole life, and the baby nursed contentedly in no time.

"Motherhood looks good on you," I said honestly. "That little lady clearly has your lungs though."

"Elijah says the same thing. I don't think that's all bad, though. If she's going to look exactly like him, it's only fair she sounds like me, right?" she said while stroking the baby's wispy hair.

"So, these theories..." I trailed off, hoping she'd open up a bit more about our previous conversation. I needed to get to the bottom of what was going on with me, and her too. If she had answers, or at least a good place to start figuring it out, I wanted to hear them.

"I don't know how you deal with it, but when someone starts telling me what they think I'm dealing with in here"—she tapped her temple with her free hand—"I get pretty defensive. It doesn't feel good when people are always trying to fix me, you know?"

"Oh, I understand that probably more than you can imagine," I muttered, but the way she held my gaze after I said it, I knew she heard me loud and clear.

"So, I processed what he was thinking might be going on with me. And mind you, this wasn't an overnight type of discussion... I checked it out with my therapist."

"Was he right?" I asked, feeling close to some answers.

She rolled her eyes and groaned. "Of course he was." The comment started with a playful inflection but turned melancholy by the end. "Yeah, he was spot on, actually."

"Can you explain it to me?" I asked genuinely.

"You know, our brains are incredible things. Not only do they get us through the day-to-day crap, but they protect us from the life-changing bad stuff too. And then it seems like a little button is pushed inside. For some reason, our brains think we're ready to deal with a bit of the truth. For me, that looks like a flashback or a nightmare." She repositioned the baby to her shoulder to coax out a burp or two.

"I understand exactly what you're saying. But it's a different type of nightmare than others. It feels so real. I can smell things, hear things in the background, and on the really shitty occasion, I feel pain or other sensations as if it's happening in real time."

"It's called PTSD, Shepperd. I'm sure you've heard that term before, right?"

I nodded. The conversation with Law flashed through my mind. "Law just said after the party that he wants to help me deal with my PTSD."

"And what did you say?"

"Well, of course my go-to reaction was anger. But I had a bad feeling he was right." I thought about him and the past day or two and couldn't stop the burning sensation behind my eyes and up my throat. I gulped as much down that would move and said, "I'm so scared. If I don't get my shit together, I'm at serious risk of losing him."

Now the tears clouding my vision were actually welcomed because I couldn't bear to see the pity in her expression.

But surprisingly, that's not what I got in return.

"You're in love..." she said with a gentle smile. It wasn't a question—and she wasn't wrong.

"Yeah, it's certainly looking that way," I said with a healthy amount of resignation.

"Why do you sound sad about it?"

I gave her the side eye. "Because, if I'm being completely honest, it scares the shit out of me. I don't know if you've noticed, but I have a knack for fucking things up."

"You're not going to fuck it up, Shep. Just be honest with him and communicate. Always communicate."

"Are these words of experience?" I teased, wanting desperately to lighten the air.

"Absolutely. Believe me, I wasted a lot of time running from my feelings for Elijah. Because I was scared too. Not of fucking things up but of getting hurt. So I pushed him away. Several times," she said with a roll of her blue eyes.

"What made you finally see the light?"

"Well, he did, for the most part. He's a stubborn man when he wants something." She laughed, and the love for her husband was oozing from her pores. It would actually be sickening if I hadn't been feeling the exact same way about Law. And damn, did it feel good to have someone to share it with.

But we still had a lot of shitty ground to cover if I was going to have any hope of feeling put together from a mental health standpoint.

"Let me go lay her down. Be right back." Hannah stood with the baby carefully nestled against her chest.

"Can I see her room?" I asked, also standing.

"I would love that," she said, and we padded off toward the nursery.

While my precious niece slept in her crib, my sister and I sat on the floor of her nursery and talked. And then we talked some more.

I finally felt comfortable enough to ask her what she

remembered about the school custodian from our elementary school. At first, I worried I had brought up a new trauma for her to deal with by the ashen color of her face.

"What do you mean? What do *you* remember?" she asked, not giving anything away about her memories of those years.

So I just let it out. "He molested me in his workshop or whatever the hell it was."

She gasped. "Oh, Shepperd, no."

"He did it to you too, didn't he?" I whispered as though speaking it aloud so close to her innocent child would tarnish her perfection.

She was quiet at first, and when I finally met her gaze, tears were running down both cheeks as she nodded. "Shep, I had no idea." She scooted closer to me on the floor to take my hands in hers.

"Why would you? I never told anyone. Law was the second person I ever told. And hell, that was only about a month ago. I've been carrying that shit around with me for what? Fifteen years?"

We were both crying then.

"The first person?" she asked.

I shouldn't have been surprised that she caught that fact in all that I had said.

"Yeah." I nodded. This next part was really going to suck. But it needed to be addressed.

"Who else did you tell? If it's too much to share..."

"I told Mom."

Hannah put her hands on her cheeks. "What did she do?"

I just made a face, because of all the shit I had to deal with from my childhood, this one fact was the absolute most painful.

"What did she do, Shepperd?" she asked again.

I just shook my head.

I couldn't say it out loud. Even though it was the truth, admitting it seemed as painful as the betrayal of our mother doing nothing.

"But why?" Hannah asked, and I prayed I wasn't about to undo any sort of progress we made today in mending our relationship. "Why wouldn't she do anything? It doesn't make sense."

I couldn't tell if she realized what the reason might be or if it was me just thinking wishfully. Her entire face fell when the truth became clear to her.

She was the reason.

I wanted to explain as much as I understood. The details were sketchy for a few reasons. One, I was young. Maybe eight or nine years old when I told our mother. Secondly, Hannah was very dramatic as a child. After the abduction attempt, she was hysterical all the time. Everyone in the family bent over backward to keep her content. And lastly, denial was a funny thing. It distorted reality, and over time, the blame I placed on her grew to such an overwhelming monster, I lost sight of what truly happened that made me feel so resentful toward her.

Now, when I thought about it, I knew it wasn't fair to blame her, but throughout the years, I needed a place to focus all those bad feelings.

"Because of me?" she croaked. Damn it, why was she pushing me to put it into words?

"I don't really remember what happened, or why." I waved my hand in the air like shooing away a pesky fly. "Or whatever."

"But it had something to do with me. That's why you've been so angry toward me for so long?" she asked, but she didn't need me to confirm it.

She was a smart girl, and I laid all the pieces of the puzzle in front of her to fit together.

"My God, Shepperd," she gasped. "I'm so sorry," she said through fresh tears.

"Hannah, stop. You were a child. And dealing with so much of your own shit." She shook her head, not hearing any of my excuses. "Seriously, I was wrong to blame you."

"I'm so sorry," she said again.

"Mom and Dad dropped the ball. They did. They were the adults in the scenario. Not you. Not me. I realize they had a lot on their plates with the abduction attempt, but they screwed up by not remembering they had four other children that needed them just as much."

I believed what I was saying even if it didn't make me feel any better to actually say it.

For a long time, we sat in the quiet nursery. Both of us so deep in thought we didn't need the additional noise of conversation.

"I'm really glad you came over today," my sister said. "This conversation was long overdue. Let's go out to the kitchen. I need some water. Nursing dries me out more than exercise, I swear."

I followed her through the enormous house to the kitchen.

After looking around the room, I said, "You must be in heaven in this kitchen."

"Well, I was before that little queen arrived. Now all I do is feed her and sleep. I couldn't tell you the last time I cooked dinner."

I didn't have a lot to add to the conversation, so I just nodded.

"Luckily, Elijah enjoys cooking and is actually quite good

at it." She smiled and offered me a bottle of water.

"Sounds like you found the perfect guy," I said, and meant it in the best way.

She smiled warmly. "Yeah, he's pretty amazing. Can I ask you something?"

"Sure, go ahead."

"Have you considered talking to someone? A therapist, I mean? And before you get defensive"—she held up her hands, but I had no intention of interrupting—"it's helped me so much over the years. I think you'd get a lot out of it."

"I've thought about it a few times, but it's overwhelming, you know? How do you pick the right person?"

"I could give you the name of the woman I go to. She's amazing. Really smart and funny too. She specializes in childhood trauma and PTSD, so I think you'd be in the right place."

"I'll take her information." Actually following through and making the appointment might be a different story, but one step at a time. "Can I use your restroom? Then I should probably get going."

Hannah showed me to a guest bathroom just down the hall from the kitchen. While I was in there, I sent Law a text.

Hi. I'm at my sister's in Malibu. Should be leaving soon.

It was a starting point at least. I owed him about twelve apologies but would rather do that in person. At least if he was worried about my well-being after the way I left the condo, he could rest easier.

Hey there. Thank you for letting me know.
See you when you get home. XO

That damn XO got me every time. I walked out of the bathroom smiling and looking at my phone until I nearly plowed over my sister.

"Ahh, one guess who that is," she teased and motioned to the phone in my hand.

"I was just letting him know I was heading back. I was a bitch to him before I left, and I didn't want him to be worried."

"I'm sure he appreciated that."

"If I didn't fuck things up today, it'll be a miracle. I was really shitty to him, and he didn't deserve that."

"Shep, listen. None of us is perfect. I'm sure he's not either. If he loves you and cares about you, he'll understand you have a lot of unsettled things you're dealing with. Yesterday was really hard on all of us."

I wasn't convinced I should be let off the hook so easily. I needed to take responsibility for my behavior and start treating people better in the first place.

But instead of getting into another deep conversation with my sister, I said, "I hope you're right. I'm going to take off. Hey, anytime you need a babysitter, feel free to call me. She's absolutely perfect, and maybe if I play my cards right, I'll be her favorite auntie."

"Are you serious? We desperately need a night out, just like adults. I'd love to take you up on the offer," my sister said hopefully.

"One hundred percent serious. Just hit me up. I may have to bring Law with me, though. He loves kiddos. Before that disaster yesterday, I was loving watching him with all the kids."

"Kind of funny how our worlds ended up being intertwined, isn't it?" she asked as we walked to the front door.

"Yeah, I guess it really is a small world." For the first time in years, I hugged my sister. Neither one of us wanted to let go, but finally she pulled back and held my gaze for a moment.

"Thank you again for coming today, Shepperd. You have no idea how much it means to me." She gave me another quick hug.

"No, I think I understand exactly. Love you, Hannah," I said and waved over my shoulder as I headed for home.

CHAPTER TWENTY

LAW

Four months later...

Pacing back and forth in front of the window, I checked through the blinds to see if she was home. Every car I heard drive through the neighborhood sounded like hers. Yet every time I checked, she still wasn't back.

Shepperd had spent the day with her sisters, and I had a big surprise planned for our six-month anniversary. Dinner was ready and on the table. Her twin, Maye, sent me a text when she left to head home, so the timing should've been perfect. I couldn't predict the traffic she'd encounter, but that particular sister didn't live too far from us, so traffic shouldn't be too bad. My nerves were toying with me in a big way, and I jumped when I heard a car door slam.

One more peek out the window confirmed she was finally home. I took a deep breath and tried to calm the fuck down so I didn't scare her when she walked in by looking like a maniac. The woman was so keenly aware of the people around her and their emotions that she would be able to take one look at me when she came through the door and know I was up to something.

The past six months had been a whirlwind. My stunning,

vibrant, intelligent girlfriend had made so much progress with her mental health and eating disorder, I couldn't wait to go through with my plans. No one deserved happiness more than Shepperd, and I planned on being a part of hers forever.

After a gentle suggestion from her oldest sister, Hannah, and heaps of support from me, Shepperd started working with a therapist to deal with her childhood trauma. I was so proud of her.

That's not to say we didn't still have bad days—or nights—or ridiculous disagreements, but we were finding our way as a couple as much as she was getting in touch with herself.

And what a funny thing for me to be ecstatic about. There was a time, and it wasn't even that long ago, that I seriously doubted I'd ever find the right woman. Someone who would inspire me to want to settle down and commit to one partner. Someone I'd eventually want to create a family with.

Then the universe brought me Shepperd Farsay. From the moment I saw her—even across the expanse of a gym—I knew she was different. So special and beautiful, inside and out.

Her key turned in the front door, and when the heavy wood swung open, I was right there to greet her. I took her purse off her shoulder and dropped it on the table just inside the door that served as the catch-all space for our home.

"Hello," I said, my voice low and resonating against the silky, smooth skin of her neck where I pressed my lips.

"Hello to you too," she said in that damn throaty, sexy laugh of hers, and I considered retooling my plans on the fly and starting our evening in the bedroom instead of ending it there.

"Dinner's on the table," I told her with a quick wink. "Hope you're hungry."

"Mmm, I am. Something smells delicious. What did you make?" she asked and stepped out of my embrace and shrugged out of her coat.

"Let me take that for you," I offered while holding my hand out for the jacket.

With a suspicious glance, she stepped out of the way of the guest closet where we kept our outerwear. "You're awfully attentive this evening, Mr. Masterson. What's going on?"

"What do you mean? Can't a guy miss his girl when she's been gone all day?" I asked and hung the jacket up and closed the closet door. I offered her a bent elbow to usher her to the dining table.

"Of course he can." She smiled up at me while we strolled through to the kitchen.

We had a small square table in the breakfast nook that we teasingly called our dining room table. The furniture was nothing like the massive masterpiece my parents had in their formal dining room, but it was the first thing we picked out together. It held more sentimental value now than anything else. Instead of sixteen, ours could accommodate four and was absolutely perfect.

The top was set with service for two. I bought a beautiful bouquet of her favorite flowers—bromeliads—in all the vibrant fabulous colors I could find. Bright pink, red, orange, and yellow, as bright as the summer sun, spikey flowers made a stunning arrangement against their brilliant green leaves. Shepperd's eyes landed on the arrangement the moment we stepped into the room, and she looked up at me as tears filled her eyes.

"Hey, hey," I said and pulled her against my chest. "Don't be sad."

"I'm not sad, Law. I'm so overwhelmed with happiness I can't hold it in. These flowers are so thoughtful. I can't believe you remembered they were my favorite."

I scoffed. "Of course I remembered."

She held on tighter and sighed. "You're just too much."

"Darling, you haven't seen anything yet," I promised and meant it more than she could imagine. The surprise I had planned for her was so over-the-top, even my sister tried talking me out of it, and she was the most diehard romantic I knew.

Dinner was fantastic. I wasn't above patting myself on the back about it, either. Shepperd worked for months with a therapist regarding her relationship with food, and we put the practices into action every time we sat down for a meal.

Viewing food as nutrition instead of a bargaining tool was the original roadblock, but my amazing woman was doing so much better with the concept now. There were times I still witnessed small backslides, but we addressed the root cause as soon as she was ready to talk about it, and if it was something I couldn't help her work through, she spoke with her doctor as soon as she could get some time with her.

I was so proud of her. My heart felt like it had expanded to at least ten times the size it was before she was a part of my life.

Actually, she was my entire life.

And that didn't terrify me like it once would have. It didn't even scare me a little. It thrilled me. I wanted to spend the rest of my life watching her blossom and grow. Supporting her through every challenge and celebrating every accomplishment.

"Did you save room for dessert?" I asked.

My girl had the biggest sweet tooth I'd ever seen, so I

made sure to have a decadent, chocolate mousse chilling in the refrigerator.

"Helllll no," she groaned. "I'm so full, you may have to just roll me to the bedroom tonight."

"It's chocolate," I sing-songed to taunt her.

"You're an evil man, you know that, don't you?" she said through a wide grin.

"You love me anyway."

"It's true. I do. Very much, as a matter of fact." She leaned over and kissed me softly.

If I didn't have a major surprise up my sleeve, I would've deepened that sweet kiss into something we both wouldn't walk away from.

But I sat up straight in my chair and looked at her for a long moment. When I reached for her hand, she willingly wrapped hers around mine.

"Do you know what today is?" I asked. I knew she would because she was one of those girls who was obsessed with dates. Our first kiss, our first date, our first fuck even. We celebrated it all!

"Of course I do," she said proudly. "It's been six months of putting up with your ass."

Shepperd, it turns out, had a wicked sense of humor. She was funny and witty too, but most of all, so sarcastic. She could come back with a one-liner for almost anything. More times than I could count, a serious conversation or even a disagreement ended with us laughing so hard we had tears rolling down our cheeks. It was just one of her many gifts.

I rolled my eyes, calling her bluff. I knew I made her as deliriously happy as she made me. All jokes aside, we were perfect together.

"Well, despite the fact that you're such a smartass, I have something for you." I went to the cabinet where I stashed the box and pulled it down from the shelf. The parcel was a flat square. A little bigger than a shirt box, and the same length on all four sides. There was a yellow satin ribbon tied into an artful bow on top that reflected the overhead light when I set it in front of her.

"Law..." she started as her eyes bounced between me and the box. "What did you do?"

"Open it and find out," I encouraged. I loved giving her gifts. Her reaction was always so humble and grateful but more than anything, happy. We both made peace with the fact that gift giving was my love language, and I was over apologizing for spoiling her every chance I got.

"But I didn't get you anything."

"Having you in my life is the best gift you could ever give me."

She rolled her eyes.

Her response coaxed a dark growl from the back of my throat. "Was that an eye roll in my direction, miss?"

She'd gotten a little taste of the darker side of my personality in the bedroom and enjoyed provoking me whenever she could. I'd be more than happy to end the night with a good discipline session.

"Maybe." She added a shrug on the end for extra effect.

"Open the present before I take you over my knee, woman."

She giggled and tugged on the ribbon, unleashing the bow into a haphazard pile of satin.

I was equally as excited as she was. Well, probably more so because I knew what was inside. As she lifted the lid, I held my breath.

There was always that moment of panic in my gut right before the recipient discovered what I gave them. What if she didn't like it? What if it was, like everyone kept insisting, too much, too fast? No, I knew it wasn't. I knew all the afternoons that led to this idea and all the effort to execute this surprise. I knew Shepperd would be blown away.

Studying her reaction, I tried to gauge if I was correct or not. She looked at the contents and then at me. Then back to the gift and right back to me once more.

"Law? What is this?" She gulped, sounding so small and uncertain.

"What does it look like?"

"Well, it looks like a real estate listing for the house we looked at a few weeks ago. This is the one in Malibu, isn't it?"

I nodded. "It sure is."

Months ago, we'd discovered we both had a secret love of touring open houses. So at least twice a month, we'd take a Saturday to look at amazing properties all over Los Angeles. Some we loved instantly. Some not so much. Then we'd spend the drive home talking about what we'd change or how we'd decorate each one to make it the perfect home.

Little did she know, I was truly in the market for a home. I knew if I'd told her, she wouldn't have been as open with her opinions as she was when she thought it was harmless fun. And then we found it—the perfect home on a perfect parcel. For weeks we had talked about that house with dreams in our heads and hope in our hearts.

So I bought it.

"Law..." she nearly choked, "What did you do?"

"Look under the flyer and tissue paper."

She pulled out a key ring with two keys attached and looked at me with a shocked expression. "Lawrence Masterson. Have you lost your damn mind?"

"After we saw that place and both fell in love with it, I couldn't stop thinking about it. So I put an offer in with the agent, but someone had gotten to it first, and the house went into escrow. Then, about two weeks ago, the agent called me to tell me the deal fell through and she wanted to give me first shot before listing it again. I think it was a sign that it was meant to be."

"I-I-I don't know what to say."

"I'd go with congratulations, personally. And then I'd say we need to get packing because I closed on the place two days ago. It's ours, babe." The shock on her face was a little worrisome, but admittedly, this was a pretty big surprise. A lot to absorb all at once.

Shepperd clutched the keys in her feminine fist. "Ours?" she whispered.

I pulled her to her feet, and she looked up at me. "Absolutely." I kissed the tip of her nose. "Are you surprised?"

"I think stunned stupid would be more accurate." She shook her head. "Are you sure you want me to move in with you?"

"Woman," I began but came up short of what more to say. Did she really not get how committed I was to her? To us?

"I just don't want you to feel obligated"—she waved her hand between us—"or whatever."

"The only thing I feel here is love, darling. I wouldn't want to live anywhere you're not. I love you, I need you, I want to share my life with you. Now—forever."

She was quiet for long seconds, staring at me with wonder

and then at the set of keys in her hand. Finally, she said, "I love you too. This is incredible. You're incredible."

"So you're happy?" I needed to hear her put words to all this.

"Law, you've made me the happiest woman on earth. You've shown me what it means to be alive. If you hadn't come into my life when you did, I'm not sure I'd still be standing here, you know?" Tears filled her eyes but didn't spill down her cheeks yet. "You've given me so much. And I don't just mean material things. You've given me purpose and joy, and I will never be able to repay you."

Emotion choked off my air supply. Through all of her healing and emotional growth, she had never expressed gratitude like this so directly. It was overwhelming in all the best ways.

Then Shepperd's entire face lit up. "Oh my God, Law," she nearly cheered.

"What?"

"I just thought how close this home was to Hannah and Elijah. We'll be able to see baby Elissa anytime we want." She smiled and clapped her hands a few times like her plans were coming together.

"That's right," I agreed. Of course, I had thought of that exact fact again and again while going through the escrow process. "It was at the top of your pro column."

She had the cutest habit of making pro and con lists whenever we would look at a house. If the cons were too numerous or insurmountable, we moved on to another house. This house only had two checks in the negative column, and I was able to address both in my offer to buy the place.

Now it was literally perfect. Like everything else in life at the moment. We were just starting our journey, and the road was sure to have bumps along the way. But with this incredible woman by my side, and the power of our growing love, we could take on whatever life threw our way.

ACKNOWLEDGMENTS

Thank you to the Waterhouse Press team, who has lent their time and individual talents to make my words shine. Special thanks to Scott Saunders, who sweats every detail and gives my words and ideas the polish they need. Shout out to the Waterhouse proofing, copyediting, and formatting teams. Thank you for your keen eye and attention to detail.

Thank you to the talented ladies on my personal team. Megan Ashley, Amy Bourne, and Faith Moreno. Your daily support and listening ears mean so much to me.

As always, thank you to the readers. Without you, stories would go untold. I appreciate each and every one of you.

ALSO BY VICTORIA BLUE

Shark's Edge Series *(with Angel Payne)*:

Shark's Edge
Shark's Pride
Shark's Rise
Grant's Heat
Grant's Flame
Grant's Blaze

*

Elijah's Whim
Elijah's Want
Elijah's Need
Jacob's Star
Jacob's Eclipse

Bombshells of Brentwood :

Accepting Agatha
Mentoring Maye
Saving Shepperd
Courting Clemson

Misadventures:

Misadventures with a Book Boyfriend
Misadventures at City Hall

Secrets of Stone Series *(with Angel Payne)*:

No Prince Charming
No More Masquerade
No Perfect Princess
No Magic Moment
No Lucky Number
No Simple Sacrifice
No Broken Bond
No White Knight
No Longer Lost

For a full list of Victoria's other titles, visit her at VictoriaBlue.com

ABOUT VICTORIA BLUE

International bestselling author Victoria Blue lives in her own portion of the galaxy known as Southern California. There, she finds the love and life-sustaining power of one amazing sun, two unique and awe-inspiring planets, and four indifferent yet comforting moons. Life is fantastic and challenging and every day brings new adventures to be discovered. She looks forward to seeing what's next!

Visit her at VictoriaBlue.com